FATE RIDES A TALL HORSE

JOHNNY BLACK—

MAN AND LEGEND

1869

GARY CHURCH

Edited by Paula Church

Cover design and book layout by Diamond Design.

In memory of

Richard 'R.D.' Church and Richard 'Dick' Riel

who enjoyed stories set in the Old West.

TABLE OF CONTENTS

FOREWORD FROM
PAUL L. THOMPSON

"In 1869, Johnny Black finds himself in a lawless, danger-filled settlement located on the Texas frontier, where Indians, criminals and nature all provide an opportunity for death as he relentlessly pursues the man who murdered his only brother. Obsessed with finding his brother's killer, Johnny makes himself very visible in a place where people often assume new identities and don't want to be found. It will require all of Johnny's experience and skills to stay alive. His man-hunt results in action, adventure and romance, which all combine to reflect life on the Texas frontier and a number of people find their fate is altered; by not only their decisions but by chance meetings with strangers, including one who rides a tall horse."

This new Western from Gary Church has all the hallmarks of a great adventure. As a Western reader you will already be aware of the fantastic novels that have been released lately. The hits from C. Wayne Winkle, Robert Hanlon, and the like have opened the door for new writers—Gary Church is one of these writers. His talent is apparent from the very first page. Give it a try!

Paul L. Thompson – bestselling author of the multi-million page selling series "U.S. Marshal Shorty Thompson."

ONE

IT WAS A COLD FEBRUARY DAY; year of our Lord, 1869 and a light rain had fallen all day, turning the hard-packed rutted streets into a sea of mud. As night fell and the rain turned into icy sleet blown by a brisk north wind, Jake Evans leaned against the bar in the Frontier saloon, trying to stay clear of the blast of cold air that came in every time someone came in or left. He was sipping on a warm beer and discussing the foul weather with the bartender, a big, hard-looking man of undeterminable age whose weather-worn face was largely hidden behind a full dark beard that served to balance an almost bald head. As the bartender, Jones, leaned in to say something to Jake over the noise, the contrast was noticeable.

Jake was a fair-haired, blue-eyed, twenty-eight-year-old with hair down over his collar, sporting at least a week's growth of a light and scraggly beard. Life had left its mark on Jake's mind, but had yet to mark his face and his natural expression made it appear he was about to smile, or that he knew something no one else knew. He was naturally inquisitive and liked to talk, although this was often frowned on in a place like the Flat, where people often did not wish to discuss themselves or why they had chosen to come here, even if they didn't intend to stay long. But often as not, he found someone he could visit with.

The place was full as it was every night, there not being much else to do at night except visit, drink and play cards or faro. It was crowded, smoky, smelly and noisy in the saloon, a wooden structure with a tin roof, one of several located in a tiny settlement located on the Clear Fork of the Brazos at the base of a plateau where the 6th Calvary had established Fort Griffin, Texas two years before, in 1867. The following year, infantry troops had been added to the fort's contingent. Originally the fort was called Camp Wilson, located by the river, but it was quickly moved up on the top of the plateau and renamed. Far as anyone knew there wasn't an official name for the settlement that had sprung up because of the fort. Some folks called it Griffin town, or Buffalo town, sometimes Hide town, but generally it was called the Flat.

The place didn't have any official law enforcement except the soldiers who occasionally policed the area. Generally, folks enforced the law themselves, as they thought proper. The result was a mix of cowboys, farmers, tradesmen, gamblers, buffalo- hunters, con-men, fallen-ladies, thieves and outlaws, all drawn to this tiny outpost on the edge of the Texas frontier. Ranches, some of them very large surrounded the town to the north, south and east, but to the west, in the area known as the Comancheria, bison, or buffalo as most folks called them, were plentiful and their hides were in high demand back east. The problem was the area was populated by Indians, some Kiowa, but primarily Comanche, who roamed the area stealing, killing, and kidnapping.

It was Saturday night and a lot of ranch hands had braved the bad weather, arriving in town with their pockets full of wages. The long bar was standing room only and a dozen tables were filled with hunters, soldiers, cowboys, drifters, prostitutes and only the Lord knows who else. Faro was the game of choice for most gamblers and there was a group bucking the tiger in the corner, but there were two poker games in progress

One was a table of rough men; cowboys and buffalo- hunters judging by their dress, which swore and drank to every card dealt to them. But then losing hands or winning hands,

It didn't seem to matter; they drank and swore to each, equally. There was lots of tough talk and threats, but there hadn't been any fights this evening. Since the place didn't have a sheriff, nearly everyone was wearing a gun or at least carrying a knife. The talk generally centered on two major subjects; money and women. Both the lack of and what was going to happen as soon as they got their hands on either. Stories abounded between the cursing and shouting, most of it somewhat enhanced if not totally unrealistic. Occasionally, someone would mention the Indians, a subject many did not want to discuss since they were a serious threat and no sane man in the area lived without a deep fear of them. And of course there was discussion of one of the main means of income - buffalo. The buffalo had reappeared in the area and demand was increasing resulting in hunters arriving almost daily to set up a base camp in the tiny settlement below the fort.

Next to a huge pot-bellied stove that separated the buffalo- hunters and cowboy's card game from the other game was a big, shorthaired dog named Flop that belonged to Johnny Black. Now, normally, dogs weren't allowed inside anywhere, but when Johnny had come in Jones had looked at him and seemed about to order the dog out, but then didn't say anything and no one had complained. The second game was higher stakes and Jake had been watching it off and on. The players included House, a local rancher, Whitt, the livery owner and operator, Birchfield who owned the general store, a hard looking fellow that called himself Clive and everyone was sure was a famous gunfighter, a lawyer, named Ladd, who had made it known he was here on business at the fort, but who Jake had seen in two other saloons during the week, and Johnny, whom Jake had met three days ago.

Jake Evans had been in town for a week staying at Brown's hotel, although it didn't resemble any hotel in the east, it was better than a tent. When Johnny took the room across the hall,

Evans had nodded to him in the tiny lobby of the hotel before formally introducing himself when he sat in on a poker game with Johnny at the Busy Bee. The custom was to use first names, many of them not the owner's real name, and it was considered bad manners to ask a man his last name, but Johnny had introduced himself as 'Johnny Black.'

Johnny wasn't a young man, and his face was leathery like he had spent most of his life outdoors, but he was handsome and charismatic, although he wasn't prone to talk. The women hired by the saloon owners to draw customers and encourage the buying of drinks and the prostitutes who frequented the saloons were constantly trying to catch his attention. His clothes and boots were clean and neat, but he wasn't dressed fancy like the lawyer. He had a relaxed, confident way about him, but he didn't waste words. His hair was dark and fell about his ears and a full, but neatly trimmed mustache gave his face a dignified look. It appeared that he shaved every day and like most of the customers, he wore a tied down double-action Navy colt on his right hip. Black favored small cigars or cigarillos popular with the Mexicans and was smoking one tonight as he played. This also tended to make him a bit different, because most fellows chewed and the favorite was the bright leaf type plug tobacco that had come from the south during the war. It was a bit milder and had gained favor amongst those that had tried it.

As Jones went down the bar to attend to some cowboys, Jake turned his thoughts to Johnny Black. Black had some tension about him, maybe anger, Jake thought. It could be he was carrying a bad memory around and when his mind was free, the memory weighed on him. Maybe he was a former Union officer. The boots he wore were high top, with the front cut higher than the back and worn with his pants tucked in and he wore a great coat of the type worn by the Union officers.

Maybe he was still suffering from the war; a lot of people, including Jake, were.

Johnny was winning, but the players at his table were all laughing and talking, eager it seemed to Jake, for Johnny to take their money. All that is, with the exception of Clive, who didn't speak and the lawyer, whose arrival a couple of hours earlier had added new tension to the game. He was a younger fellow himself, well dressed and wearing brown and white city shoes, with a striped wool suit, but he didn't smile and his eyes seemed to bore into folks as if he were trying to read their mind when they spoke to him. He seemed to be a fairly good player, but he stared at each man for what seemed forever before he would make his play. Everyone, except Johnny and Clive, seemed to be made uncomfortable by the lawyer. Whenever he looked into Johnny's eyes, Johnny would look back at him and smile a little smile, his mouth just turning up at the corners. The talk at this table was a bit different as it touched on politics, money, cattle and San Francisco. It was pretty varied and entertaining, considered Jake.

Jake was enjoying the evening and the warmth of the stove so he had been putting off a visit out back, but nature called and he pulled on his coat, eased out the back door, stepped into the mud and slogged his way to the row of outhouses. It wasn't necessary to wait; the weather was discouraging visits. Finding his way back to the bar in the dark, Jake stopped at the back door and took the time to knock most of the mud off his boots and shake the ice off his hat before coming back in. He had just pulled off his coat and slung it over the back of a bar stool where it began to drip water on the wooden floor, when the front door burst open and a gust of cold air rushed in followed by a huge lumbering man who smelled like he hadn't bathed for a good year.

He was closely trailed by two men who smelled equally as bad, but both were a good head shorter than the big man.

The giant had arms as big as a normal man's legs and was clothed from head to foot in buffalo skins. He had a large brimmed hat on his head whose brim curved both up and down. A huge buck knife was strapped upside down on his chest and he had a big pistol on his right hip, Jake wasn't sure, but it looked like a Colt .44. But it was his face that Jake would remember.

His nose was flat and listed badly to one side as if he had been crushed by a press and a dark puckered spot on his upper left cheek was definitely an old gunshot wound. Men automatically moved aside as he and his crew approached the bar. Jake didn't know if it was the man's size, the smell or his menacing look, but there was suddenly plenty of room at the bar. He and his friends ordered a bottle of whiskey, and then stood drinking and everything seemed to return to normal.

Observing the big man and his friends for a bit, Jake noted they were definitely buffalo-hunters; probably just in from somewhere out on the Comancheria. As it began to get late in the evening the beer and whiskey began to take its affect and the crowd thinned a little as some of the harder drinkers stumbled out into the sleet and mud to find their way home, back to the fort or down the street to the hotel.

But it was still crowded when the giant's booming voice rang out. "What you staring at Mex?" he yelled at a Mexican cowboy, standing a few feet down the bar.

The owner of the Frontier allowed Mexicans, but not Negroes in his place. Indians were also barred, no exceptions, not that one would likely try to enter. The giant had been putting away shots of whiskey at a rapid rate and was, Jake reflected, probably pretty drunk.

The Mexican shrugged his shoulders and turned his head away; he probably didn't speak English. But the big man moved with cat like speed taking two quick steps and hitting the Mexican cowboy in the side of the head with his huge right fist. The Mexican dropped like a load of potatoes, his head making a terrible noise as it hit the hard wooden floor. Another Mexican he was with jumped back and drew his gun pointing it at the giant who, in one quick motion drew his knife and backhanded the knife blade across the man's throat. Blood gushed as the man gurgled, dropped the gun and clutched his throat. The big man kicked the Mexican in the chest sending him flying across a table to crash and die on the dirty floor.

Returning to his beer, the giant looked at Jones. "You seen it. Clear case a self-defense."

Jones, an empty beer glass in his hand, looking stunned, just nodded.

"Damn right" said his two buddies, almost in unison.

Things kind of froze for a minute, and then slowly returned to normal. The giant wiped the blood on his knife on his pants leg and sheathed it as he returned to his place at the bar. A couple of Mexicans helped the hurt one to his feet and they took hold of the dead man, now soaked in his own blood and began to pull him out the door. The area around the giant got much larger and a goodly number of fellows decided to call it a night. Johnny turned and looked, but didn't seem to take much notice.

The card game had just got going again when the giant's voice boomed again. "What the hell is that bag-a-fleas doing in 'ere?" he bellowed, looking at Flop who immediately raised his head and bared his teeth. Flop had moved away from the stove and was now lying beside Johnny's chair. Johnny reached a hand down and touched the dog's head without taking his eyes off of his cards. Flop stopped growling, but kept his eyes on the giant.

The giant banged his glass down on the bar and yelled. "No damn dog bares their teeth at me!" Then he lumbered over to Flop and raised one of his huge legs to stomp him. As soon as the giant began to move, in one lightning fast motion, Black tossed his cigarillo toward the floor and dropped his cards to the table as he jumped to his feet, flung his chair aside, stepped over Flop and directly into the path of the giant. Johnny's momentum carried him into the chest of the huge man as he brought his right knee up and into the giant's groin. Screaming, the big man stumbled backward into his two buddies.

The giant grabbed for his gun, but it wasn't there. He clutched at his chest where his knife was supposed to be, but it was gone also. He looked up, his breathing ragged. Johnny had the knife in his right hand and the big .44 in his left. One of the giant's friends stepped out from behind the giant with his gun drawn and Johnny shot him left-handed, the bullet hitting the man at the point where his arm met his shoulder. He was slammed backward by the force of the shot. His back hit the bar and he sank to the floor. The giant, recovering, let out a blood-curdling curse and charged.

Everything seemed to happen in slow motion. Johnny stood frozen in place. The giant, his face twisted in pain and rage, his huge arms swinging, charged toward Johnny. The huge man seemed about to ram into Johnny, but at the last second Johnny stepped aside and the man crashed into the card table causing cards and money to fly everywhere, but nobody tried to grab any of the money because everyone had backed well back against the walls and they stayed there. For such a big man the giant was quick. As he turned back his monstrous sized right hand swung a killing blow aimed at Johnny's head. For an instant Jake thought it was over. He was watching a show in slow motion, but so fast he didn't have time to think. Johnny didn't move, nor did he raise the gun or knife, just held them at each side, but as the potential death blow approached his head, Johnny leaned back, just enough so the blow missed him by an inch. Johnny pivoted on his left foot and slammed his right boot into the giant's right knee. The big man crashed to the floor as he filled the room with an agonizing scream. In the same motion Johnny looked right and pointed the pistol at the man's unwounded friend, who was frozen in place, his arms held at waist level, as he stared at Flop, who stood five feet away, his teeth bared, a low growl emitting from his throat.

Johnny whistled and Flop backed up. The man, still holding his hands up moved slowly to help his wounded friend. Johnny walked over to the bar and placed the giant's knife and gun on the bar. Everyone began to recover from the shock. The man that Johnny had shot in the shoulder had passed out or was dead from shock or loss of blood, Jake wasn't sure which. The giant was rolling around on the floor holding his busted knee with both hands groaning and calling for help. Some folks began to straighten out the chairs and tables and pick up the cards and money. Talk began again. Johnny walked over and squatted down by Flop. He started talking to him in low tones. Someone handed Johnny his money. He nodded a thank you.

There must have been an army patrol in town because suddenly five armed troops, including a Captain waving a pistol burst through the door. The men, obviously trained, spread out in the room.

Captain Bates stood looking down at the giant who, seeing the Captain gasped "I need a doctor."

The Captain's eyes scanned the room. The man shot in the shoulder was sitting up against the bar holding a dirty rag to his wound, trying to staunch the bleeding. There was a huge amount of fresh, but drying blood where the Mexican whose throat was cut bled out.

"Jones, there's a Mexican lying out in the street with his throat cut. Blood trail leads in here," the Captain's statement that was really a question was firm and loud and directed at the bartender.

"Well Captain Bates, sir," said Jones, "no soldiers was involved, that big feller on the floor there hit a vaquero in the head, but I don't think he killed him, but then he cut a Mex's throat and then he was going to kill a dog I guess, but, well, as you can see, he isn't doing so good. Oh and the guy down there," pointing under the bar "is the big man's buddy and he pulled a gun, but as you can see, he isn't doing so well either."

The Captain looked at Jones and then around the room, confusion evident on his face. "You're not making any sense," said the Captain.

People were leaving. The show was over and no one wanted to get involved with the soldiers. Finally, the Captain spotted a table of non-commissioned soldiers that had been drinking beer and throwing some dice. He walked over to their table and talked to them in a low voice. The men began gesturing. Jake looked around for Johnny, but he and Flop were gone. Who the hell was Johnny Black, Jake thought to himself. As Jake eased out the door he heard the murmuring. "Never, ever seen nothing like that."

TWO

THE MORNING AFTER THE FIGHT between Johnny Black and the giant at the Frontier saloon found Jake at Kirk's cafe having breakfast as he had every morning since arriving in town. There were other places serving breakfast, but even as a young man he'd taken some comfort in habit. It was still cold as blue blazes, but the weather had cleared, in fact the day was sunny. The coffee was a little stout for his taste, but it was hot and after he finished his eggs, ham, biscuits and grits Jake called for another cup, sat back and turned his thoughts to the events of last night.

That Johnny Black fellow was a mystery. He had moved around town and asked about buying cattle, discussed the area a bit, asked some about buffalo hunting, but this wasn't really cattle buying area. Ranching and buffalo hunting were the two big trades in these parts, with some folks just hanging out or living off business with the fort or the soldiers, but generally the cattle were sold to the fort or driven up to Kansas. Maybe he was a cattle buyer, or maybe he was really a gambler - that was Jake's first thought, but that seemed unlikely. If a man wanted to earn his keep gambling there were much better and a hell of a lot safer places. The Flat sat on the edge of the frontier and Indian raids were common. The town was full of rough men many of whom were here because of some indiscretion somewhere else. Some had left a family or were running from legal trouble. There wasn't any law here except for the soldiers and the vigilantes so in the case of criminals it wasn't a bad place to be. Of course, there were some who had come to seek their fortunes. Yeah, Jake thought, maybe Black was running from something, but a well-groomed man like Johnny Black could change his name and get by in Austin or New Orleans. You were who you decided to be in the West and generally people minded their own affairs.

Jake's thoughts turned to his own situation. A New Yorker by birth, Jake had celebrated his twenty-eighth year on this earth in January. Events had led him to this unlikely place on the Texas frontier with more or less honest employment as a reporter for the Dallas Herald. The editor had offered him the job based on a friendly debate they had engaged in at a saloon in Dallas. Shortly after hiring him he had explained to Jake that he had a great opportunity for him. In fact he had stated it pretty clearly as he proffered the assignment.

"Well, Jake, the army's built a new fort out on the western frontier. I understand there is no shortage of bad men, fallen women, Indians, disease and hard-living out there. A gold mine for a reporter - if you don't get shot, knifed, beaten to death, scalped or catch a disease from the water or the women."

A couple of weeks or so later and here Jake was on the edge of civilization.

THREE

MONDAY, EAST OF THE FLAT, on the bank of the Clear fork of the Brazos, Pete watched the stick carefully as it floated out away from the muddy bank. It seemed to hesitate and then it turned and headed against the current. Pete hauled back on the long tree branch in his hand and after a frozen moment, a three-pound catfish sprung from the water fighting madly as the boy swung the fish upon the bank. Pete's dog, Dandy, a small mutt of unknown origins, began to bark excitedly.

"He's a good one, Dandy!" exclaimed the boy, grabbing the catfish with both hands. "Look Alvin!" he said to his uncle, a slight young man whose nearly baldhead, white hair and lined face gave him an eerie look. Alvin, sitting on the bank feeding wood to a small fire, looked at the catfish, but showed no emotion. Pete unhooked the fish and retrieved a line from the water that held several smaller catfish and one large perch. Stringing the newly caught catfish on the line, he picked up his pole and called to Dandy. "Come on boy, we have enough." Pete walked over to a nearby tree and grabbed an old single shot shotgun leaning against it. Then he turned to his uncle. "Come on Uncle Alvin, it's nearly dinner time."

As Alvin struggled to his feet, the left arm of his coat blew in the wind as he snatched a large flat brimmed hat from a tree branch, jammed it on his balding head where some white hair blew about and grabbed a walking stick leaning against the tree, he followed Pete and Dandy. Pete, Alvin and Dandy the dog struggled up the bank and

13

down the trail. They soon came into a clearing in the trees. Smoke rose from the cabin. Besides the cabin, the clearing held a small barn with a fenced corral on one side and not far from the house sat a smokehouse and a chicken coop. As the group entered the clearing they passed a small fenced enclosure holding a couple of hogs. Alvin had returned to the family farm after losing his arm at Shiloh and had not spoken a work since he had awoken from the operation.

Danny, Pete's step-father and Alvin's brother, was out on the range with what he called his 'crew'. They were branding a few head of longhorn maverick cattle they had found out on the range, along with the occasional calf, but most heifers would birth their calves as the weather turned warmer. Of course it wasn't much of a crew, just the two Lowery brothers and three Mexicans. The Lowery boys were colored teenagers whose family had all been slaves just a few years before, but now sharecropped a little truck farm to the east on land held by their prior owner, while living in a small shack with their mother. Danny hired them by the day to help him round up what mavericks they could find and to cut out his own cattle running the open range with the other area rancher's cattle. He had tried to hire regular hands, but nobody would hire on, and once when he had hired a drifter, the man had worked a few days and disappeared.

The problem was James Baggett whose ranch joined Danny and Alvin's on the north side. Baggett was a mean son-of-a-gun, who, Danny was sure, was stealing his cattle, butchering them and selling them to the army up at the fort. Baggett had the largest spread in the area and saw himself as some sort of land baron. He offered below value for the local land, but other ranchers had sold out to Baggett after their cattle had been run off or stolen and their hands hired away from them or threatened. Danny knew Baggett was threatening and paying off people to keep them from working for him, but there wasn't much he could do. There wasn't a local sheriff and besides, he really didn't have any hard proof.

Barbed wire and the railroad had yet to make it this far south and west, so the cattle were free to roam. In spring and fall, the cowboys would round up the ranches branded cattle and brand the new calves and the mavericks, lone cattle without a brand and not running with a particular herd. The maverick cattle were open to whoever put a brand on them. In fact, sometimes, a cowboy might get a bonus of four bits or so, for every maverick he branded for his owner. This worked sometimes, but often, cowboys would register their own brand and while out on the range, being paid by the ranch owner they were working for, they would put their own brand on strays, trying to build a herd for themselves. Times were hard in Texas. Some folks farmed a little, growing oats and corn, but generally, cattle ranching was the norm. The Civil War had destroyed much of the South and the political and legal structure was a mess at best.

Soldiers were returning from the war, which had ended in 1865. Some after fighting for the Union, most returning to Texas after serving with the Confederate Army and so very many were wounded and damaged by their experience. Northern "carpetbaggers," men hoping to take advantage of the disorganization and opportunity brought on by the end of the war were flooding in. Many of the carpetbaggers were finding jobs in government, closed to those who had fought for the Confederacy. Criminals, cowboys and freed slaves were going hungry as they looked for work or an opportunity to make some money, anyway they could. But also resented and feared were the "scalawags," southern Republicans who had backed the Union during the war and now were in favored positions.

Danny and Alvin Anderson's family had settled in the area before the war and began to ranch when old Camp Cooper was operating north and west of their place. The old Butterfield Stage Route ran through until it was shut down in early '61. After the Homestead Act of 1862 had passed, they waited about a year and then, using their life savings paid one and a quarter dollars each for 160 acres. As the war progressed, both Danny and Alvin had gone to fight leaving their elderly dad and mother to hold on to the property.

Danny had met Rebecca, a southern belle, in Atlanta, Georgia, at a church service while recovering from a war wound. Rebecca's husband had been killed at Gettysburg and left Rebecca a widow with a young son, Pete. Danny courted her and they had married a year after the war ended. Danny had been working on Rebecca's parents' farm, but Danny had felt guilty about his parents and felt he should be home helping them and Alvin, but Rebecca was accustomed to the large city close by. However, after his dad died, Danny felt the overwhelming need to return home. Soon after he returned, his mother had passed. Their parent's stock had gone to almost nothing during the war. They had kept a few hogs, a couple of milk cows, some chickens for the meat and eggs and a big garden, but without the boys help, they couldn't keep the cattle going.

"Over there!" Danny yelled, pointing out a young long- horn that he had spotted not thirty feet from the oldest Lowery boy, Tom.

Danny cut his horse hard, but the horse stepped on a rock and stumbled, then fell, Danny still in the saddle, his right leg under the horse. His leg snapped and Danny screamed even as his horse, terrified, but unhurt struggled to its feet and bolted. Tom and his brother, Jim, slapped their horses and were at Danny's side in less than a minute, both coming out of their saddles with lightning speed. Danny lay on the ground groaning in pain. Using Danny's rifle as a splint, they ripped his shirt up and splinted his leg before easing him onto his horse and leading him home.

The army doctor from the fort had ridden out and set Danny's leg and assured Danny's wife, Rebecca that in time, Danny would be okay, well, as long as some sort of infection didn't set in. Rebecca went outside into the garden and sobbed. It was too much. Life in this horrible place was unbearable. But, after a minute, Rebecca regained her composure. She was Southern born and bred. A lady. Danny had taken her as his wife even though she was not only a widow, but one with a son. If he wanted to make a life on the edge of the frontier, then her place was here.

FATE RIDES A TALL HORSE

FOUR

"BREAKFAST ALL" EXCLAIMED REBECCA from the main room of the small cabin, the room that served as everything except bedroom and outhouse, although occasional visitors did use it to sleep in. Danny, awake for what seemed like hours, reached for the crutch he had carved out of a tree limb, hoisted himself up and then propelled himself out of the bedroom; swinging his splinted and swollen leg. He had just reached the table his daddy had made himself when Alvin and Pete came through the door, Pete carrying a pail of milk.

"Hey pa," said Pete. "Can Alvin and I go fishing today?" he asked.

Struggling to settle at the table with his bad leg, Danny looked at him. "Not today son. I need you and Alvin to go to town with your momma for supplies. I just don't think I better go with this leg." Rebecca sat a bowl of eggs on the table and a towel covered plate of hot biscuits. Then she stepped to a mantle over the fireplace where she picked up a large Bible and handed it to Danny. "Okay, everyone, find a seat and let's pray. Heavenly Father we ask your blessing and guidance. In Jesus name, amen." Handing the Bible back to Rebecca to put up, Danny turned to Pete. "Pete, your momma has the list. Now don't go running off when you get to town. Your momma will need your help loading and counting everything and all."

"Yes pa," answered Pete, happy to go to town, put disap- pointed that he wouldn't be able to play with the other kids that he might see there.

Rebecca was a beautiful young woman and the men looked at her as she drove the wagon through town, Alvin and Pete on the seat beside her. A few people she knew waved. Everyone knew about Danny's leg, because the doctor, who traveled about to help the ill and hurt when he wasn't traveling with the army patrols or treating the endless problems of injury and disease that seemed to be a large part of army life, did his part to spread the local news and gossip.

Pulling up in front of the general store, two young cowboys, covered in dust bumped into each other trying to get to Rebecca's wagon first to help her down. She awarded them with a dazzling smile as they both extended a hand. "Thank you gentlemen," she said, as Pete jumped from the wagon and dashed into the middle of the street, dodging wagons and horses, to greet his friend Adam who was waving excitedly.

"Hey, come on, I found a dead polecat," exclaimed Adam. "I got to help ma," said Pete, his voice pained.

"It'll just take a minute," said Adam, excitement in his voice.

"Let me ask ma," said Pete, turning and rushing into the general store, only to come rushing out only seconds later and the two boys headed off almost as one to look at the dead polecat.

Across the street, on the opposite corner, stood Kirk's restaurant. It was still busy this time of day, although breakfast would be over soon. A young man stood outside, his hat pulled down shading his eyes, which missed nothing as he slowly smoked a hand-rolled cigarette. Men were coming in and leaving the restaurant, but no one looked at or spoke to the man. Everyone in town knew who he was though most had never spoken to him and no one wanted to meet him. He was however, the topic of much of the gossip in town. His name, or at least the name he used, was Clive and he could be found most evenings at one of the saloons, usually playing poker with some success. But it was generally considered an open secret that Clive was nothing more than a gunfighter for hire whose reputation as both a ladies man and a gunfighter was legend. Of course most of what folks thought they knew about Clive came from gossip, but somebody in town had a year old copy of a paper, its headline story about how a gunfighter whose description pretty much matched Clive had stood up to four gunmen at the same time and come out of the gunfight untouched while his four opponents were all dead as doornails. The story went on to talk about other exploits of Clive, who the newspaper story called a man of exceptional skills. The reporter, deep in his story, mentioned that he didn't have time to verify all of the stories about Clive, due to his deadline and all, but he was pretty sure they were all true. According to the story, which in two days, everybody in the area had heard the details of, Clive had killed as many as forty men, always in self- defense, and during the big war, the Civil War, he had fought for the South, making a name for himself as a man who didn't know the meaning of fear. There was other talk too, of stories, rumors really, of a fellow named Clive leading a gang of outlaws back east, of bank robbery and murder, but no one had any real facts. It was all third- and fourth-hand information, passed along.

Clive was watching Rebecca with a keen interest when James Baggett emerged from the cafe, red-eyed and rumpled. Baggett's condition was the result of a late night at the poker table and the faro game in Shane's saloon where the whiskey flowed faster than the gambling action. Baggett was a coarse, heavy set man and the most feared scalawag in six counties. Baggett's foreman, a man known only as Smith and often seen with Baggett when he was drinking, was sitting in a chair someone had left outside of the building, waiting on Baggett. Rebecca was just entering the general store as Baggett stepped out of the restaurant doorway, but when he saw her, his already scowling face turning even harder. "Smith," he spoke, his voice the sound of coarse paper. "There goes that Anderson woman from the Rocking J. Is her husband with her?"

Smith didn't look at Baggett or seem to hear. Then quietly he spoke, "No, just the cripple and the sprout."

"Come on," said Baggett, as he lurched down from the wooden step, still slightly drunk.

Smith tossed his cigarette butt into the street, watched Baggett stagger along for a moment, then rose from his chair with the grace of a cat and without seeming to move, he was one step behind Baggett as they headed for the general store.

Entering the general store, Baggett sees Rebecca reading out loud from a list as the store's owner, Birchfield, an elderly man whose family had come to Texas in the early days, placed items on the counter and yelled orders at a young boy who worked for him. Alvin stood in the corner, staring at a display of garden seeds. "Why good morning," exclaimed Baggett, somehow imagining himself as a friendly looking amiable fellow. "How's your husband faring?" he asked in the general direction of Rebecca.

Rebecca turned and stared at Baggett. "Hello, Mr. Baggett," she said, her voice neutral. "He's getting along well thank you."

"Well, I heard he broke his leg bad," stated Baggett. Rebecca studied him without smiling. "Yes, Mr. Baggett,

he broke his leg, but it is mending well, and thank you for inquiring," she said, turning back to the written notes in her hand.

"Ah, listen here," said Baggett gruffly. "I made your husband a generous offer to buy him out, maybe he didn't tell you."

Without looking up, Rebecca answered. "Oh, he told me Mr. Baggett and the answer is still no thank you." She turned to smile at him then, noticing Smith, leaning against the counter, for the first time, felt the old fear of Baggett and the men that worked for him. Smith's mouth turned up just slightly at the corners, just a little, to let her know he saw her looking at him. Rebecca's face flushed just a bit and she trembled slightly as she turned back to her list.

"You and your husband might want to rethink your position," said Baggett, a hint of a threat in his voice.

Suddenly, Rebecca whirled around. "Why is that?" she demanded.

Surprised, Baggett seemed stunned for a moment before he replied. "I own all the land around you folks. My cattle and my men are gonna be all over your place keeping up with my cattle. I just don't want anybody to get hurt, accidentally I mean, what with all the confusion and all."

"I trust you will continue to be a good neighbor Mr. Baggett, as will we," she replied, smiling then turning once again to her shopping.

Baggett stood there for a minute, and then he smiled broadly. "Well, tell your husband I hope he mends well, good- day." With that, Baggett strove out the door, shoving his hat on his head as he stomped out, Smith followed without a word.

FATE RIDES A TALL HORSE

FIVE

A WEEK HAD PASSED and, having accomplished nothing, Jake was headed down to Kirk's for breakfast much later than usual, but he hadn't fallen asleep until nearly three in the morning. As he neared his destination he noticed an attractive woman in front of Birchfield's general store. Although he noticed her beauty, it was something else that caught his attention. The woman looked like she should be in New York or Atlanta maybe. Her clothes and manner were different. City like, was what he realized at once. Another city-dweller who had come west, but had yet to adapt, he considered. But she carried herself with a confidence and self-assurance he had seen often in women. Strength of character, a trait missing in many of the men he had known.

"Welcome Mrs. Anderson, how are you today?" announced Birchfield, opening the door to his store to let Rebecca enter.

Jake kept walking, thinking about the Anderson woman and wondering what had brought her to this place when he entered Kirk's. Establishing himself at his usual table he enjoyed his breakfast and after lingering long enough to drink three cups of coffee, decided to visit the fort. Jake had posted three stories back to the Herald, but they weren't really news and his boss wasn't happy. He was expecting stories about outlaws, gun-fights and Indians. Jake's stories had been about life at the fort, the local settlement and the weather. He sat thinking maybe he could interview someone who had actually seen some Indians. It was a bit of a walk back down to the livery which was located across the street from the hotel. As he walked down the street he passed a number of tents and open fires as men began their day. It seemed like there were a dozen tents filling spots that had been bare the day before, he thought as he looked at the black cloud mass building in the north. Arriving at Whitt's livery, now wondering if he should go back to the hotel for his slicker, Jake encountered Black. He was talking intently to Whitt and pointing to his ear. Strange, he thought. Whitt shook his head no, and Black turned away toward a stall to fetch his horse.

A few minutes later, having saddled his misnamed horse, Hurricane, Jake led him out and found Black atop a horse that must have stood 18 hands and had a huge barrel of a chest. Jake, stunned at the size of the horse, noticed with horror that he had on a halter and reins, but no bit. Flop came out of the building as he greeted Black. "Good morning Mr. Black," Jake said.

Johnny looked at him for a moment, then said "Morning reporter."

"Jake. Jake Evans."

Johnny nodded, "I remember you from the Busy Bee," he said. Then, looking at Jake for moment, "and the Frontier. You following me?"

"Why no," Jake said, a bit stunned. "I'm looking for stories, so I've been moving around and now I'm headed out to the fort for the same reason." Black nodded. "Mr. Black," said Jake, admiring the horse, "That is, without doubt, the biggest horse I have ever seen."

"Johnny," he corrected Jake, leaning forward and stroking the big black horse's neck. "Name's Loco; just a shade over 19 hands."

"Loco, that's Spanish for crazy isn't it?" Jake asked, staring warily at the big horse.

"It is," Johnny said. "I got him from some fellows down San Antonio way. They couldn't break him or even get him to take a bit. Called him caballo loco, meaning crazy horse, so I called him Loco for short." As it turned out, Johnny was on his way to the fort also.

"Going to visit around a little," he said, so they rode toward the fort together.

Johnny was, as noted earlier, a quiet man, not prone to talk, but the silence made Evans uneasy somehow and he wanted to know this man. Most folks, including Jake, weren't keen to discuss the war, but he had heard quite a bit of talk about reconstruction in Texas so he eased into the subject as he and Black walked the horses up the hill toward the fort, not sure where Black stood and not wanting to offend him. Johnny was noncommittal for the most part, not saying much, but talking in general terms when he did comment, so he revealed little about himself. Inquisitive by nature Evans guessed that was why he had agreed to work as a reporter, he wanted badly to ask this man who he was, where he was from and what he was doing in this god-forsaken part of the country. But that would have been bad manners. When they first met at the poker table he had tried to draw Black out by talking about how he had hired on as a reporter. Black had listened politely, made a few comments, but didn't talk about himself.

They arrived at the top of the hill to find a small plateau covered with humanity, smoke, noise and activity. Jake took in the pleasure of the smell of fresh bread coming from a large stone building on the east side of the fort's area. Things appeared to be chaotic at first glance, but as Jake and Johnny eased the horses along between tents and tiny wooden buildings they would see workers building permanent stone structures, soldiers drilling in formations and women scrubbing clothes in large tubs placed over open fires. A wagon eased by carrying large stones from the river area. He was so taken with the scene

Jake rode right past Johnny and Loco. Realizing it, he turned back. Johnny had dismounted and Loco had drifted over to a patch of grass. Johnny, with Flop laying a foot away, was talking to a group of soldiers standing around a very large hole in the ground with a structure built of large tree branches and ropes and a pulley built over it. A rope disappeared down into the hole and several men were pulling on the rope. He wasn't sure about turning Hurricane loose, so holding the reins in his hand he eased up to the hole and looked down into it. There were a half a dozen men in the hole with picks and shovels digging. "What the devil," Jake said to no one.

"Water. The witching stick says there's water down there," growled an older soldier with sergeant stripes on his arm standing nearby. "Damn it" he suddenly bellowed, causing Jake to jump. "Beauchamp, you haven't filled a bucket all morning. Get to work afore I come down there and kick your skinny ass!" The sergeant turned his head in Jake's direction and spit a stream of tobacco that came within inches of his muddy boots. Jake moved back and looked around. Johnny was still conversing with the soldiers digging the well and he led Hurricane toward a structure with an American flag hung on a pole in front of it. It had to be the headquarters. Entering the building, Jake was confronted by a soldier busy with paperwork at a desk just inside the door of a larger building. Jake asked to see the Commander. "The commander is a very busy man," stated the soldier, barely looking up as he spoke. Jake used the magic words. "I'm a reporter."

The soldier looked up and quickly stood. "Let me see if the Commander can see you."

The fort Commander turned out to be a Lieutenant Colonel, a career Calvary officer who was an experienced Indian fighter. After Jake expressed interest in a story about Indians, the fort's commander suggested Jake join him for lunch in a couple of hours, but in the meantime he suggested Jake talk to the Sergeant Major who had recently led a patrol that had engaged a small raiding party of Kiowa. The Sergeant Major was supervising the construction of a building to hold the fort's weapons and powder. As Evans left the commander's building, huge, black clouds in the north were blocking out the sun and that meant rain and maybe a storm, he noted with some concern. As he waited for a wagon to pass so he could cross the road he saw soldiers breaking away from their duties to stare at something coming down the road. Standing transfixed he watched a lone rider coming toward the headquarters building with soldiers gathering and walking along side, staring at the man on the horse. As he reached the headquarters and turned his horse in Jake looked at the man on the horse - and vomited.

There were many horrific sights during the war and Jake had personally seen more than his share of them, but the man on the horse was missing his scalp, his nose and both of his ears. Surprisingly, there wasn't much blood. The man's eyes were open, but glassy looking. Shirtless and barefoot, he pulled the horse to a stop and slumped in the saddle. It was then Jake noticed the man had been tied to the saddle with rawhide strips. The doctor arrived and pushed people back as soldiers cut the man loose and lowered him to the ground.

"Comanches," someone stated in a flat, final tone.

FATE RIDES A TALL HORSE

SIX

REBECCA STOOD IN THE STREET along with a number of others watching the big, dark clouds in the north. A storm was coming. Maybe she should stay in town, but then Danny would worry. Better to get on across the river. It could become swollen when it rained heavy in the north. Rebecca, Alvin, Pete and Dandy the dog began the long ride home, the wagon heavy now with the supplies, which had been carefully loaded and covered with an old tarp to keep the rain out and the dust off as much as possible. Having broken out the fried chicken she had packed for the trip and passed it to Alvin and Pete, Rebecca, lost in thought, let Pete take the reins, a fact that thrilled him. Her mind was trying to recall the exact words Mr. Baggett had said, something about people getting hurt and that Smith man, a dangerous man according to the town gossip, but he seemed nice, although he hadn't actually said nor done anything. Maybe the gossip was, as usual, just people trying to put some excitement in their lives, the thought of a dangerous man moving about town somehow added to the routine of everyday life. Oh God, she thought, this is such a terrible place. The heavily laden wagon churned slowly down the hill, creaking and groaning under the weight as it followed the hard, rutted trail. Dandy was happily perched in the back, barking at numerous unseen animals and smells. Alvin sat, his face impassive, chewing on a fried chicken leg, while Rebecca thought and Pete clucked at the horses and imagined himself a stagecoach driver trying to get away from a bloodthirsty gang of Indians.

Back at their cabin, Danny struggled to his feet, using the crutches that Alvin had made from a dead tree. He hobbled to the front door, having to lean against the wall to get the door open and propel him outside to the porch. His leg was hurting badly, but he refused to take the laudanum the doctor had left him. Finally, getting on the porch, he looked out toward the west at the building black clouds. Rebecca and the others would have to cross the river at a shallow ford on the way back, one that became a raging creek when there was a heavy rain. Surely they were well on their way back and hurrying as they saw the clouds building. He looked at the sun, almost covered now by the building thunderclouds. He began to figure the time in his head. They would have reached town by mid-morning. Two hours perhaps to buy the supplies and load the wagon. They had packed a lunch, but surely they wouldn't stop to picnic after seeing the sky. Okay, if they left by noon, it would take a good two hours to reach the creek; it would be close. Maybe they saw the clouds building and stayed in town. Danny's brow crinkled in worry as lightening flashed across the sky. He was so concerned he almost forgot about the horses. He had to get the barn open and let them get in. Gripping the crutches hard he eased down the porch and began to work his way toward the corral.

A tremendous clap of thunder and a flash of lightening broke Rebecca's concentration. She looked up at the darkening sky as rain began to fall heavily. "Oh no," she said, reaching to take the reins from Pete, who, shook out of his daydreaming by the thunder, was staring in surprise at the sky. "We've got to hurry," she said, more to herself than the others, as Dandy began to bark incessantly at the sky. It has probably been raining in the north; the river may already be awash, thought Rebecca as she shook the reins trying to hurry the horses. As she urged the horses to move ever faster, Alvin looked at her and then the sky, his face never changing expression, as though it was somehow frozen, his now stripped chicken bone still grasped in his hand and rain running down his face. "Let's go!" Rebecca shouted at the horses.

• • •

At the Rocking J, the storm had put the horses on edge. They stomped around the corral, shaking their heads and neighing loudly. Danny managed to reach the barn, enter the side door and work his way to the wide doors that opened to the corral, but his leg was hurting so badly he began to feel faint. Perhaps he should have taken a shot of the laudanum, but it was too late now. He managed to push one of the doors open and immediately three of their four horses bolted through into the safety of the barn. Danny called to the fourth horse, a sandy- yellow dun with a dark brown mane, that stood a good 16 hands they called Mule, because he was so stubborn. "Mule," he yelled, "come on boy!"

Mule, shaking his great head and whinnying, ran around the perimeter of the corral, but wouldn't come near the door to the barn.

Clutching his crutches, and glancing at the ever-darkening sky, Danny moved out into the corral to herd Mule into the barn. As he reached the center of the corral, another thunderclap and bolt of lightning erupted, causing Mule to rear up on his hind legs and then charge toward the barn. Had he not been dependent on the crutches, Danny could have easily moved aside, but the huge horse hit him full force as he went by, spinning Danny around and off balance. His hands reaching for something to grab, but finding only air, Danny's head hit the hard packed earth hard and he did not notice the rain that began to fall.

• • •

The clouds had turned the sky completely black, the winds blowing strong now, with the smell of rain and Rebecca's face was strained as she urged the horses on down the hill and toward the river. Dandy continued to bark, Pete felt his mother's fear, but he really didn't understand it. He had no reference never having seen a dry creek bed turn into a raging river in minutes. There! Rebecca could see the trees that lined the creek as they began to reach the bottom part of the road that ran from the flat land up the hill to the fort. Rebecca continued to slap the reins and now began to yell at the horses.

Water was already running knee deep in the formerly dry creek bed when they reached it. Rebecca eased the rain drenched horses to a halt. Then Rebecca yelled and slapped the horses with the reins and they plunged into the creek, stepping sluggishly in the deepening water; the wagon following seemed to sink, then began to rock. They moved forward, Rebecca slapping the reins and screaming, Alvin and Pete hanging on for dear life and even Dandy quiet now.

Everything seemed to be in slow motion, but they were moving, then just as Rebecca began to feel relief, the wagon stopped and she could feel the wheels sinking. "No!" She screamed, to no one in particular. Tears began to stream from her eyes, mixing with the rain. Everything was frozen in time and then as if in a dream, she saw Alvin in the creek, tugging at the horses with his one arm. How had he gotten there she wondered, just as the wagon began to move again. "Hyaaaa!" she screamed at the horses.

In a minute the horses had made the far bank and the wagon rolled from the creek, but even as it erupted onto the bank, rain was falling so heavy it was hard to see. The horses tried to rear up, but Alvin still

34

had a hold on the harness. He guided them away from the creek and then climbed up onto the wagon bench, took the reins from Rebecca who was sitting motionless, crying and as Alvin slapped the reins causing the horses to lurch forward toward the ranch and home.

• • •

Danny saw a winged horse flying toward him. And everything was red. Was he in Hell he thought? Then he realized he was very, very cold. Wasn't it hot in Hell? As he opened his eyes he was further confused. Everything was very blurry. He was in the water, no wonder he was cold. Then he realized his head was hurting very badly and something was hitting his face. He covered his face and head with his arms and hand and began to shout at them. "Stop, for God's sake, stop," he cried out, but they continued to hit him. His head was hurting so bad he hardly felt the blows, and then he realized they were no longer hitting him, but he was cold again and his head was hurting so bad. He moved his arms and opened his eyes. It was raining very hard.

He was soaked and lying in the mud in the corral. Suddenly he remembered. He was trying to get Mule in the barn, because the storm was coming. He must have hit his head. It hurt. He had to get up. One of his crutches was lying a few feet away. Slowly he crawled over to it, grasped it and managed to get to his feet. He was halfway to the house struggling with the one crutch, trying to convince himself that Rebecca, Pete and Alvin were okay, waiting out the storm in town when he heard them yelling at him. He looked and saw them all, as wet and muddy as him waving from the wagon as the horses sped up, sensing food and shelter. "Thank you Lord," he said out loud.

Covered in blankets, sipping coffee, everyone, except for Alvin of course, was talking. They were going over the details of the great storm that was still raging outside. The terrible wind, Alvin jumping into the creek to pull the horses through with his one arm, Danny awaking in the corral, thinking he was in the river. Pete couldn't wait to tell Adam about it and his mom and dad had let him have coffee with lots of cream and sugar. Normally, he only got coffee at Christmas. What an adventure! Finally, as the excitement died now, Danny insisted they all pray and thank God for delivering them safely through the storm.

SEVEN

FIRST THE WIND PICKED UP and then rain began to fall. Slow at first and then it was coming down in a torrent as the soldiers and civilians at the fort ran for cover. Jake cursed himself for not bringing his slicker. The disfigured man who had ridden in had been given some morphine by the fort doctor and although he was in shock and the doctor said either the shock or infection would soon kill him, he managed to get out some of his story. He and two fellow buffalo-hunters had been camped some five miles northwest when they were suddenly attacked by a small band of Comanche. He didn't know how many. The band had charged their horses into the small camp at dawn and he had been knocked out after being run over by a horse. When he came to, he was being scalped.

The Indians had killed and scalped his partners, tied him to a horse and ran it off. The horse found its way back. The rain stopped about 2 a.m. and Johnny and Jake, along with a couple of soldiers and a handful of buffalo-hunters joined an army patrol intent on seeking out the renegades. Although he had ridden south with an 1860 Colt Army revolver in a saddle pommel holster and had a holster rig in his saddlebag, Jake didn't wear or carry a gun around the Flat. He had explained to Johnny that he thought as a reporter he should try to show a neutral state. With great reluctance, Lieutenant Angleton had loaned Jake his personal 1866 lever-action Winchester, known as a "yellow boy" in reference to the gold colored loading gate on the side and after promising to take good care of it, Jake had tied it and its scabbard to his saddle. Jake admired it, remembering that it was the same type rifle Johnny carried, except it was longer. The Lieutenant had explained the model came in three versions. A long barreled musket model was available, while he had the rifle, which sported a barrel just over twenty-four inches long. Johnny had admired it and mentioned to the Lieutenant that he carried the carbine which had a twenty-inch barrel.

Other than a brief stop for hardtack and biscuits while they rested the horses, they had been riding all morning and Jake was regretting his decision to come. He was daydreaming, writing the story about the disfigured hunter in his head, when the air was filled with screams, smoke, gunfire and arrows. The posse was immediately thrown into chaos.

A low dip in the plain had hidden the horse-mounted Comanches who fell upon the posse like a pack of wolves. It happened so fast at first Jake wasn't afraid, just confused as his mind struggled to understand what was happening. Out of the corner of his eye an Indian, his knees clammed to the sides of a pony, was charging him from a few yards away, as he drew back a big tomahawk decorated with feathers. Jake yanked the rifle from its scabbard, swung it and levered it at the same time, then turned and fired. The Indian's horse continued to charge as the Indian, a look of surprise on his face, slowly leaned backward as the tomahawk fell from his hand. Jake jerked hard on his horse's reins pulling him to the left and his horse reared up just as it collided with the Indian's horse and seemed to bounce sideways. Jake saw the Indian flying through the air. His own horse collapsed and fell forward pitching Jake onto the ground where he tumbled, the breath knocked out of him. As he struggled to his feet, he saw an Indian on the ground raise his bow when suddenly the Indian's head exploded. A wave of fear swept through Jake's body as he looked around for his rifle, but hearing a shout over the din he looked up to see Loco bearing down on him.

As the huge horse flew by, Johnny reached down and grabbed Jake by the back of his shirt, dragging him several feet before lifting and swinging him, flopping and waving his arms, one-armed onto Loco's broad back. Jake grabbed onto Johnny with all his might, trying desperately to hang on as Loco charged into the fray.

Having hoisted Jake onto Loco's back, Johnny began firing handguns with both hands. Jake couldn't see very well clinging to Johnny's back, but as Loco turned and jumped and dashed, he saw a cowboy grab an arrow protruding out of his arm and break it off. An Indian was flung from his horse. It was mass confusion. Smoke, gunfire, shouting, screams and dirt flew through the air. Then without warning, Loco stopped and Johnny turned in his saddle, reached around and grabbed Jake with his right hand. Suddenly Jake found himself sailing through the air and saw Loco bounding away. He hit the ground hard, but came up fast he was so surprised, not to mention terrified. The Indians were retreating in a dead run with Johnny and the patrol in hot pursuit.

Jake surveyed the area. Three horses were down. One was kicking and whinnying. Two cowboys he did not recognize were on horseback. One of them fired a shot from a rifle into an Indian lying on the ground. The other jumped down, fired his handgun into the injured horse's head and then holstered his gun, kneeling down beside an unmoving cowboy in a red shirt. Noticing a rifle lying on the ground he was surprised to see it was his borrowed one. Jake picked it up, walked over to his own horse that was breathing heavily and trying to get up, but could not. Jake saw at once its front legs were broken. He squatted down by Hurricane, stroked his neck, spoke softly to him and then stood and shot him in the head, ending his pain. With tears stinging his eyes, he went to see if he could help the cowboy on the ground. Jake was surprised when he noticed Captain Bates had not joined in the pursuit of the Indians. He was sitting on his horse and appeared to be in shock.

The cowboy was dead and in a few minutes Johnny and the remainder of the patrol rode up. The riders were in high spirits. Four Indians had been killed for sure, and it was generally accepted that several more had been hit by gunfire, but hung on to their horses. Jake's gaze picked Johnny out of the group. Johnny looked like his normal self. Relaxed, but unsmiling. Unhurriedly, Johnny pulled out one of his little cigarillos and lit it with a match.

Entering the fort the group was treated as conquering heroes, but the mood was contained by the death of a ranch hand from the Easy L, and a soldier. Besides the two deaths, there were two wounded. A buffalo-hunter named Petrie had a bad gash in his thigh and the other wounded man was the cowboy Jake had seen with the arrow in his arm. Everyone was reminded of the dangers of living on the edge of the frontier. Jake felt as weak as a new born kitten. Johnny found Flop, whom he had left in the care of the cook at the fort and then he and Jake rode into town, with Jake on the back of Loco, hanging onto Johnny, who let him off at the hotel as he walked Loco on down to the livery, Flop trailing along.

Jake entered the hotel on wobbly legs, glad to have a real story at last, but a little shaken, his youthful thoughts of invincibility, confirmed in part because he had survived the war, were now shaken.

EIGHT

JAMES BAGGETT WAS IN A FOUL MOOD and the more whiskey he drank, the fouler his mood. He couldn't seem to think of a way to force the Andersons to sell to him. He had even paid that shyster, Ladd, that idiot that called himself a lawyer, to look into the deed, and the fool said not only was the deed solid, but the Andersons owned the place free and clear. How could that be, he wondered? The fact that they didn't owe any money on the land was going to make it a little harder to use his money and power to squeeze them. The money he was passing to the politicians in Austin was of no help either. This just didn't seem to be a situation where they could help him, but he had to keep paying them, because as he moved forward on his plan to be the biggest, richest rancher in Texas he knew they would come in handy. He got up and poured himself another drink.

Oh, he had been thrilled when he heard that Danny Anderson had broken his leg. It seemed like there had to be some way to take advantage of that. Then, it occurred to him. The parents must have come into some money and passed it on to the kids. He made a mental note to himself to have Ladd see just how and when the land was paid for. How were they going to pay the taxes on the place? The government had thought up all kinds of taxes to help pay for the reconstruction of the South. Well, maybe they planned to put together enough cows to sell. Now, that was something he could put a stop to.

But if the Andersons had money, it must be buried somewhere on their place. Probably around the house somewhere.

Well, by golly, he would think of something, and of course there were always the alternative methods, ones he had been forced to use on a couple of other reluctant families. Patience wasn't one of his virtues.

Quite drunk now, Baggett had talked himself into taking action regarding the Andersons. He needed to get that land and move on with his expansion plans. Besides that, the railroad was coming and nobody seemed to know exactly where it was going to pass on its way west, but wherever it was, Baggett planned to own the land. Hoisting himself to his feet, he staggered out the door and across the yard to one of the ranch's three bunkhouses. It was the one where his foreman, Smith bunked.

Yells and curse words flowed from the bunkhouse as Baggett neared it. Inside he found ten or so men, some of them sitting or standing around a rough-hewn pine table where five cowhands were playing poker. A couple were cleaning guns, one was reading a dime novel and most were smoking, so the place had a blue haze about it.

"Smith," yelled Baggett, over the din in the room.

Smith, sitting at the card table, but obscured by several of the men watching, slowly turned his head toward the sound of Baggett's voice. "Deal me out for a bit, boys," he said, slowly rising from his chair.

Baggett, swaying as he tried to pick Smith out of the crowded, smoky room, was startled when Smith appeared in front of him.

"Let's step outside," said Smith, taking Baggett's arm and leading him out the door.

"I want you to send a few men over to the Andersons place tonight and burn 'em out. Make it look like an Indian raid," demanded Baggett, drunkenly, "I want to find their money."

"Well, I don't think that is a very good idea," stated Smith calmly, "but tell me about the money," he encouraged the drunken Baggett. "I'll look into it."

NINE

NOTHING LIKE SHARING A BATTLE to make friends was something Jake had read somewhere and he figured there was some truth to it. It had been three days since Johnny and he had joined the posse. They had eaten breakfast together each morning since and had greeted each other in one or other of the saloons each evening. During the day Jake was generally busy trying to find a news story that would satisfy his editor and Johnny was usually 'visiting around a bit' as he would say.

They were buttering hot biscuits when Johnny spoke, catching Jake by surprise. "You did well." Jake looked up. "When the Indians hit us. You stood your ground, didn't panic. You an experienced Indian fighter?"

Jake smiled. "No, Indian fighter I'm not. Frankly, that was the first time I've seen an Indian, well, except for the Tonkawa around the fort."

"The war then" asked Johnny?

"Yes" said Jake. "I was there, mainly towards the end. I didn't fight. I was sort of support."

Johnny nodded. Then, "I'm looking for a man," he said.

After a moment Jake stupidly repeated what Johnny had just told him, "You're looking for a man." Johnny went on eating his breakfast.

Finally, Jake recovered enough to make some sense. "Did you come out here to find him?" he asked.

"Yep."

"Do you know for sure he's here?" "Nope."

"Oh," said Jake, confused. Finally, he asked, "This fellow a friend of yours?"

Johnny looked up from his breakfast, he said, "No, I'm going to kill him."

He had Jake's full attention now. "Kill him, huh. Bad blood between you then."

"You don't seem all that bright for a reporter." "Sorry, I'm just surprised is all."

"The man tried to shoot me in the back, but it was dark and he shot and killed the wrong man. The man he killed was my younger brother, Billy. By the time I got after him he had realized what he had done and had taken off out of town. That was a nearly a year ago. I've been trailing him ever since. I missed him by about a month in Tyler, and a couple of weeks in Dallas, but picked up some information that he was headed out here."

"Dang," was all Jake could think to say.

Johnny looked at him for a long moment, slowly chewing his breakfast ham. "Fellow's name is Kyle Stephens or at least that's the name he was using. Fancies himself a gambler and a gunfighter, but really he's just a bottom-feeding low-life that preys on the weak. He had a reputation around town as a bully. I had seen him around, in some saloons and horse sales, and he was sort of a foreman for an old man that raised quarter-horses in Tennessee. I went out to the old man's ranch looking to buy a horse and I rode up on Stephens using a blacksnake on a young Mexican woman. She was lying on the ground crying and a wash pail full of laundry was turned over in the dirt. I guess she was a housekeeper. He had peeled a good bit of skin off her with the whip. He was yelling at her. Asking her what made her think she was too good for him. I told him enough. Well, he stopped for a minute, looked at me and told me to mind my own damn business. Johnny took another sip of coffee, set the cup down and continued.

"When he reared back with that bull-whip again I shot off a goodly part of his left ear. Well, actually, to be fair my shot was a little off and the bullet cut a deep grove in the left side of his face before it took off most of his ear. That stopped him, but left the man a bit peaked at me." Shaking his head and frowning, he said, "I should have done the world a favor and killed the bastard where he stood."

FATE RIDES A TALL HORSE

TEN

THE DAY AFTER THE STORM, Danny and his family took the wagon into town and up to the fort so the doctor could take a look at Danny. Rebecca, Alvin and Pete were in the general store to get a candy. Danny was hobbling across the street alone, headed over to the feed store, when Baggett stepped off the sidewalk, and walked straight toward him, causing Danny to stop in the middle of the street, supporting himself on his tree branch crutch. A buffalo-hunter's wagon full of buffalo hides had to stop so as not to run them down.

Confronting Danny, Baggett spoke loud enough for everyone on the sidewalks to hear. "I'm missing some horses. Thinking maybe they found their way down to your corral."

"You know I am not a thief, "said Danny quietly.

"Well, I'm thinking maybe you are. So what do you say to that?"

Danny started at Baggett silently. Suddenly, Baggett slapped Danny hard across the face. Danny simply stared at him while his cheek turned bright red. Baggett grinned.

"What the hell? You really not gonna fight back?" Baggett turned to his left, looking at his small army of paid underlings watching from the sidewalk. "You knot heads ever seen anything like this?" he asked.

"I saw a guy wouldn't fire his rifle during the war," said a fat dirty man wearing a hat that was covered in grease stains.

Turning his head back toward Danny, Baggett spit a stream of tobacco juice onto Danny's shirt, some of it bouncing back on Baggett himself. Danny didn't move. Silence hung with a stillness that felt heavy while the tobacco juice slowly spread down Danny's shirt. Danny stood motionless, staring into Baggett's face. Suddenly, tired of the game, Baggett turned and started for the saloon, his motley crew following him. Danny stood frozen for a minute, and then crossed the street. A few men watched, but said nothing.

Standing in the door of the hotel, Johnny and Jake, just arriving back from their breakfast at Kirk's watched the scene play out.

"That's Danny Anderson works a spread up north. The Rocking J. He's a coward," exclaimed Jake, "and married to that breathtaking beauty. It doesn't make sense, a woman like that."

"You got it backward," said Johnny. "He's a very brave man. I hear he's a religious man and it takes a lot of courage to stand by your convictions in a situation like that; especially out here on the frontier. I admire him."

ELEVEN

IT WAS ONE OF THOSE THINGS you can't account for. The sun had set only an hour before, but a low cloud cover created an unnatural darkness. The day had been uncommonly warm for early March and the heat had caused the horse droppings and the outhouses to smell something terrible. The streets were still packed with people, horses, oxen, donkeys and wagons trying to get somewhere as if night had caught the town by surprise. The Flat was exploding with growth and all of the stores were doing a brisk business.

Johnny and Jake had just stepped out of the hotel and taken a step or two toward the street with Flop at Johnny's heels when a fellow coming down the wooden sidewalk in a hurry looked back and bumped into Johnny who turned just as a flame flashed across the street as a shot ran out and the man jerked, a red hole appearing in his white shirt.

Before Johnny could react a second shot rang out hitting Johnny in his left side, just under his ribcage. Instinctively, Johnny pulled his revolver, even as his legs gave way. He toppled off the wooden sidewalk onto his face, even as he tried to see where the shots had come from. Flop began barking loudly as everyone on the block ran for cover.

Random gunshots were not uncommon in town as cow- boys, buffalo-hunters and drifters got drunk day and night and would sometimes take out their weapons and fire into the air or have an impromptu shooting contest. And there was the occasional accidental discharge, but two quick gunshots, this early in the evening was likely to be trouble.

Jake had taken to wearing his revolver after the Indian fight. He drew his weapon and jumped down behind a water trough set up for horses. He peered over the trough but couldn't see anything. He looked back just in time to see the blood stain spreading across Johnny's back. Jake jumped into action, quickly crawling back to Johnny, throwing himself down beside him and pulling a handkerchief from his pocket, he clamped it over the hole in Johnny's back, staunching the flow of blood. Jake slid his hand under Johnny and felt for the wound. He found a small hole in the front and blood was bubbling out slowly, but he was bleeding pretty badly from the larger hole in his back where the bullet had exited. Jake glanced at the man shot in the chest who appeared dead. He turned his focus to Johnny. He was still bleeding badly from the exit wound and Jake's hand was slippery with his blood.

"You're okay," Jake said, mostly to himself.

"Are you a doctor?" someone asked from a small crowd that had gathered after determining the shooting was over and someone had realized that at least one person had been hit.

"No, I'm a reporter" Jake said, not looking up from his work. "Can you fellows help me get him upstairs?" he asked, looking at the group of onlookers. No one moved for a moment, then one started forward and in a few seconds, Jake held the handkerchief in place as two men lifted him up and carried him up the stairs to Jake's room, Flop trailing close behind. A woman followed, telling Jake she had been a nurse during the war.

"Please come and help," he said.

On the rooftop across the street, Kyle Stephens smiled. He'd killed the son-of-a-gun, he thought to himself. Now he could go into town, have a drink, play some faro. No more hiding out on Baggett's spread pretending to be saving his money to start his own herd and staying behind when everybody went to town. He could tell nobody believed him, but he didn't care. Nobody's business why he stayed behind. He pulled his tobacco pouch out, then thought better of it, instead taking a flask from his boot and taking a long drink. Wiping his lips with his shirt sleeve he peered over the top of the building and cursed.

"What the hell," he muttered to himself. The fellow that got in the way was being ignored, dead most likely, but people were carrying Black inside. "Did he not kill the bastard?" he thought.

Well, now he'd have to lay low, ask his half-brother Smith to find out what was happening with Black. He'd asked Smith to kill the man, but Smith refused. Said he needed to deal with his own problems. Of course, Kyle Stephens wasn't his real name. In fact he was currently using Kyle Lambert, but his real name was Kyle Smith.

Johnny was lain on the bed and Jake leaned over to look at his wound. Gunshot wounds were often fatal, he thought to himself, but then that was often from infection and he had read Lister's paper that had been published in a medical journal, the Lancet, a year before about cleaning and disinfecting wounds. He asked the men to step outside and asked the woman to hold pressure on the wound with a towel as he removed the handkerchief. Hurriedly, he washed his hands and reaching under the bed, he removed a leather bag. Quickly, pulling a pair of scissors from his bag, he cut away Johnny's blood-soaked shirt. He told the woman to step back as he washed Johnny's wound and poured a mixture of water and carbolic acid in and around it. After drying it with a clean towel, he stuffed some cotton soaked with the solution into the wounds, and sutured the wounds front and back with silk thread using a flat, curved suture needle. Then pulling a roll of cloth and tape from his bag he dressed Johnny's wound.

"There," he announced to no one.

"You're a doctor," the woman stated, a note of surprise in her voice.

"Not really, ma'am," Jake said. "I picked up a bit here and there during the war."

"But you have a doctor's bag," she insisted.

"Won it in a poker game, during the war," he stated flatly. "Oh, I see," she said.

"Thank you for your help," he said, taking a gold three dollar coin from his pocket and handing it to her.

She didn't object, just looked at the coin in her hand and said, "Thank you doctor."

Johnny opened his eyes and looked at Jake. Jake could tell from the expression on Johnny's face he was in a lot of pain. "Here," he said, rising from the only chair in the small room, "let me get you some laudanum."

"What about the other one?" Johnny asked, as Jake spooned some laudanum into his mouth.

"The fellow that bumped into you died on the spot."

"Am I bad hurt?" asked Johnny, reaching over with his hand to touch the bandage. "Hurts like hell."

"Just a scratch," Jake said. "Hardly worth noticing."

Looking at the blood covered Jake, Johnny said, "Were you hit?"

"No, all this blood is yours," Jake stated calmly. "Bullet went through clean, but it bled a lot."

"There's a lot of blood. You sure I am not dying?" said Johnny with a hint of a smile.

Jake smiled at him. "Pretty sure. You'll be weak for a few days, and then you'll be good as new."

Johnny started trying to rise up. "Whoa!" exclaimed Jake, jumping up. "Got to see to Flop."

"I'll get it done." At the sound of his name, Flop, who had been lying on the floor in the corner of the room, jumped up and padded over to where to Johnny sat.

Easing back on the bed, Johnny ran his hand over Flop's head. "Good boy," he said softly to Flop. "Who patched me up?" he asked.

"I did." said Jake softly, hesitating, then "helped some in the war."

Johnny stared at Jake for a long moment, then said "I owe you reporter," and closed his eyes.

'Who is Johnny Black?' thought Jake, not for the first time, as he stared at Johnny's scarred torso. There were faded tattoos on both forearms, knife wounds, old gunshot wounds and some scars from shrapnel, he noted as he covered him with the blanket.

Johnny thrashed about in the bed and Jake, trying to sleep in a chair, rose and fished a bottle of morphine out of his bag. Using a dropper, he squeezed a few drops into Johnny's mouth. Johnny opened his eyes and looked at Jake.

"That you reporter, or have I crossed over?" he asked.

"It's me," said Jake. "I gave you some morphine, you'll feel better in a few minutes."

Johnny closed his eyes and Jake eased back into the chair.

The candle casting a dim light over the room had burned low when a scream split the air and Johnny, his system in shock, his senses dulled by laudanum and morphine, instinctively tried to rise, but the pain stopped him and as he gazed around, Johnny saw Flop was on his feet, but did not appear alarmed. Jake, still sitting in the chair, a blanket over his legs, was thrashing and talking. It took a moment, but Johnny realized Jake was having a nightmare and had screamed in his sleep. Flop let out one sharp bark.

"What?" asked Jake, his voice thick with sleep. "You screamed in your sleep," said Johnny said.

Sitting up in the chair, Jake shook his head. "Sorry," he said, "I was a doctor in the war," began Jake, somewhat hesitantly.

"I had completed my training and I thought as a doctor I could deal with the wounds, but I just wasn't prepared for the carnage. I have nightmares." Johnny stared at him.

"I'm from New York," Jake continued. "I volunteered as a contract surgeon for the Union." He stared at Johnny, knowing that in Texas, someone siding with the North was considered a traitor, as though Texas was its own country.

Johnny didn't speak for several minutes, then, "I spent most of my youth in the San Antonio area." He seemed about to say more, but he closed his eyes and soon Jake could hear his ragged breathing.

TWELVE

THE SUN WAS SETTING in the western sky, two days since the storm. The weather was so warm and sunny the storm seemed almost like a dream. Rebecca was clearing the table while Danny, more or less recovered from his adventure during the storm, read from the Bible with the last light of the day. Pete lay among the hay in the barn's loft, playing with one of the five or so cats that lived in the barn. He looked out a crack in the boards and saw Alvin on his evening stroll out to the woodshed. Although smoking and drinking were harshly condemned in the Anderson household, every evening Alvin would go out to the woodshed and sit, sometimes for hours, where he would smoke a long-stemmed pipe and sometimes drink moonshine from an old fruit jar. Pete knew about this because he had heard his parents talking about it when they thought him asleep. Pete's dad - Alvin's brother, Danny, had said he was going to ignore it because Alvin wasn't right in the head since the war. Pete would have liked to go and sit with Alvin, but he had been told to leave Alvin alone when he walked.

"Everyone needs time to himself or herself," Rebecca had told him.

It was a beautiful evening and Danny hoisted himself up with the help of his handmade crutches and made his way to the porch, where he propped his broken leg up on the railing. The sun had sunk below the skyline. Devoutly religious, Danny's faith was unwavering, but he was still deeply concerned.

What, he thought to himself, for the thousandth time, should he do? Was God telling him to sell the place to Baggett, for him and his family to move on? His parents had lived here. It just didn't feel right, to think of giving in and moving. But if they stayed, he would have to have help and with Baggett scaring off every honest man in the area, finding reliable help wasn't going to be easy. Maybe he could hire some more freedmen, but many of them had been farm hands and didn't know anything about working cattle. Some cowboys came through town from time to time, drifters mainly, many of them running from past troubles. It was hard to know whom to trust. He was so deep in thought he didn't even notice the two men on horseback coming toward the house along the lane until he realized that Dandy was barking.

Rebecca came out of the house holding the rifle. He reached for it. "Please," he said, "go inside."

She hesitated for only a moment before handing him the rifle and going back into the house. "It's alright boy," he said to Dandy, who stopped barking but began a low growl. The two men were very young, Danny noted, seizing them up as they rode into the yard and hailed him.

"Yo there!" said the blonde one.

The dark-headed one held up his hand in greeting.

Danny watched them wearily. Normally, he would have welcomed visitors, it was the custom in the West, but with all the problems since the war, and with the threat of Baggett hanging over him, Danny was cautious. "Howdy" said Danny, a neutral tone in his voice.

"We're looking for work sir," said the blonde one. "I'm Chase and this fellow with me is Rusty. We met a colored fellow on the road, he said you might be hiring."

Danny didn't say anything for a minute. He just sat there sizing the two boys up. He looked at everything including their clothes, their horses, and their gear. Well, thought Danny, they are down at the heel, but their horses and gear look cared for. Actually, he was almost beside himself to think he might have a couple of hard working young fellows that hadn't been scared off by Baggett, well, at least not yet, but one thing held his enthusiasm in check, and that was the fact that Dandy was still growling deep in his throat. But he couldn't see a downside. Worse case, first time they went to town, these two kids might get scared off by Baggett.

Finally, Danny spoke, "Well, boys, why don't you take your animals to the barn and settle them in, and I'll see if the wife can rustle you some dinner. Then tomorrow, after breakfast, we'll talk."

Rebecca had never seen two men of any age eat with such enthusiasm. You'd have thought they hadn't eaten for a month. But the fact was she liked them both. They were well mannered and full of energy. Rusty, the dark-haired one didn't talk much, but Chase made up for it. Their story came out slowly as they concentrated on eating. They were from Alabama and both had joined the Confederacy as soon as their families would let them go, but by then the war was in its last throes and although they had marched a lot, neither had fired a shot. After the army released them they had gone home, but soon took off looking for the adventure they had failed to find in the war. They had worked off and on between Texas and Alabama, but Texas had been their goal and here they were.

FATE RIDES A TALL HORSE

THIRTEEN

REBECCA, WALKING OUT of the general store, which also held the local post office, was so excited she was trembling. She had received a letter from her younger sister Charity, still living in Georgia. Never married, her fiancé killed in the last year of the war, she had no children of her own and had suffered from serious melancholy since his death. She tore the envelope open and began to read.

Danny, using a cane now, watched as Rebecca walked toward him reading a letter. He smiled to himself. News from home always cheered her.

A smile broke across Rebecca's face as she read. "Danny," she said, almost out of breath with excitement, "Charity is coming to stay with us, to live with us," she hesitated, "if we have room for her." She stood, almost trembling, staring at her husband.

Danny didn't even hesitate. "Of course she'll come," he exclaimed. "I'll have the boys start adding a room today."

FOURTEEN

THE EARLY MARCH WEATHER had been warm and clear. People were arriving in town every day, but most were busy conducting business or working. Johnny and Jake had eaten breakfast and strolled down to the livery. Johnny had brought Flop some beefsteak and a hambone and Jake visited with the livery owner, Whitt, while Johnny brushed down Loco and then Flop.

Jake needed to work up a story for the paper and Johnny wanted to read a week old copy of the Daily News, a one page paper published in Galveston, that had come in the mail with an army patrol, charged with delivering the mail to the frontier forts, had brought and someone had left at the restaurant. So they drifted down to the Busy Bee and took a corner table where Jake pulled out his notes and began to scan them as Johnny read. The bar was almost empty. Johnny waved at the bartender and made a hand like he was drinking coffee and the bartender brought two cups over to their table.

Three Mexican vaqueros were standing at the bar, drinking beer and talking to each in low tones in Spanish. Since he did not speak Spanish Jake barely noticed them, but when he looked up to say something to Johnny he was looking intently at the vaqueros. Did the man speak Spanish?

Johnny motioned to the barman and when he approached Johnny handed him some money and motioned toward the three vaqueros.

The barman nodded, showing no surprise or interest in Johnny's buying the three a beer. Upon arrival of the beer, the three looked at Johnny, surprise on their faces, but then caution. "Mucho gracias senor," said one, lifting his beer up in a salute, the others nodding, but not smiling. Johnny nodded and turned back to his paper. The three Mexicans resumed talking.

Presently Johnny got up and eased over to where the three were standing. "Buenos Dias," he said.

Jake understood good morning, but when Johnny continued to speak in low tones in Spanish he was completely lost. It was obvious that Johnny was fluent in Spanish, even though he spoke it slowly and occasionally seemed to search for a word, gesturing with his hands, but he seemed to be communicating with the three men. Would this man ever stop surprising him? He tried not to stare, but glancing at the group he saw one of the vaqueros pull his bandana down exposing what looked to Jake like a rope burn on the side of his neck.

Johnny nodded and turning called to the bartender to bring another round for the group.

Jake watched as Johnny asked the bartender for a pencil and the bartender, after rummaging around under the bar produced a pencil and a scrap of paper, which he handed to Johnny. Johnny drew on the paper as the vaquero gestured and taking the pencil from Johnny's hand, made some marks on the paper.

As Johnny returned to the table, "Somebody try to hang the fellow?" Jake asked, without raising his head as he focused on completing a sentence on a story about the progress at the fort.

"No," said Johnny. "Somebody ran a blacksnake around his neck and jerked him off his horse. He didn't get a good look at who did it.

He was traveling with a couple of other Mexicans, but he was suffering from stomach trouble and he had broken off and gone into the bush alone, told his friends he would catch up. Whoever did it took his horse and gear and left him there. He thinks there were at least two men that set on him."

Jake looked up at Johnny. "Blacksnake, huh? Not many people use a bullwhip," he said, stating the obvious. "It could be the fellow you're hunting."

"Could be," said Johnny, sipping on his coffee. "Could be." "So, where did this happen?" asked Jake.

Johnny pointed at the scrap of paper he had lain on the table. There was a crude map drawn on it. "Well, the Mexicans were traveling, coming from the Northeast, headed down to the Flat. They were following the old Butterfield route and at some point had broken off and headed south, down toward the town. It looks like they might have crossed over part of Baggett's spread. Could be my man is working for Baggett or his honcho, the one calls himself Smith. Do you know Smith's given name? "Let me think, no, I've not heard anything but Smith, but

I doubt he's using his real name anyway. Lots of people around here seem to be using new names."

FATE RIDES A TALL HORSE

FIFTEEN

RUSTY AND CHASE HAD QUICKLY been accepted into the Anderson family. Danny's leg was healing well, but the extra help was making a difference. The new room for Charity was almost finished and they had branded a couple of dozen maverick cows from out on the Comancheria. For a while Danny had been suspicious of the two, mainly because Baggett hadn't hired them away, but they were so much help, he soon forgot his misgivings. With the new boys out chasing wild cattle, Danny hired the Lowery boys to plow up a few acres for corn. They had a mule and a plow and were accustomed to farming, so this was working out well. The winter had been mild, so Danny was gambling that a late frost wouldn't get his corn. He had a pretty good little herd now and soon he would get the new boys to help him round them all up and band with some other local ranchers to drive them to Fort Worth. There, they would be able to sell them to a buyer who would add them to his own herd and drive the lot on up to the new stockyards in Abilene, Kansas.

SIXTEEN

EARLY EVENING FOUND JOHNNY SITTING in the lone chair in Jake's hotel room smoking a cigar and looking out the window onto the street, while he idly stroked Flop's massive head. Jake was sitting on the bed holding a letter he had received that day from his editor requiring him to show up in Dallas as soon as possible as, the editor pointed out, Jake seemed to have run out of news to report at his current location. It had been ten days since Johnny was shot and he moved slowly with some overall weakness about him, but his wound was healing nicely. The slug had gone through him missing vital organs. Jake had cut the stitches out the day before.

"My editor wants me to shift back to Dallas," Jake stated, without enthusiasm.

Johnny turned his head toward him. "Well," he said, "enjoyed your company."

Always the gentleman, Johnny Black, Jake thought. "Thing is, I feel like I have unfinished business here."

Looking at Jake again, Johnny asked, "What business is that?"

"Well, I think there are some more stories out here. A few at least."

"You hadn't seen enough death to suit you?" Johnny asked. "Cause people die at a pretty brisk pace out here." He looked at Jake for a moment. "Look what happened to that unlucky fellow that took the bullet to the chest. No," he said, shaking his head, "you'd be better off going on to Dallas."

"Yea," said Jake, "I reckon I'll try to find another story or two and then head for Dallas, see where life takes me."

"I may not be far behind you," said Johnny. "I don't plan to hang out here any longer than I have to."

"Well, you need to heal up some before you try to confront the man you're looking for."

"Might not get the chance. Truth be told, I should be dead."

"Could be the person that took a shot at you was that mountain man, the one you took down at the saloon," said Jake.

"Don't think so." "No?" queried Jake.

"He isn't the type to back shoot a man. If I see him again, it'll be face to face."

"Yes, I'm sure you're right," said Jake.

"Well then reporter, I'm going down to the Busy Bee and see if I can find a game and keep my ears open. Haven't heard anything at the Frontier. You're welcome to tag along."

• • •

Two hours later, Johnny was playing cards, Flop lying at his feet while Jake asked the bartender about cattle drives - the bartender had worked as a ranch hand until he broke his leg badly after being thrown- when screaming and yelling from upstairs, where a few rooms were rented out to the ladies that worked the saloon crowd, caused the room to go quiet. Jake looked up to see a woman, her face twisted in pain, her dress torn, her face bloody, stagger out of a room and head down the stairs. It was Katie, a popular young girl who was kind and sweet to everyone. How she ended up working in the Busy Bee was often a topic of discussion, but no one seemed to know the real story. Jake had spoken to her a few times and recognized her instantly.

Suddenly, an older buffalo hunter stepped out of the room carrying a pistol. "Bitch!" he screamed as he pointed the gun at her.

At that moment there was a tremendous explosion as a shot rang out and Jake expected Katie to be thrown down the stairs by the impact of the bullet, but to his astonishment the hunter's head seem to explode in a cloud of blood and gore before he topped forward and fell part of the way down the stairs. There was a stunned silence in the room and as Jake turned his head he saw Clive standing at the end of the bar with a drink glass in one hand and a smoking pistol in the other. Jake turned to see Johnny, sitting at the poker table, calming smoking a cigarillo while his left hand, dangling by his side, stroked Flop's head, his face showing no emotion as he gazed at the staircase where the now very dead buffalo hunter lay.

Finally, the air returned to the room and everyone began to talk at once. Women rushed to assist Katie and a couple of men ventured up the stairs to remove the body of the buffalo hunter. 'His friends,' looking to pick his pockets after they get him outside or out to the local cemetery, thought Jake. There wasn't any law in town but a natural order ruled. If someone stole or attacked a family, a group of vigilantes always seemed to form up to deal with the offender. Even among this very tough crowd there were certain unwritten rules and most men had friends about who could be counted on to retaliate against a perceived wrong. In the case of the man who had hurt and then threatened Katie, the public had made its approval clear by its lack of action when Clive blew the fellow's head off. Such was life in the Flat where justice was often swift.

SEVENTEEN

THE NEXT DAY DAWNED clear and warm as Jake and Johnny stepped outside to have a smoke, having just finished breakfast. Jake figured he had a week or two before he would be forced to start the several week's long journey to Dallas or quit his job as a reporter. He guessed there was plenty of adventure to find in other places, but he didn't feel like he had completely covered the stories here. With those thoughts in mind, he decided to see if he could tag along with a buffalo hunting crew. He figured that should be an interesting story and would, maybe, keep his editor happy for a bit longer. Then maybe a cattle drive might be coming through on its way to Kansas. The cowboys generally had a few stories to tell, and if they were exaggerated some, so much the better, thought Jake.

After smoking and watching the small town come to life, they parted ways. Johnny on his way to the general store, planning to outfit for a few days of riding out among the ranches looking for a lead on the man he was looking for, while Jake headed down to the Frontier saloon in search of a buffalo hunter.

Jake found Jones setting up drinks for a gaggle of cowboys just in from the Baggett spread. His interest was instantly peaked as he thought of what Johnny had said, that maybe the man he was looking for was working on the Baggett spread. Jake ordered a beer and tried to see if any of the cowboys were missing part of their ear, but as far as he could tell, none were.

When Jones stopped by to see if he wanted a refill, Jake asked him about local buffalo-hunters. There were quite a few around, but nothing like the area would soon see. Smith pointed at a table of rough looking men drinking from a bottle of whiskey. There were three of them, all wearing buffalo hides and had large knives strapped to their bodies.

Jake moved to their table. "Gentlemen," he said. The hunters looked at each other and then at Jake. Nobody spoke and nobody smiled.

"Jones there," said Jake, pointing at the bartender. "Said you boys are some of the best buffalo-hunters around. I'm a reporter for the Dallas Herald and I'd like to write a story about you." This brought grins from the three men. Feeling encouraged, Jake pulled out a chair and sat down.

EIGHTEEN

JAKE WAS FREEZING, but he was so scared he didn't pay the discomfort much mind. Only a day after he met the three buffalo-hunters he found himself out on the Comancheria, the area west of the line of forts set up to protect settlers and ruled by the Indians, primarily the Comanches. After seeing what happened to the man that he had seen at the fort, Jake was, frankly, terrified. But he was also in awe. The three hunters were crouched in a small group just in front of him. One of them had a v-shaped stick stuck in the ground with a huge .50 caliber Sharpe rifle balanced in the v pointing at a massive herd of gigantic buffalo. Lord, thought Jake. There must be a thousand or more pawing and grazing on the frozen grassland. Jake crawled up to the group.

"We gotta take down the leader," said one of the hunters." Then the group will kind of drift around, lost like and we can commence to shooting em."

Suddenly an explosion of sound as the big .50 fired! Jake involuntarily jerked as he saw a huge buffalo stumble and drop. The buffalo nearest pulled back, ran a few yards, but then stopped and began to circle, wary. A couple came up to sniff at the downed buffalo. Then the group began to graze.

"Got him," said the man who had fired.

Without a word, the man began to reload and methodically shoot, dropping a buffalo with almost every shot. Buffalo were dropping to their front knees and keeling over. Some were walking a step or two before falling. Occasionally, a big bull would shake his giant head and trot a way like he had been stung by a bee, rather than shot by a large caliber rifle.

In a matter of hours, Jake looked up from his notes to see nearly a hundred buffalo lying dead or dying on the frozen ground.

"Come on," said the shooter to the other two as the three quickly moved out to the killing field, knives in hand. "Reporter, you keep an eye out, you hear?" said the shooter.

"Okay, sure," said Jake, still writing on his pad.

NINETEEN

THE SUN WAS JUST COMING OVER the horizon, but breakfast was over and Rusty and Chase had mounted up and headed northwest, their assignment to see if they could locate a few mavericks to add to the Anderson herd and to be on the lookout for unbranded calves. But they didn't go far. As soon as they were out of sight of the house they turned into a grove of trees and dismounted. They let the horses graze as they rolled cigarettes.

"How long we gonna wait?" asked Chase, touching his lit match to Rusty's cigarette.

"A couple hours should do it," said Rusty, blowing smoke slowly. "Gotta make sure they're gone."

Danny helped Rebecca into the wagon as Alvin checked the harness. Looking around, Danny didn't see Pete anywhere. "Pete!" yelled Danny.

"Coming!" was the response, as Pete and Dandy came tearing around the corner of the cabin.

"What were you two up to?" asked Rebecca, suspiciously, staring at Pete as he lifted Dandy into the back of the wagon.

"Looking for grasshoppers," replied Pete, pulling a small jar with two large grasshoppers in it from his pocket. "We're going to need some for fishing tomorrow."

Twenty minutes after the Andersons' wagon disappeared down the road, headed for town, Chase and Rusty appeared, walking their horses slowly down into the homestead. "Make sure you leave things as they are," Rusty said, as he and Chase entered the house. "We don't want to raise any suspicions or nothing." Quickly, the two began to tap on boards and look under the rugs, moving quickly through the cabin.

TWENTY

RUSTY AND CHASE SAT ON a large downed tree trunk, smoking, watching their horses graze. Chase was nervously jerking his head around as if he expected Indians to charge out of the trees at any second. "He's late," stated Chase.

"He said meet him here, we're here, so shut up," said Rusty tersely. Ten minutes later Smith, riding on a beautiful Palomino, appeared in the clearing.

Both boys jumped to their feet. "Mr. Smith," they said, almost in unison.

"Morning boys," said Smith, then, looking at Rusty, "You have something for me?"

Rusty started shaking his head no. "We didn't find it Mister Smith." Smith sat atop his horse and stared at the two.

"Oh yea," said Rusty, suddenly. "We found $80.00 in a coffee can in the root cellar."

Smith's eyes narrowed. "But we didn't take any of it," exclaimed Rusty. "We just counted it and put it back, like you said."

Smith nodded. "Good, good. Has Anderson paid you boys yet?"

"No sir," they answered in unison. "Anderson said first day of the month. April. Thirty dollars each."

"Okay," said Smith. "They've been going to town for supplies every couple of weeks, and you two are going to have to be paid, so they are going to need some more cash by the first of the April." Looking closely at Rusty, "Watch them very close towards the end of the month. That money is somewhere close."

"Yes sir," said Rusty as Chase nodded his understanding.

Smith looked lost in thought. Rusty and Chase were starting to get concerned, when suddenly Smith focused on them again. "Listen, you," he said, pointing at Rusty. "On Saturday, beginning the last week of the month, I want you to 'get hurt'."

"What?" Rusty stammered.

"I need you around the homestead when they'll be digging up the money. Tell Anderson you throwed out your back, you need to lay up for a few days. Make sure you walk like you got a stiff back. You getting it now?"

"Oh, yea," said Rusty, understanding on his face.

"Watch 'em close," said Smith, as he turned his horse, then he stopped and turned back to the boys. "Gents, don't get no ideas if you want to live to see another year," and with that he turned away and nudged his horse into a trot.

TWENTY-ONE

JAKE AWOKE STIFF AND SORE. He had gotten in from the buffalo hunt the night before and was too exhausted to eat or drink. He had pulled off his coat and boots, climbed into bed and fell fast asleep. Painfully, he sat up and reached for his boots. A week of sleeping on the ground and riding in the wagon as it bounced across the prairie, all the while scanning the horizon for Indians, had taken its toll on Jake. How the old guys did it weeks at a time, he had no idea. The group had decided not to stay out long, given the recent Indian attack.

Well, he thought to himself, he had never really been the outdoor type. Born to a wealthy family, his father having made considerable wealth as a trader, Jake had learned to ride and shoot, but school had been his strength and learning was what interested him. He had really found his interest in medicine and after graduating with a medical degree from Harvard at the age of 21, but feeling that America was behind in medical knowledge, had gone to London, where he entered the Royal College of Physicians of England. He returned to the states in '64 and volunteered as a contract surgeon becoming an irregular serving the Union army. His real training, he thought, took place during the war. In fact, treating the never-ending health issues and injuries encountered by the troops had challenged him, but the horrific war wounds had left a mark deep inside him. He had not carried a gun or fired one during the war, but the camps he had been in had been shelled and fired upon many times and he had found himself in the middle of the chaos that battles wrought as he tried to tend the wounded. That was why, after the war, he decided to travel, to seek some adventure that didn't involve dealing with sickness, injury and severe wounds. He didn't want anyone to know he was a trained doctor, because, and rightfully so, people would seek him out for help.

The hunt, according to the three hunters, had been a success. For one thing they were alive and well, not having seen any Indians or suffering any misfortunes. They brought in over 100 hides, some buffalo tongue and a wagon load of buffalo meat the hunters had sold to the army as they came back into town. The only problem was that they had run out of whiskey on the last day, a fact the hunters complained bitterly about, blaming the one responsible for supplies. He countered that the other two had drank more than they should have. The argument continued until they hit town and laid eyes on the first saloon.

TWENTY-TWO

DANNY STOOD STILL, ALMOST MESMERIZED as he watched the Lowery boys prepare the corn field. One of them was holding the harness while the other held the mule's bridle, slowly leading the old mule while he talked softly to her. The plow turned the soil over slowly and steadily. Danny felt a calmness and optimism he hadn't felt for months. Rebecca had bought corn seed on her last visit to town and the weather had been mild, so Danny was betting, well praying actually, that there would not be a late frost this year. The sooner he could get the corn started, the better. Rebecca, Alvin and Pete were pulling weeds and turning over the garden, Danny's leg was pretty much healed and Rebecca's sister, Charity should arrive soon, they weren't regular, but the occasional stagecoach came with mail and the payroll for the fort. Rusty and Chase were out checking on the calves, branding the new ones and trying to get a count.

He felt so at peace, growing his own food, teaching Pete the things a man should know, spending his evenings on the porch with Rebecca, sometimes reading the Bible, sometimes just talking quietly and sometimes just sitting. His only concern was rounding up his cattle, which as best as he could tell was probably over 200 head now. He would keep the young ones to rebuild his herd, but he should have at least 150 to sell. Soon, he would have to find someone to partner with or someone to sell the herd to so they could be driven to Kansas to the cattle sales. They wouldn't bring a lot, maybe four or five dollars a head, but it would get them through the winter. 'Well, he thought to himself,' the corral needed work and he reluctantly turned away and headed for the horse pen.

As he neared the house he saw Rebecca hoeing in the garden and his mood shifted. She was so beautiful and belonged, longed really, to be back in Georgia. To attend tea parties and galas. To be the Southern Belle she was. Well, perhaps Charity coming will make a difference, he thought. At least he hoped so, because no matter how much he told himself Rebecca was happy, he knew better.

TWENTY-THREE

WHILE JAKE WAS RECOVERING from the buffalo hunt, Johnny had returned from spending a few days riding up toward the old Butterfield Trail. He had shot some rabbits and a wild turkey and had enjoyed the solitude. In the evenings he had built a fire, prepared coffee and supper. It had given him time to enjoy nature and time to reflect. Flop and Loco seemed to have enjoyed themselves also, he thought to himself. He had seen no sign of bushwhackers in person or old campfires; nothing.

He finished up his breakfast and strolled back to the hotel, deep in thought. Arriving on the porch, he sat in a chair and reached in his pocket for his cigarillos when he remembered he had smoked everyone he had brought out from Fort Worth and the general store didn't have any -he had asked them to order some- so he'd had to settle for a sack of tobacco and some papers. He pulled out a bag of Bull Durham, recalling that 'Bull' had recently been added to the name, a paper and slowly tapped out a line of tobacco onto the paper before licking the edge and folding it over. A quick twist of one end and he stuck it into his mouth, fished a match from his pocket, scratched it on the side of the chair and lit his cigarette, taking a deep drag as his thoughts focused on what he thought of as the lay of the land. It was something he did often. A sort of reassessment of his current situation and goals.

He was blowing out the smoke when Flop appeared, having returned from a mission known only to him.

"Hey Flop" said Johnny absently. It wasn't until Flop nuzzled his pocket that Johnny remembered he had wrapped a piece of ham in some paper and put it in his pocket for Flop. He reached over and rubbed Flop's head as he pulled out the bundle and unwrapping it, handed the ham to Flop who took it gently in his mouth and walked away to enjoy it.

Johnny, a man of many interests and a hard scrabble past, enjoyed life and worked to enjoy each day even as he lived with both physical and mental pain. His thoughts turned to his current goal. Find Kyle Stephens and kill him. Nothing else matters at this point, thought Johnny as an image of his brother laughing just before he was shot in the back flashed in his mind. Johnny had looked back to see Stephens turn and run as his brother fell into his arms.

Johnny considered his conviction that Stephens was still somewhere in the area. According to witnesses, Stephens had left Dallas running from debts owed to the general store, the hotel, two saloons and several gamblers who held IOUs from Stephens and would love to have a word with him. He had in fact, used the name Kyle Lambert, but the damaged ear, which he had tried to hide by letting his hair grow long, and the scar on his face gave him away when Johnny described him. Johnny had ridden over to Fort Worth, where he found a scattering of houses and buildings and few people. The Fort had closed in '59 and after the war, the settlement almost ceased to exist as families moved on, in fact its existence seemed to depend almost entirely on large herds of cattle and the cowboys who herded them, who found the area to be a good resting place on their way to the market in Abilene, Kansas.

Johnny had described Stephens in a low-rent saloon that opened whenever a herd came through usually with 12 to 15 hands looking for a drink and the bartender had remembered the man with the scarred face. He had drank heavily and alone, paid and left, never uttering a word except for ordering his whiskey. Yes, thought Johnny, he's holed up around here somewhere, probably broke, maybe living rough trying to accumulate some money working as a bushwhacker. If he was robbing travelers, he probably covered his face, but most men would recognize the horse, or maybe his voice, so he wouldn't chance coming to town if he was robbing travelers. What else did he know about Stephens? The man was a terrible poker player, had a fondness for faro and whiskey and had experience working with horses and cattle.

Johnny had mimicked the trail the vaqueros had taken as he worked his way up to the old Butterfield trail and although he came across a few travelers, there was no sign of Stephens.

"It's just possible he's working horses or cattle on the Baggett spread, using an alias," said Johnny softly to himself, as he weighed the idea. But, thought Johnny, he would be in town, drinking and gambling - unless he had spotted me. That was definitely a possibility and it would explain his being shot. Taking a deep drag on his cigarette, Johnny went over it all once again in his mind.

TWENTY-FOUR

THE SKY WAS JUST BEGINNING to lighten in the east as Baggett stepped out on the porch of his large ranch house carrying a tin cup of coffee. He had china cups, but Baggett wasn't born to wealth and sophistication. He came to where he was now from a wretched and poor childhood, where even food was often hard to come by. He had escaped early and found himself punching cattle at a tender age. He had fought hard and often dirty, and truth be known, had killed to get where he was, but he couldn't shake some of his habits-like the tin cup-it felt comfortable in his hand.

As the sun rose he looked out at the corral out by the barn where some of his hands, breakfast over and the sun rising, were taking turns trying to break some wild horses. From the look and sound of it they weren't having much luck. As he sipped his coffee his mind turned to the Andersons. He had finally made up his mind to run them off and be done with it. He was sure they had some money hid, but he wasn't sure how to find it. The main thing was to take over their spread, to expand his holdings. If they did have money, and he couldn't steal it, then he wouldn't be able to starve them out, but there was one thing that all folks had in common and that was fear. Anderson was really an easy target, thought Baggett. His family made him very, very vulnerable. The difference between Baggett and his victims was that Baggett wasn't afraid of using violence to get what he wanted and in fact considered it a natural part of life, especially out here on the edge of civilization.

FATE RIDES A TALL HORSE

TWENTY-FIVE

JAKE WOKE FROM A DEEP SLEEP to a moment of fear, near panic and confusion as he heard shouts and the thunder of horses close by and in the distance a volley of gunfire. His first thoughts were that he was back in his tent during the war and an assault was underway. He glanced around his hotel room and his breathing began to return to normal as he realized where he was. The noise had abated, but another round of gunfire echoed from the direction of the fort. Indian attack was his next thought, but then Jake realized from the timed volleys the soldiers were taking target practice at their range southwest of town. Relief flooded him as he realized he had been having nightmares again and the current sounds had intervened and caused him to awaken.

Jake sat up in the bed, gathering his thoughts. Nightmares, all of them involving the war and the horrific wounds he had seen and treated, were his constant companion, but they seemed to come most often when he was very tired. Finally, he climbed out of the bed and walked barefoot over to the window, pushed the curtain aside and looked down on the street. Jake was surprised to see a stagecoach sitting on main street surrounded by people and a troupe of buffalo soldiers. Then he saw that it was part of a wagon train. Several freighters were easing down through the people. It must have come in from Dallas carrying provisions and the payroll for the fort, thought Jake. That would explain the soldiers. Travelers and wagon trains were often attacked and robbed as they made the long journey west.

It was always exciting when a stage came in. Since the Butterfield had stopped running in '61, there wasn't any kind of regular service to this part of the country. Jake was about to turn away from the window when he saw a woman step from the stage. She was wearing a worn, long blue and white dress. The only women who would come to the frontier were the wifes of soldiers or fallen women following the men. But Jake was captivated as soon as he saw her face. She didn't, at first glance, appear to be what one would call a beautiful woman, but she was attractive, with good facial features, but none of this registered consciously with Jake. He wasn't sure why he was so captivated. He stood transfixed as two men and another woman emerged from the stage, but he didn't really see them. He had eyes only for the dark-haired woman in the blue and white dress. She turned toward the stage, looking up as the driver and assistant driver began to untie the luggage from the roof of the stage. She didn't look like the type that was drawn here to earn money, thought Jake. A soldier's wife then. He felt disappointment flood him, but Jake continued to watch when suddenly the Anderson woman ran up to the woman in the blue and white dress and embraced her. A young boy appeared with the one-armed, white-haired man he had seen in town with the Anderson woman. The boy and the one-armed man grabbed the girl's trunk and hauled it away as the two women, arm in arm followed. What the heck, thought Jake.

Jake found Johnny sipping coffee, the remains of his breakfast pushed aside. "Mind if I sit?" asked Jake.

"Take a load off reporter." Jake pulled out a chair and waved at the waitress who was moving from table to table with a coffee pot, filling cups as fast as she could.

"You appear a bit flushed," stated Johnny flatly. Smiling, Jake said, "A wagon train come in."

"Yes, I saw it," said Johnny, sipping coffee. "Let's hope there are several boxes of cigars on board," he said as he studied Jake.

Before Jake could respond the waitress arrived with a cup and the coffee pot. "You want the same, sweetie?" she asked.

"Huh," said Jake.

"I asked if you wanted the same order you've made every time you've been in here. Two eggs, ham, grits and biscuits."

"Oh, yes, I do," said Jake as the waitress turned away. "You feeling alright?" asked Johnny.

"I'm fine," said Jake, "how the cards been treating you?" he asked, trying to change the subject.

Johnny didn't answer, but sat, sipping his coffee and looking at Jake. Something was up with the boy. The waitress arrived and quickly placed Jake's breakfast on the table and re- filled the coffee cups before charging off. Jake attacked his breakfast. Johnny took out his fixings and rolled a cigarette.

Finally, Jake broke the silence. "What do you have planned today?" he asked, his mouth full of eggs and ham.

"Well," said Johnny, "I got a pretty exciting day planned. I'm going to stop by the general store and hopefully pick up some cigarillos and then I plan to ride up to the fort and drop my laundry off with one of the washerwomen up there. Then I'm going to ask around the soldiers one more time, see if anybody has run across a man with a scarred face and missing a good part of his ear."

"Mind if I trail along?" asked Jake. "I'm going to see if I can interview the fort Commander, the Lieutenant Colonel, get an update on the Indian activity and see how the fort itself is progressing. I can knock out a story for the freighters to take back with the mail. Then I thought I'd interview some of the local folks in regards to life on the frontier."

"I thought you were set on heading back to Dallas." Johnny smoked and looked at Jake. "But then, maybe something has changed," he posited.

"Ah, I am headed back soon, but as a reporter I feel I should try to…"

Johnny interrupted with, "Something special come in on one of those freighters this morning?" Jake stared at Johnny. "Reporter, your poker face isn't working," said Johnny.

"Alright then," said Jake. "My reporter curiosity was peaked this morning and I aim to satisfy it before I head out."

"That so," said Johnny. "Well, let's see. What could've come in that is so very interesting. A famous gunfighter maybe. That's very possible and would no doubt make a good story. Or maybe a famous politician." He stared at Jake. "Well, maybe some rumor and you want to investigate it." Johnny smiled and lifted his coffee and sipped it, his eyes never leaving Jake. "No, I don't think so. You look like you might be holding aces. That can only mean money or a girl."

Jake picked up his coffee cup and looked away. For the first time since he had met him, Jake heard Johnny laugh.

TWENTY-SIX

EVER SINCE THE FIGHT with the Indians when Hurricane had broken his legs and Jake had shot him to stop his pain, Jake had been renting a horse as he needed one from Whitt. While Johnny saddled Loco, Jake sought out Whitt.

Flop had picked up a friend in the form of a skinny short- haired dog a third his size and the two of them ran out front checking out smells and noises as Johnny and Jake walked their horses up the road to the fort. The plan for the fort included all stone buildings, but that took time, so tents had been replaced by wood barracks and buildings, all except for the bakery. The horses had been suffering due to a lack of stables, but the men themselves had suffered through the winter as the green wood warped and provided little protection from the elements.

As they entered Fort Griffin, the early March morning was warm, and a stiff breeze whipped the United States Flag in its place on a flagpole in the center of the compound. The troops were already performing drill on the large parade round located on the south side of the road that started in the Flat and ran up through the fort located on top of the plateau. Watching them, and seeing the troops that had accompanied the wagon train, Jake recalled some Negro units that had served with distinction in the war, but all of the officers and NCOs, he remembered were white. Well, thought Jake, time will mean progress on all fronts, including, hopefully, the human one. As a doctor he knew all men were essentially the same, with the same hopes and fears as they lay injured, death a very real possibility.

Johnny and Jake walked their horses through the camp to the far edge where women were thrashing clothes in large pots sitting on fires and filled with boiling water. Wet clothes flapped in the strong winds and the women's housing, tents, appeared in danger of blowing away as they bowed and relaxed under the same wind gusts.

After Johnny had reached an agreement with a washer- woman, drill had ended and the troops began what was known as fatigue, a period of work parties assigned to various tasks. This worked for Johnny as it allowed him to drift around the fort speaking with small groups in his quest to find someone who had seen a man with a scar on his face. In the meantime Jake headed for the headquarters' building to see if he could speak with the fort Commander about the progress of the camp.

• • •

A buffalo-hunter, named Harry, camped just north of the Flat, near Collins Creek, with a couple of hunting partners, had walked down to the creek to gather water for coffee and had just filled the pot when he saw the horses, three of them, watering in the creek. They wore no halter or hobbles. The hunter knew them because they belonged to a fellow hunter and his group, the one they called Mountain Man. He quickly walked back up to his camp, set the pot on the fire, picked up a rope and walked back to the creek. One of his partners hollered at him, but he ignored him. Reaching the creek the hunter eased up to the largest horse and speaking softly to him he put his rope over his head. Then he led the horse slowly back to camp as the other two horses followed. Once there, he eased out the length of the rope on the lead horse and the three horses began to graze. The man rummaged in the wagon, finally pulling out several lengths of looped leather straps. Slowly, he approached each horse in turn, speaking softly to them then reaching down and slipping the leather straps over their front legs as he twisted them. Having hobbled the three so they couldn't venture far, but still graze, he walked over to the wagon and found his rifle. He checked to ensure it was loaded.

His two partners were at the fire preparing breakfast. They stared at him silently as he worked to hobble the horses, then, "What the hell are you doing?" asked one.

"Did you steal the Mountain Man's horses?" asked the other, his voice revealing his total disbelief and fear.

"Be right back," Harry hollered back as he strove away. As he approached Mountain Man's campsite he could see the smoke from the smoldering fire and just make out the three men still in their blankets close to the fire. "Hello there!" he said. He purposely kicked at some rocks as he got closer. Nobody moved. "Mountain Man, it's me, Harry," said the hunter, but no one stirred.

Reaching the campsite, Harry stood and stared. He knew the men were dead, but he was having some trouble accepting the fact. Finally, he walked up to Mountain Man and using the rifle he pushed the blanket back to reveal a lot of blood and a huge gash in Mountain Man's throat. Both of the other hunters had their throats cut as well. All murdered in their sleep. Harry knelt and patted Mountain Man's pockets. Empty. He got up and looked in the wagon. The guns were there. Someone had murdered them, robbed them and cut the horses loose. Someone who cared about horses but knew better than to steal them. People knew their horses in these parts and knew who owned them. Well, he had no intention of being hung for stealing horses or murder for that matter.

Harry walked back to his own camp to have some coffee and tell his partners what had happened. He would skip breakfast as he had lost his appetite. An hour later, grim faced, Harry and his partners hitched the Mountain Man's team to his wagon, tied his spare horse behind and drove to the fort to report the murders to the Lieutenant Colonel.

Jake was visiting with Lieutenant Angleton when Harry came in. There wasn't any law in the Flat, but the army took an interest in the major crimes such as horse theft or murder.

Harry explained what he had found and added the fact that it had been the Mountain Man who had slashed the vaquero's throat perhaps a month ago, when Captain Bates had come by with a patrol. Lieutenant Angleton told him to wait while he briefed the fort Commander. Ten minutes later he returned.

"The Commander feels that the army should have the horses, needs of the government, but that you should take the wagon and weapons, in return for burying the dead men. Make sure you take the bodies out to the graveyard."

Harry stood silent.

"Is that satisfactory with you sir?" he asked.

"Oh, yes, yes," said Harry. "I'll see to it straight away."

Later, on the way back down to the Flat, Jake told Johnny what had transpired.

"The Mexicans tend to be loyal," said Johnny, his only comment, as they finished the ride into town in silence.

GARY CHURCH

TWENTY-SEVEN

JAKE AND JOHNNY DIDN'T DISCUSS IT, but Johnny tended to take his evening meal around six each evening and Jake often joined him. Johnny had just sat down when Jake appeared and pulled out the chair opposite Johnny. "Evening," said Jake.

Johnny nodded his greeting and turned his head as the waitress appeared.

"What'll it be boys?" she asked, not bothering with a pencil. "Good evening Maybelle," Johnny said with a smile. "I

guess I'll try the beefsteak with potatoes if you have them." "The same, please," said Jake.

"I'll put in your order and be back with coffee in a sec," she said as she turned away and hurried off.

After testing the coffee, Johnny said, "I think I'll try my luck tonight at Shane's."

"Your luck at cards or information?" asked Jake.

"Both," replied Johnny. "If the man is around, he's got to be itching to come to town."

"Well," stated Jake, "I've not been there, but I heard the place draws a rough crowd."

This brought a smile from Johnny.

"I mean, I know the whole town is rough, but…" his voice trailed off.

"I know," said Johnny, as Maybelle thrust plates of beef- steak and potatoes between them.

• • •

Jake and Johnny entered the saloon and stood in the door, letting their eyes adjust to the dim light. The place was crowded and filled with noise. A faro game had a large crowd, both players and watchers on one side, while a poker game was in progress on the other side. The center of the saloon was filled with men, drinking beer and whiskey, talking, swearing and laughing. There was a loud crash, yelling and cursing as two men in the midst of an arm wrestling contest somehow managed to turn the table over, sending glasses and bottles crashing to the floor as everyone jumped back to avoid the spillage.

Johnny found a place at the poker table while Jake managed to wrangle a spot at the bar by easing in sideways and ordering a beer. The bartender, a red-headed fellow with an accent that made him a little hard to understand, was a friendly sort named Clancy. "Me name, it means red-headed warrior,' he stated proudly.

Jake nodded, smiling. As the fellow seemed obliging, Jake decided to engage the man a bit. "I'm a reporter for the Dallas Herald," he said. "Name's Jake. Doesn't mean anything I know of." Jake smiled.

"A reporter, you say," responded Clancy. "That's good. Can't read much myself, but it's important, the news." Clancy turned and went off down the bar to refill some glasses. Jake turned and looked around. Johnny had left Flop at the stable with Loco, but otherwise he appeared the same as always, reflected Jake, watching him at the poker table. Calm and relaxed but doesn't miss a thing. A little later, having drank a couple of beers and one whiskey, Jake, and he wasn't sure why he did it, asked Clancy if he had noticed a man with a scar on his face and a damaged ear.

Clancy's face lost its pleasantness. "It can be unhealthy to be asking after people around here," he said very quietly.

Jake placed a silver dollar on the bar and pushed it toward Clancy who looked at it for a second, placed his hand over it and slid it off the bar into his other hand. "Funny story," he said, in a normal tone of voice, "a couple of nights ago a fellow playing faro won. The fellow was so surprised he stood there a minute, stroking his beard and then asked the dealer if he was sure!" Clancy and Jake laughed.

An hour later, Jake was nursing his third beer and thinking about going to the hotel and working on his story about progress at the fort. He wanted to tell Johnny what he had learned from Clancy, but he wasn't about to interrupt a poker game. He drained his beer, sat his glass on the bar, nodded at Clancy and glancing over at the table where Johnny was playing, realized everyone at Johnny's table was sitting very still. Not a good sign. It soon became apparent that a skinny man, missing most of his teeth, tattoos on both hands, looked angry. A sailor guessed Jake. The man was glaring at Johnny who had four cards turned up in front of him and one turned down. It appeared Johnny had been winning, as he had quite a bit of money stacked neatly by his left hand.

Jake eased slowly away from the bar, not attracting any attention, turning to avoid a man pushing to take his place at the bar, he made his way over toward the wall, where he could see the table better.

There was a large pile of paper and coin money in the center of the table. Five card stud, thought Jake, with a large pot, a very large pot.

Johnny was returning the sailor's stare, his face a mask. Everyone had five cards in front of them. The man on Johnny's left had rearranged his cards to show a pair of queens and a high card of a ten of diamonds. The man to the left of him had turned his cards over and tossed them toward the pot. Then Jake realized Clive was sitting across from Johnny. How he hadn't noticed he didn't know. Clive also had a pair of Queens, but he had a high card of a Jack. Clive was breaking off a chaw of tobacco. A rough looking hunter, dressed in buffalo skins tossed his cards into the middle, turned and spit toward a spittoon missing it completely.

The sailor's hand included two kings. Finally, the sailor turned over his hole card, a worthless nine of hearts, but with two kings showing, he had the others beat. Jake leaned forward and he could see Johnny's hand included an Ace, but Johnny had not yet turned over his last card. So, thought Jake, if Johnny turns over an ace…. Johnny's hands were resting on the table, but the skinny man had his hands under the table. Oh no, thought Jake.

As Jake watched, it all unfolded in slow motion. Johnny pulled his cigarillo from his mouth and placed it carefully on the edge of the table, then he slowly turned over an ace. The sailor reached behind his back, screamed something in a foreign language, pushed the table away with his left hand and half rising, moved sideways slashing at Johnny's face with a long knife held in his right hand. Johnny quickly stood, moved left and faced the sailor, who was now grinning as he stood in a half-crouch holding his knife.

"Thief!" the man grunted in broken English. "Go for your gun cheat," he hissed as he lunged at Johnny who, stepping back, reached down into his right boot and withdrew his own knife.

"No sir," said Johnny calmly, "I never cheat, but you, however, are a very bad poker player."

By now, the saloon had become quiet. Even the faro game was suspended as everyone made room for the two combatants. The sailor stayed close, Jake reasoned he didn't want to give Johnny a chance to pull his gun, as he and Johnny began to circle to their left.

Everything seemed surreal to Jake. It had happened several times during the war in times of extreme stress and chaos. The details seemed so clear to Jake. Clive had put his chaw in his mouth and was standing and chewing as he watched as though he was at the theater. The buffalo skin clad hunter was thoughtfully chewing and spitting on the floor, ignoring the spittoon. Johnny and the sailor had moved out away from the table, to give themselves room to move, but still very close to each other, both in a crouch, holding their knives in front of them.

The sailor was obviously an experienced knife fighter. He lunged and slashed left and right cutting a six inch slit in Johnny's shirt at his stomach. The shirt began to darken with blood. It seemed like an hour, but only a minute or two passed as the two slashed and stabbed at each other. Blood was soaking Johnny's shirt and spreading to his trousers. He wouldn't last long, thought Jake.

In the end, it wasn't knife technique that ended the fight, but tactics. Having watched the sailor carefully, Johnny did the unexpected and as the man slashed left, rather than jump back, Johnny stepped in, just as he had when he had fought the Mountain Man and when the sailor slashed back to his right, Johnny blocked his arm with his right arm and slugged him in the side of the head with a looping left hand. Then, stepping back, Johnny slashed the sailor's knife hand cutting the wrist deeply and the knife dropped to the floor as the man screamed and lunged at Johnny, who rather than stab the man, dropped his own knife and buried his right fist in the man's stomach then bringing his knee up into his face knocking him up and back. The sailor hit the floor, out cold. Blood poured from the deep cut on his right wrist and his broken face.

Johnny picked up his knife and slid it into his boot, then he picked up the sailor's knife and holding it close to the floor stepped on the blade until it broke. He then walked over to the sailor and used his boot to turn him on his side as the man appeared to be drowning in blood.

No one moved. Johnny picked up his money including the pot, walked to the bar, blood dripping on the floor, as men stepped aside to let him through. "Can you get someone to take him up to the fort to see the doc and to clean up the mess?" he asked Clancy as he placed some bills and coins on the bar.

"Aye," said Clancy.

Jake followed Johnny out of the saloon, caught up to him and put his arm around his shoulder just as Johnny sagged, his knees giving way. "Looks like you're in need of my services yet again," said Jake, smiling.

Back at the hotel, Jake sat in a chair staring at Johnny who was lying in bed, his stomach wrapped in white bandages. "I have benefited from keeping company with you," said Jake grinning.

"How's that reporter?" asked Johnny, his voice spiked with pain in spite of the laudanum Jake had given him.

"Well, I was a might worried about getting out of practice as a doctor, but you've provided ample opportunity for me to keep my skills sharp. It took over a hundred sutures to close your wound. Seriously though, you can't ride or walk about for at least two weeks, maybe longer."

"Glad I been able to help," said Johnny dryly. "And reporter," he started, but had to stop as a pain spasm hit him. "I truly appreciate you asking about Stephens. I was beginning to doubt he was still here and the beard, I hadn't thought of that, but," he hesitated again, "you can get killed asking about a man like Stephens. Better you leave the man-hunting to me and I'll leave the doctoring to you." He turned his head to look at Jake, who nodded.

"Okay," said Jake, "how about I see if the hotel owner knows a woman can fetch your meals and something for Flop and his new friend. I'll see Whitt about Loco."

"Appreciate it reporter. There's money in the top drawer, take what you need to cover things, including your services. You can't be getting rich as a reporter."

"I'll take the money for the woman, livery, food and that, but don't worry none about me. I got a little put away."

"Somehow reporter, I get the idea there's things about you I don't know."

This caused Jake to laugh. "Me!" he chuckled. "If ever was a mysterious man, it's you my friend." Johnny smiled.

TWENTY-EIGHT

JAKE HAD BREAKFAST ALONE and strolled back to the hotel where he found Flop and his new dog friend Johnny was calling Perro, in the lobby. He hollered at them and they followed him up the stairs to Johnny's room. The door was cracked open and the dogs charged in, but Jake stopped and knocked.

"Come on in reporter," said Johnny.

Jake stepped in and looked about. A breakfast tray beside the bed held the remains of Johnny's breakfast and Jake saw the dog's water bowl was full and a plate beside it was dirty, but empty. "Well," he said. "Looks like you and the boys have had breakfast already."

"That we have," said Johnny, "and thanks for taking care of things."

Jake walked over to the bed, reached under it, extracted his medical bag and removing some scissors, began to cut and remove Johnny's bandages, soaked through with seeping blood. He examined the wound. "You staying still?" he asked as he worked.

"Yes momma," said Johnny.

"Okay," said Jake. "The wound is doing okay. Infection is our enemy and we have to watch it. The girl doing to suit you?"

"She is," said Johnny.

"I'm going out to the Anderson spread like I was saying the other day, get their take on life on the frontier. I'll be back this evening. Check in on you then."

"Leave the door cracked if you will so the boys can go in and out."

"See you tonight." Jake rubbed Flop's head, picked up his hat off the dresser and strolled out of the room.

• • •

Arriving at the stable, Jake looked in on Loco, feeding him an apple he had brought, rented his usual horse from Whitt, a gentle mare named Girl and headed out toward the Anderson spread, not sure what to expect. He wanted badly to see the girl in the blue dress, if for no other reason than to get over the memory of her that he couldn't shake. He saw smoke first and then as he rode up out of a low area he saw the cabin sitting on a high spot, the immediate area cleared of trees, but there was a thick stand of mesquite off to the east. It was the typical homestead, he thought to himself. A small cabin, barn, corral, chicken coop and although he couldn't see it, he guessed there would be a hog pen a ways back from the house. As he got closer he realized the smoke was coming from out behind the cabin. Maybe they were burning something. A small dog appeared and watched him approach.

Reaching the house Jake eased Girl to a halt and sat taking in the cabin while the dog stood and watched him. Finally, Jake hollered out a greeting, "Good morning!"

He was greeted with silence and he continued to sit until a female voice hailed him from one side of the cabin.

"What can I do for you mister?" she asked.

Jake turned to see Rebecca Anderson pointing a rifle at him. "Ah, Mrs. Anderson?"

Silence followed. Then, after removing his hat, "I'm Jake Evans, a reporter with the Dallas Herald. I've seen you and your family about town. I came out to ask your husband about the cattle trade. For a story," he added, speaking too quickly, his voice displaying his surprise at being greeted by a rifle.

The rifle remained steady for a minute, then, "Step down Mr. Evans, we're out back making soap. Please join us." A young boy appeared beside the woman. "Pete," said Rebecca, "please see to Mr. Evans horse."

The boy ran out to where Jake sat on his horse, still hold- ing his hat in his hand. Jake replaced his hat on his head, eased down off Girl and handed the reins to Pete before striding toward the house and the waiting Mrs. Rebecca Anderson.

As Jake neared Rebecca, she said, "Women on the edge of civilization have to take care."

"Oh, of course," said Jake, "I didn't mean to cause alarm."

Rebecca smiled. "I have seen you in town and although we don't have any close neighbors somehow gossip finds its way to us. We had heard there was an important newspaper man about."

Jake shook his head smiling. "Well, I'm a newsman, but important I'm not." He might have said more in the way of making conversation, but as they approached an old, fire darkened kettle sitting on a fire, a woman in an old dress was using a long pole to stir the pot. The woman turned to look at Rebecca and Jake, causing Jake to completely lose his train of thought. He actually stopped walking while Rebecca strove on the last few steps to take the staff from the woman who stepped back from the fire and blinked her eyes to clear them of smoke. Jake stared. It was, as he had hoped, the woman from the stagecoach, and he felt an instant connection to her. Another would say it was simple physical attraction because the woman was beautiful, but the sadness on the women's face hid her beauty. And Jake wasn't thinking of beauty or anything else for that matter, or at least he couldn't think later what he was thinking. As he stood and stared, Rebecca began to stir the pot and the woman stared back at Jake, finally tilting her head a bit in curiosity at the behavior of this handsome young man.

Suddenly Jake remembered his manners and grabbed his hat from his head. "Good morning," he stammered.

Rebecca turned, "Oh, my manners, Charity, this is Mr. Evans, a newspaperman. Mr. Evans, this is my sister, Charity Chapin."

Jake stepped forward and still holding his hat in his left hand he extended his right hand, "Jake," he said.

Charity grasped it with a firm, almost manly grip and gave it a shake. "Would you mind taking a turn?" Charity asked, pointing at the kettle. "It is tiring and the smoke is very irritating."

Rebecca appeared about to speak, but seemed to think better of it as Jake stepped forward and took the pole, saying, "Allow me please," as Rebecca stepped back.

"My husband is in the field, but he will be in for lunch Mr. Evans, would you be kind enough to join us?"

"That would be great," said Jake, "Thank you." A bit later, using an old spoon, Jake scooped the mixture in the kettle into old gourds Pete brought from the barn and handed them to Pete who carefully set them in a neat row to cool. The women, satisfied he had the hang of the final stages of soap making, had excused themselves and disappeared into the house.

Pete introduced Jake to Dandy who had never barked at Jake, but had kept a respectful distance, watching him carefully. Jake rubbed Dandy's head and made an instant friend. As Jake visited with Pete, he saw Charity gathering tomatoes from the garden and then he heard a noise and turned to see Danny and Alvin walking their horses toward them.

After introductions, Danny asked Pete to see to the horses and he led Jake out to the pump to wash up. "We're blessed to have a well," said Danny as he worked the pump level while Jake washed his hands. "My parents had it done."

Jake stepped back and taking the pump handle, nodded his agreement.

Danny sat at the head of the table, Alvin to his left, then Pete and at the other end of the table sat Rebecca with Charity to her left and beside her and on Danny's right, sat a happy man, Jake Evans.

Danny said a prayer and then beefsteak, boiled potatoes, cornbread and fresh slices of tomatoes were passed among them. As Charity handed Jake the cornbread basket his hand brushed hers and he felt a thrill run through his body. Steady boy, he thought to himself. She's likely to have a husband or at least a suitor somewhere.

After everyone had filled their plate, Rebecca spoke. "I know you men have business to discuss after lunch, but I thought we might get to know each other a little. Besides, I've heard that newspaper men are very curious."

Jake smiled. "It's a fact."

"Mr. Evans, I am Rebecca Anderson, formerly Rebecca Chapin of Atlanta, widow of Raymond Taylor and mother of Pete. Mr. Taylor, an officer in the Confederate Army died at Gettysburg." She hesitated, her voice had cracked just slightly. Then, she smiled and looking at Danny said, "I met Danny in Atlanta. He was recovering from a wound, I was grieving and we found ourselves seated beside each other at a church service. Danny looked up and smiled at her.

Rebecca looked at Charity. "Sis?" she inquired very softly. "I, like everyone it seems, am a product of the war. Whatever I was or perhaps would have been was changed by that horrific madness."

Jake, his face a mask, stared at her, his fork, a bite of beefsteak dangling from it, was frozen in place a few inches above his plate.

Charity was quiet for a moment, then continued, "My fiancé died, I am told, at the Battle of Saylers Creek in Virginia, in '65. We were engaged for the entire war as he didn't want to marry until the war was over. He died just months before it was over," she said, almost to herself, bitterness apparent in her voice.

To fill the silence that followed, Jake spoke up. "Well," he said, "I hope you won't hold it against me, but I'm from up North. I, ah, wasn't a soldier, I did volunteer though," and he looked right at Charity, "to help with the wounded. I didn't carry a gun or fire a shot." He sat in silence for a moment, then shrugged his shoulders. "So anyways," he continued, "after it was over, I decided to see some of the country and while I was in Dallas, I met the editor there, he offered me a job if I would come out here to Fort Griffin and do some reporting, so…" his voice trailed off.

He glanced around the table to measure their reaction to his being a Northerner. Everyone was staring at him in silence as though he were some unexplained object they had run across. Danny spoke. "The war was an evil, horrible event, but God expects us all to forgive and serve as examples of Christians," he said with sincerity. "No one has escaped the effects, North or South," he continued. "But it is imperative we move on." He looked at Alvin. "I introduced my brother Alvin, but since we're getting all this out of the way, he lost his arm and his voice at Shiloh. Now, is there any coffee and pie?" he inquired, smiling.

Danny and Jake sat on the porch, drinking coffee. Jake could hear the women clearing and washing the dishes. Jake was trying to get his mind around his attraction to Charity, that she, as far as he knew, was unattached and the fact that she had not spoken to him or looked at him since he had admitted to being a Northerner and involved in the war that had killed her fiancé.

Danny speaking interrupted his thoughts. "Rebecca tells me you came out here pursuing a story. Is that right?" he asked. "Yes," said Jake. "Folks are interested about life out here, and I've written some stories about the fort, the Indians and the buffalo-hunters, but I thought maybe I would write one about life out here for families. It's my understanding you're a rancher."

Danny sipped his coffee, thought for a moment and said, "Well, I'm trying in that regards. My folks had a decent herd of longhorns when the army was up at Camp Cooper, before the war. But when Alvin and I left they began to struggle and then daddy died and mother couldn't deal with the cows. Really, daddy couldn't either. There wasn't anybody around to help."

"Mind if I take some notes?" asked Jake.

"Please yourself," said Danny, "but there's not much to tell. When Alvin and I came back there were maverick longhorns everywhere. So we started catching and branding them. The idea is to sell some, but also to keep some bulls and build a herd of cows that will calf in the spring. The market is small here, only the fort really and a few families that are trying to farm, but drovers are driving herds through the old Fort Worth settlement and on up to the new stockyards at Abilene, Kansas." He sipped on his coffee, lost in thought. "I'm thinking of trying my hand at farming though. Maybe corn."

Jake waited expectantly for him to continue.

"Look, Jake, we're probably not the best folks for you to interview. We're sort of, well, unusual I guess. Sort of a mixed up situation. Now there's a family a few miles south of us, the Franklin family. Bill and Eloise. They have a covey of kids and they been out here forever." He smiled.

"I think the war has affected almost everybody," Jake responded soberly.

Abruptly, Danny stood. He held out his hand to Jake. "I don't want to be rude Jake and I enjoyed meeting you, but I need to get back out in the field. Pete's out at the barn, he'll help you with your horse. Go with the Lord."

Jake, a bit stunned at the sudden end to the conversation, stood and shook Danny's hand. With that, Danny turned and walked quickly toward the barn. Jake stood there a minute, looked at the door and trying to decide if he should knock and say his good-byes, but then he remembered neither of the women had spoken directly to him since they found out he was a Yankee. He hesitated another minute, then looked out toward the barn where Danny was already riding back out to the north. As he neared the barn Pete came out leading Girl. "She had some oats Mr. Evans," said Pete, handing Jake the reins. Jake reached in his pocket, pulled out a two-bit piece and offered it to Peter. "Oh, I couldn't sir," said Peter. "You're our guest."

"Please," said Jake. "Get yourself some candy next time you're in town."

Smiling Pete took the coin and thanked Jake.

Jake took his time riding back down to the Flat. His mind played the scene over and over of his telling the Andersons he was from the North and that he had served with the army, their faces still. The problem was he felt a strong attraction to Charity.

"What are you, sixteen?" he asked himself out loud. Well, he thought, it don't matter, I don't have a hope. Of course, he could have told her he was a doctor, maybe that would have made a difference, but somehow he wanted her to accept him for, well, for him. It was dark when he got back to the stables where he found Flop and his new friend Perro laying in the hay by Loco, who was enjoying some oats. Jake turned Girl over to Whitt along with a dollar and headed to Kirk's for dinner. A bit later, entering Johnny's room, he was surprised to see the barber shaving Johnny, who was sitting in the room's chair. He had knocked at the open door and Johnny had hollered for him to come in and wait his turn. Jake had entered and sat on the bed without speaking.

"You feeling alright reporter?" Johnny asked. "You look poorly."

"Just tired," said Jake.

"That a fact," said Johnny, obviously not buying Jake's explanation.

They sat in silence as the barber finished up. Jake paid him with a fifty-cent piece lying on top of Johnny's dresser and then changed Johnny's bandages before helping him back to the bed. "I saw Loco, Flop and Perro down at the stables," he said. "They were all good, so you just take it easy. The girl come by today and see to you?"

"She did and thanks again Jake," he said, groaning a little as he settled into the bed.

"You're welcome," said Jake, "I'll stop by tomorrow."

TWENTY-NINE

RUSTY ACTUALLY FELT GUILTY. HE had informed the Andersons that he had hurt his back and they had been so sympathetic it was embarrassing him. Ms. Anderson had the boy bring him his meals. It was getting on to late March and Smith wanted him to keep a close eye on the Andersons, especially at night. So Rusty was hanging around the barn where he and Chase bunked, walking slow and holding his back and at night he was sitting in the loft watching until he saw the lamps go out in the house. Smith was sure the Andersons had some money buried and that they would need to dig some up soon.

In fact, Danny personally had no money, but Rebecca's parents had given them some when they got married. Her parents had been prosperous and had money hidden even as their farm was ravaged by the Union army. Danny had lived in fear of it being stolen as they made their way west and now it was safely buried. It was all in silver and gold coins and he had to move it every time he moved the outhouse because he always dug an extra hole for the money. He figured it unlikely that a thief would consider the outhouse a hiding place. They used the money sparingly and only to tide them over.

After Danny paid Rusty and Chase at the end of the month Rusty had reported the fact to Smith along with the fact that he hadn't seen anyone come out of the house at night. Smith told him to tell the Andersons he was better but would need a bit longer before he started riding and for him to search the house again when they left for town to buy supplies.

Rusty did as he was told and three days later Pete brought his breakfast and told him they were going to town and asked if he wanted them to fetch anything for him. Rusty said he was good. Chase came out of the house after breakfast and saddled his horse and rode off but returned an hour later. Rusty told him he had seen the women and the boy in the wagon and Anderson and Alvin riding horses as they all rode off down the road toward town. Chase said he had been watching from the thicket. Quickly, he and Rusty strolled up to the house and began to search. They didn't want to disappoint Smith, frankly, the man scared them, but although they made three searches, including tapping on the bricks around the fireplace, the only thing they found was the same coffee can in the cellar with a single dollar in it. Rusty didn't spend much time in the new room built for the sister, but he did give it a quick look, taking a minute as he ran his hand over her underthings.

"They got no money," said Chase. "Let's get out of here. Matter of fact, we been paid, lets ride out, to hell with Smith. I don't even like the man."

Rusty considered a minute, looking around. "I think we ought to square up with him though. He's the kind to hold a grudge."

"You know," said Chase, "these folks been nicer to me than anybody I've ever known."

"That right," said Rusty. "So, you want to tell them what we been up to? Maybe confront Smith and the boys?"

"No," said Chase, but I think we should ride. Smith ain't likely to..." He stopped talking, confused, as he saw Rusty reach for his sidearm and then freeze. Chase looked over toward the door and saw

Alvin standing there, a double-barreled shotgun pinned under his arm, his finger on the triggers. Chase froze. He and Rusty slowly raised their hands. At this range they would both be cut in half. Nobody moved for ten seconds, then Alvin moved slowly away from the door, waving the shotgun just slightly. Rusty and Chase, their hands held up and in front of them eased toward the door. Alvin followed them outside. The two boys slowly turned to face Alvin, then started to slowly turn toward the barn. Alvin shook his head no and motioned again with the shotgun, this time toward the road.

"You want us to walk?" stammered Rusty, his voice display- ing his total disbelief. "We was just going to leave a note. We was looking for a pencil."

As Rusty spoke, Chase turned just slightly, slowly lowering his right hand so he could grab his gun. He practiced quick draws all the time and felt that if Rusty could distract Alvin for just a second or two he could get the drop on him. Now, if Rusty would just keep talking.

He did. "Why the hell are you pointing that scattergun at us, huh? Mr. Anderson is going to be one mad man you run us off. We ain't done nothing wrong. I'm better and was gonna go to work."

Chase had gotten his hand down, just inches from his gun and he was drawing a breath in preparation to draw when a shot rang out and hit so close to his boot dirt sprayed over it. Chase jumped and so did Rusty. Just as sudden as the shot, a voice rang out strong and clear.

"Don't move a muscle." The voice came from the side of the house. Rusty and Chase recognized Danny's voice, but they didn't move. Danny stepped out from the side of the house, a rifle held steady and pointed at Chase.

"You watch Rusty," he said to Alvin. "I got to say I'm disappointed in you boys. Rebecca and I thought the world of you, but Dandy knew from day one. Yep, that's why I been a little uneasy you see. Cause Dandy has never liked either of you, so this bad back business seemed a little odd and yes we noticed some things moved last time, but didn't want to believe it was you Rusty or you Chase. I guess it was Baggett sent you. Well, you can tell Mr. Baggett you didn't find no money. Now, I would appreciate it if you would take your guns out with two fingers and drop them on the ground."

The two pulled out their guns and dropped them to the ground as ordered. "Now, if you boys start now you'll make town by nightfall. I'll leave your guns and horses at Whitt's in a day or two. Now go. And boys, go with the Lord."

Neither of the two had walked more than a block since they were young boys. It didn't take long before both were suffering badly from pain in their feet and their legs. They argued constantly. Blaming each other for what happened and they couldn't agree on what to do when they got to town. Should they just take off or try to explain what happened to Smith and then they began to wonder what they would say if anybody came along or when they got to town. They couldn't exactly tell people what they had been up to. Chase came up with the idea to tell people that they were attacked by a band of Negro outlaws. Rusty wouldn't hear of it. "I ain't gonna tell people I was bested by Negroes!" he exclaimed.

"I got it," said Rusty, "we'll say we fought it out with an Indian raiding party."

"Everybody knows the Indians don't come in here behind the fort," Chase explained calmly. "What if we said we quit the Andersons because he was always preaching to us and during the night we were fallen on by bushwhackers?"

"Yeah, that sounds good," said Rusty. "But we gotta see Smith. I don't want to be having to watch my back for next ten years. We didn't do nothing wrong. There wasn't any money. We just tell him. It isn't our fault the one-armed guy hid out and caught us. And besides, we didn't tell on him. Anderson thinks Baggett sent us."

"You're right by gosh!" said Chase. "For all anybody knows we was just gonna leave a note and take off. Which is what we say, see? And Anderson got mad, called us heathens and we left."

They looked at each other and smiled, but they never did catch a ride. When they limped painfully into town, long after dark, they went to the stable and bedded down in the hay, falling asleep almost instantly.

The next morning Rusty and Chase, both flush because they had been paid just days before by Danny, ate a large breakfast at Kirk's and then limped back down to the stable. They made a deal with Whitt to rent out a couple of horses and rigs for the day. Whitt had never seen them, but he didn't ask any questions although he asked for a large deposit. They grumbled, but paid it and headed out to the Baggett spread, dreading it, but becoming more confident as they discussed and reinforced each other's thoughts.

Smith had hired them one day when they came across him as they worked their way out west on the old Butterfield Trail. Smith had been out there alone, deer hunting. He made it clear they worked for him and not the ranch owner, Mr. Baggett. After giving them some money and instructions, he had sent them to the Anderson spread. In fact, they had heard a lot about Baggett in town, but had never seen him or spoken to him. When they saw the large stone house Baggett lived in they stopped, undecided as how best to find Smith.

"Well," said Rusty, "he said he was foreman, so we just ask the first person we see for the foreman."

123

They didn't approach the house, but walked the horses toward the corral where they could see some hands sitting on the fence. As they got close, Smith, who had been smoking and watching some cowboys working horses in the corral, saw them, turned and began walking toward them. His face was tight. Rusty and Chase got down from their mounts, and stood holding their horse's reins, both boys fidgeting nervously.

"Can I help you boys?" asked Smith when he was ten feet away, his face a mask of warnings.

"Yes sir," said Rusty. Then softly, "Could we have a word?" "I have an office out at the bunkhouse," said Smith loudly.

"Let's go out there and discuss your experience."

Smith looked around and assured no one else was about turned on the two boys who had followed him, leading their rented horses. "What the hell are you two idiots doing here!" he spit out between clenched teeth.

The two looked at each other. Rusty started explaining.

Five minutes later, Smith's face was hard, but he was calm.

"A one-armed man got the drop on you two and then a coward faced you down. Have I got it straight?" he asked pleasantly.

"Honestly, he didn't act like no coward," said Rusty, defensively. "But anyway, there weren't no money and Anderson thought Baggett had sent us. We didn't say nothing."

Smith thought for a minute, then, "I want you two to clear out of the area. Clean out of the state. I got friends. Any word comes back to me…"

"We're gone!" said Chase with enthusiasm.

Smith glared as the two mounted up, turned their horses away and spurred them into a trot.

"Woo wee," said Rusty, as he looked over at Chase and grinned.

The two were surprised and thrilled when they returned to the stable and Whitt told them he had their horses and kits. He even had their guns, but all of their bullets were gone. They settled up with Whitt, who didn't mention how he had come by their horses, and after a brief conference decided to forgo having another meal or another drink in the Flat. With that, they stopped by the general store for some supplies and decided to see what San Antonio might hold for two young men.

.

THIRTY

JAKE WAS NATURALLY A HAPPY go lucky man. Although his war experiences had made him rethink life to a certain extent, he generally approached each day with an optimistic outlook and a certain humor, never taking himself seriously, but he had been out of sorts ever since he had been out to the Anderson ranch. He knew it didn't make sense, but he felt a strong desire to get to know Charity better. His interest in writing news stories was waning. He had sent one off about progress at the fort with a freight wagon headed for Dallas, but hadn't taken a note or written a page since. He had spent the last two weeks visiting Johnny twice a day, changing his bandages and taking care of odds and ends for him.

He rode Loco twice, although he was terrified both times, but Johnny said the horse needed exercise and assured him that Loco knew him and wouldn't be a problem. His evenings he spent at the Frontier, drinking beer and visiting with Jones. He finally decided to ride back through Dallas, resign from the paper and then to head south, to seek out some new experiences. Sometimes, when he'd had an extra beer or two, he told himself he was running from his experiences in the war. Of course running did no good, because he still had nightmares several times a week, when he would awaken, terrified, often soaked in sweat.

The weather was turning pleasant and Johnny was healing well, thought Jake as he stepped into the Frontier one evening just as a fistfight erupted in the vicinity of the bar. It didn't last long because the bar patrons were more interested in drinking than watching the two slug it out, so one was quickly put out of action by a burly man wearing a coonskin cap who kicked one of the brawler's feet out from under him and the other one was hit in the back of the head with a pistol. It didn't knock him out, but sent him groaning and stumbling out the door.

Jake moved to one side and worked his way to the far end of the bar. Jones spotted him and brought him a beer which arrived just as Betsy, a working girl, came up behind Jake and hugged him. Betsy was a regular and although she was probably in her early twenties, she looked much older.

"Hi sweetie," said Betsy. "How about some company?"

With difficulty, due to Betsy's bear hug, Jake turned around. "Hey Betsy," he said.

"I'm going to have to pass, but thanks." She instantly let him go, her face frustrated. "What's with you? You're young and I'm young. Is there a problem?" She looked at him, her face a question.

"Well," said Jake, "it is not you Betsy, I'm spoken for."

That set her back for a moment. "Oh," she said. "A girl back home?"

"Yep," said Jake. "Childhood sweetheart. I came out west to make my fortune before I get married."

Betsy looked at him for a moment and then walked away. Jake sighed and turned back to his beer. A few minutes later he saw Betsy sitting in the lap of a cowboy, her arms around him. This was a strange place, thought Jake. Its very isolation attracted people, many of them running from something, often the law, sometimes debts and he felt sure, many were running from the damage the war had done.

So many had lost everything in the war. But some, he reflected, were seeking their fortune or like him, adventure. To add to the mix were the freedmen, the Mexicans, many who still considered this area part of Mexico, and the soldiers who were ordered to this isolated outpost.

Jones appeared at his elbow, but Jake shook his head no. He and Johnny had agreed that Jake would arrive before breakfast tomorrow at Johnny's room to remove the sutures. Johnny had been a terrible patient, but had healed in spite of himself.

THIRTY-ONE

BAGGETT HAD SMITH UP to the main house for breakfast so he could discuss dealing with the Andersons with him. The two sat at a large table alone eating well before daylight.

"I've lost patience with the Andersons," said Baggett, "but we have to be very careful. The local landowners all buy into that religious crap he's always spouting. And the simpletons are all impressed by the airs his wife puts on like she's special."

Smith didn't look up from his food; only grunted his acknowledgment.

"Now, I'm a businessman," said Baggett, "and seeing as how we may have to take some extraordinary measures, I'm going to double the bonus I promised you when they sign their land over to me."

At this, Smith looked up and smiled. "Well, I do appreciate that Mr. Baggett," he said, his mouth full of eggs.

"So," continued Baggett, "I'm thinking we put some pressure on them. Now, we've tried cutting out their cattle and hiring away their help, but the land's paid for and they keep hanging on. So it's time for some new tactics. I've been thinking they might have some money hid, but if they do or not, money isn't going to help if they're living in fear." He smiled.

Smith looked up from his plate again, set his fork down and picked up his coffee, sipping it while he waited for Baggett to continue.

Smith was a hard man, but he was afraid of Baggett. He wanted the money Baggett had promised, however, he didn't plan to go back to prison, hang or get himself killed trying to collect it. After the experience with Rusty and Chase, Smith wasn't sure the Andersons were going to be as easily intimidated or were as defenseless as Baggett seemed to think.

"What I plan to do," said Baggett, "is make life so uncom- fortable for them they'll come to me to buy their land. The key," said Baggett, "is for me to be totally and completely beyond suspicion.'

Smith frowned.

"I mean you too," stated Baggett, irritated. "Now," he continued, "last Saturday night, while you and the boys were in town," he stopped to look at Smith, who nodded. "I had a few drinks with that new fellow you hired, what's he call himself? Lambert I think. Yea, well anyway, strange duck I was thinking, man says he's saving his money, not going to town. He's hiding, but no skin off my back. But then I got to thinking. Nobody knows him or knows he works for me. Right?"

Smith's first reaction was to tell Baggett that Lambert was really Kyle Smith, his half-brother, but he thought better of it. "That's right," he said. "Fellow's hiding out I guess, but nobody except our boys know about him."

"Well," said Baggett, grinning. "Mr. Lambert seems to be in need of money and don't seem all that concerned about how he earns it. Add that to the fact nobody knows he works for me, hell, nobody except our crew knows he exists, well, truth be told, he's the key to my new plan."

THIRTY-TWO

JOHNNY WAS WAITING when Jake arrived in the pre-dawn to remove his stitches. It didn't take long and there was some scar tissue built up, but when he pushed on the still red and puffy wound, it appeared to be healing well. Johnny's stomach muscles were still very sore and he moved stiffly, but he was able to get around and Jake knew there was no use in telling him to take it easy any longer.

The two walked slowly down to Kirk's for their breakfast. A number of men nodded or said 'morning' to Johnny. Johnny had always been accepted and respected, but his two saloon fights and his role in the Indian skirmish had earned him a reputation in the small settlement.

After breakfast they stepped out of the restaurant and made their way down to the livery where Loco began to toss his head and whiney upon seeing Johnny. Flop and Perro were sniffing around the outside of the stables and both ran to greet them. Johnny fished out a piece of ham for both of them and rubbed their heads before turning his attention to Loco. As Johnny talked to Loco and brushed him, Jake stepped outside to build a cigarette. The day had dawned clear and warm and it appeared that the area had escaped a late frost. It hadn't rained much though and the streets were hard as rock. Jake pondered this for a moment, wondering how this might affect the wheat and corn some were growing or even the grazing for the longhorns. Well, he decided, spring generally brought rain so it would probably rain soon enough.

As he stood and smoked the street began to fill with more and more activity as people began their days. His thoughts turned once again to the Andersons, but now he began to wonder about the abrupt ending to his conversation with Danny Anderson. Why had he said their situation was different, he wondered? Well, it didn't matter. He considered his decision to move on and although he wasn't really satisfied with the idea, he knew it was the right thing for him.

It was then he caught a glimpse of a wagon making its way down the main drag. He was sure he had seen a flash of blue dress like the one Charity had worn the day she had arrived in the Flat. Dang, he thought to himself, you're losing your mind boy. Better you get gone before you go completely crazy. But just the same he tossed his butt down, stepped on it with his boot and started walking down to the corner where the Busy Bee Saloon stood. Arriving at the corner, he looked up the street and saw the end of the wagon stopped in front of the Birchfield general store, but he couldn't tell if it was the Anderson's or not. It was too far. He stepped into the street, totally unconscious of his actions. Like a man sleep walking he crossed the street, two men on horses yelling at him as he stepped in front of them, but he ignored them, crossing over to Shane's Saloon on the other side before turning right, his eyes focused up the way. Arriving in front of Birchfield's, Jake stopped, trying to peer inside. He stepped up to the window to get a better look.

"Mr. Evans!" said a voice behind him as he leaned forward to peer into the window.

Jake, startled, jumped like he was shot. He turned to see Charity staring at him, her mouth set, her face displaying, not its usual sadness, but something between anger and unhappiness.

Jake grabbed his hat from his head. "Ms. Chapin?" It came out a question as though Jake couldn't quite place her, as though she hadn't filled his thoughts since he first saw her.

"Yes, Mr. Evans, Charity Chapin," she said. "I'm sorry, but I couldn't help myself. Your behavior last week was unforgivably rude. My sister told me not to concern myself, but then she is a Southerner, and always shows class. I realize full well that you are a Yankee, but surely even Yankees learn to say thank you and goodbye after being fed." She stared at him.

Jake found himself unable to form a coherent thought. He wanted to kiss her. Instead, he asked, "Would you like a cup of coffee? Kirk has it on all day. It's a might strong, but you could add some water."

Charity stared at him in disbelief. "It's my sister that you need to make amends to," she said stiffly.

"Oh," said Jake quickly. "She can come too."

Charity stepped past him, opening the door as she said, "Good day Mr. Evans."

As the door closed and she disappeared from sight, Jake stood there holding his hat trying to figure out what had happened. He thought to follow her into the store, but then thought better of it. He considered himself a smart man, but he now realized that his smarts were book smarts and that he knew nothing, absolutely nothing about women. Maybe Johnny did, he thought as he placed his hat on his head and started making his way back down to the livery.

Jake waited till the middle of lunch before approaching the issue with Johnny. "Can I ask your advice?" queried Jake as he and Johnny ate fried chicken.

"I don't tend to giving advice," said Johnny. "I figure a fellow should do whatever strikes him and probably will no matter what I say. Least that's my experience."

Jake ate on his chicken for a minute, then broached Johnny again. "What I mean is, I'd like to know what you would do if you was me."

"I am not you," answered Johnny. "And no matter how well you know a man, even your own kin, every man and woman has to walk this earth and live their life themselves. Nobody can do it for them. A person can feel some for those suffering or be glad for someone's happiness I guess, but at the end of the day, we're all alone."

Jake stared at him. "Thanks Johnny, for the philosophy lesson, but I would really appreciate you hearing me out."

"Well, I'm going to finish my chicken and gravy, have a cup of coffee and apple pie and then I'm going to have a smoke. After that I plan to take a nap. I don't plan to shoot you - unless you interfere with my nap, so if you can get it out before then, go ahead and explain what's troubling you. Probably be beneficial anyway. I'm tired of seeing you looking like your dog died. Let's hear it reporter."

Jake took a deep breath and relayed the story of his visit to the Anderson farm, his introduction to Charity, Danny Anderson's abrupt departure and how he had left without saying anything, thinking he had brought up bad memories and wasn't welcome as a former member of the Union. Johnny was working on his apple pie and coffee. He looked at Jake, but offered no comment. Jake continued, explaining the morning's events in front of Birchfield's.

"What I can't figure," explained Jake, "is why Charity, I mean Ms. Chapin, is so mad."

"Reporter," said Johnny, pushing away his pie plate and drawing his coffee closer. "If you plan to leave in the next few days, why do you care what the Andersons think about you? I doubt they have time to give you much thought, to be honest."

Jake looked down at his unfinished chicken dinner. "I'm not sure," he finally got out.

Johnny sipped his coffee and then leaned back as Maybelle stepped in and refilled his cup before darting off again. Johnny pulled out a cigarillo and a match, struck the match on the bottom of his boot and lit up.

"Okay," said Jake, "I'm attracted to Charity. I'd like to get to know her better. There, you happy now." He glared at Johnny.

"Did you just figure that out, or you been holding back?" asked Johnny.

"Sorry, I've, you know, desired some women before, and slept with a few at school, but I've never felt, you know, like I wanted to protect a woman."

"What I would do, reporter, is finish up here, go down to Whitt's, buy a horse and head either east or south, but either way, I wouldn't look back." Johnny drew on his smoke and studied Jake's reaction.

"That's your advice?" asked Jake, as though he couldn't believe he'd heard correctly.

"I told you, I don't give advice," said Johnny flatly, "but you asked what I would do and if you were listening, I just provided you with that information." With that, Johnny laid some money on the table, rose and walked out the door.

Nightfall found Johnny and Jake back at the Frontier. Flop had seemed hesitant to leave his new buddy, so Johnny had told them to stay with Loco at the livery. Jake had planned to play some poker and even considered going to the Busy Bee so as to avoid Johnny, although he wasn't sure why. He wasn't sure if Johnny had taken him seriously or made fun of him, but in the end he found himself at the bar sipping on a beer and telling his story to Jones, who nodded and seemed to be enthralled with Jake's story.

Johnny was at the poker table enduring some good-natured joshing about his adventure with the knife wielding sailor at Shane's.

"What you get, going to another saloon," joked Birchfield.

Johnny smiled and the dealer, a fellow now provided by the Frontier's owner so as to discourage claims of cheating, called five-card stud and began dealing.

Having finished his story, Jake looked expectantly at Jones who smiled the smile of a wise man who knew all the answers. "Well, Jake," said Jones, "given your youth I can understand your confusion, but it's as plain as day."

Jake waited, but Jones was enjoying himself. Finally, Jake exclaimed, "What's plain?"

"First off," explained Jones, "Anderson isn't a drinker, I've never met the man and men tend to be close mouthed about themselves in these parts, but gossip is steady fare here as you know. The word is that he's under a lot of pressure from Baggett, rough fellow owns the place north of the Andersons. He and his foreman, Smith, drink in here occasionally, but generally they and their crew prefer the company at Shane's place. Been buying everybody out, cheap. Rumor has it he plays rough. Just a minute" Jones turned and went down the bar to see to some customers.

Jake sipped his beer and didn't have to wait long for Jones to return. "So, anyway, Anderson's married to that Southern beauty, well, I guess you saw her up close. Word is she isn't all that happy out here on the edge of civilization."

"That could well explain Anderson's reluctance to talk," said Jake. "I saw him, Baggett I mean, spit on Anderson."

Jones shook his head in disbelief.

"But what about Ms. Chapin, acting all mad and such?" Jake asked.

"Why that's easy Jake, you lucky sod," said Jones smiling, "the girl's sweet on you."

It was late when Johnny pushed away from the poker table, but Jake had waited and when he saw Johnny stand, he pushed his glass away, nodded to Jones and joined Johnny on the walk back to the hotel. They walked in silence, both lost in their own thoughts as lightning and thunder split the sky. Just as they reached the hotel the first rain began to fall.

THIRTY-THREE

JAKE LAY IN BED, listening to the crash of thunder and pounding of rain on the roof. Lightning flashes cast eerie shadows across his room. He was thinking about what Jones had said about Charity. Was it possible he asked himself? Did she feel the same attraction he did? If so, why had she been so hostile toward him? At some point in the night he fell into a deep sleep, his first in a week. He woke a few minutes later than usual and while he was shaving, with cold water, he heard Johnny's door close. He would be on his way to breakfast, thought Jake, who was still not fully awake.

The rain had stopped in the early hours, but the streets were a sea of mud. As he fought the mud, trying to hurry up the street for breakfast, Jake heard the bugle blowing from the fort, but it seemed out of place. For one thing, the timing just didn't seem right. Jake suddenly realized the bugler was signaling a call to arms. His first thought was that the fort was under attack. As he entered the restaurant there was a stillness, a certain quiet while men listened to the bugle call. Then when it ceased, excited talking broke out.

Jake worked his way over to the table he and Johnny shared most mornings. Johnny had coffee, but his breakfast had not yet arrived. Jake nodded and turned to wave at Maybelle as he pulled out his chair. Jake looked questioningly at Johnny who was sipping his coffee and looked like he hadn't heard the bugle call.

"Morning reporter," said Johnny. "I see you didn't take my advice," he continued, but with a smile.

"Good morning Johnny," said Jake, mystified at Johnny's lack of concern. "Did you hear the bugle call?" he asked.

"I did," said Johnny. "Thank you, Maybelle," he said, as Maybelle, barely slowing down, sat his breakfast and Jake's coffee on the table. "I'm guessing there's been another Indian attack in the area. Reckon I'll ride up to the fort after breakfast. It'll take them an hour or so to mount up."

As Johnny began to eat, Jake's mind flashed with thoughts of the last time he and Johnny had ridden out with the army in pursuit of Indians. He was startled back to the present when Maybelle dropped his plate on the table before dashing away. Jake was just finishing up and Johnny was having a final cup of coffee when Whitt came through the door.

"The Indians raided the Starnes's place last night," he exclaimed loudly. "Stole their horses and took their boy!" Silence filled the room. "Starnes is hurt, but he'll live."

Johnny and Jake reached the fort less than an hour later. It was a beehive of activity as the army was organizing its response. A group of Tonkawa Indians sat on the ground, off to one side, smoking, holding their horse's reins. Supply wagons were being loaded and extra horses were being readied. Army non-commissioned officers shouted orders. Jake saw a handful of civilians gathered to one side, either looking for news or planning to join the rescue, Jake wasn't sure.

Jake had stopped at the hotel for his revolver, now in place in its pommel holster. He had hesitated, but grabbed his medical bag and shoved it into his saddlebags. Reaching the livery, he asked for Girl, the mare he rented from Whitt, but Whitt said she wouldn't be up to the pace. Instead he helped Jake bridle a young black gelding called, reasonably, thought Jake, Blackie. Johnny had saddled Loco and spent several minutes talking to and stroking Flop, who, disappointed walked back into the livery followed by Perro. The gelding has been edgy and a bit contrary on the way to the fort, but Jake knew horses and easily kept up with Johnny and Loco. Jake had borrowed a rifle from Whitt and offered to pay him when Whitt handed him a box of cartridges but Whitt had shook his head. The Indians were a common enemy and having a child or a woman stolen was everyone's nightmare. It was possible the Indians might try to ransom the boy, but many children, taken by the Indians had never been heard from again.

It was nearly two hours since the first bugle call when the army patrol, sixty troops and officers, accompanied by two supply wagons, twenty extra horses, fourteen civilians, including Johnny and Jake, was led out of the fort by five Tonkawa scouts. Jake rode along-side an older farmer whose wife had been killed in an Indian raid several years before. The man told Jake that he had spoken to Starnes. During the raid, his teenage son had ran out to the corral to try to save his horse. Starnes and his wife had prevented the raiding party from setting fire to their barn or house, but their son and all of their horses were taken. Starnes had gone to the corral during the fight after seeing his son trying to get to his horse and had been cut badly, a long gash down his left arm, when an Indian on a horse came up behind him and tried to stab him with a long spear. The heavy rain had left the ground soft and it made for slow movement.

By the time they reached the Starnes's home, it was lunch. Word was passed that the wagons and a security force would follow, making the best time they could and after resting and eating, the main force, carrying only weapons, water and a day's rations would move out in pursuit. The Tonkawa were nowhere to be seen. Captain Bates was in charge and he was anxious to catch up with the Comanches and less than a half-hour after reaching the Starnes' spread, they were on their way, following the tracks first by the Comanches and then the pursuing Tonkawa.

They rode hard all day and when the horses were near total exhaustion, they made camp in a clearing atop a small rise that gave a good view of the surrounding area. It was windy and cold, making it difficult to start the fires, and the soldiers grumbled, but the Captain had no intention of being trapped in a draw.

While it was still light, Johnny walked the perimeter, his long black duster blowing in the wind, smoking a cigarillo while his rifle dangled from his left hand. Jake had unbuttoned his duster, identical to Johnny's, and after pulling a notebook and pencil from his saddlebags, sat by a small fire he had built and took notes. If he lived he figured he would write up the story and send it in. His mental state was better. The sleep had helped, but it had come only after he made up his mind to ride out to the Anderson spread and confront Ms. Charity Chapin, face-to-face. She wouldn't catch him unawares this time, he thought. This thing would be settled, at least to his satisfaction. He'd explain why he had ridden off after lunch without expressing his appreciation. He would apologize to Mrs. Anderson. In fact, but for the Indian raid, it would have been over by now. He had convinced himself that the problem stemmed from the fact that it had been too long since he had enjoyed the company of a young woman. That was all there was to it, at least until Ms. Chapin had verbally attacked him just because he was trying to spare their feelings. All he wanted to do now was to explain things, apologize to Mrs. Anderson and then he'd take Johnny's advice and be on his way to whatever new adventures awaited him. He might even head down to Mexico where he would hang out and drink with the pretty young senoritas he had heard about. The more he thought about it, the idea of heading to Mexico seemed like a good one.

They were running low on water late the next day and Johnny knew they would have to stop and wait for the supply wagons if they didn't hit a creek soon. Suddenly two of the Tonkawa scouts appeared out of the trees. One minute there was nothing and the next the two Indians were riding toward them. Captain Bates was very glad to see them.

Johnny watched and smoked while the Captain conferred with the Scouts. Perhaps twenty minutes passed before word came to move east in single file for about a half mile to a small stream. They found it well shaded by cottonwoods and willows growing close to the creek bed. As they dismounted and led the horses to the water, everyone filled their canteens. Another conference and word was passed to make camp, but no fires and everyone was warned to make no noise. The enemy was close by. A guard was posted, and the troops began to break out their hardtack and jerky.

Johnny walked over to Captain Bates who recognized him from the fort. "Sir," said Johnny who touched his hat with his finger. "Don't mean to bother you," began Johnny.

"I'm glad to see you. You were with us during the last little skirmish," the Captain observed. "The Tonkawa scouts have spotted the raiding party and the horses. This creek bed widens about three miles west, sort of an arroyo, but there is still some water. According to the scouts, the Comanche have the horses penned up there." He smiled. "I figure we'll split into two groups, one goes north and one south," as he used his hands to describe a circling motion. "I'm forming the battle plan, but I'm thinking it'll be light about five and I want to be in place so we can hit them at first light."

Johnny nodded, then spoke. "That sounds like a sound plan Captain, but I suspect a raiding party will hit the supply wagons tonight."

The Captain smiled again. "Well, I doubt that Mr. Black, but if you took note, I left ten troops with the wagons and extra horses and all of the civilians stayed back except you and your partner. The Sergeant in charge of the group is an experienced man. He'll see they set up in a defensive position, so you can rest easy."

Captain Bates nodded and turned away, striving off with purpose, not giving Johnny a chance to respond. Johnny joined Jake who put away his notebook and they ate in silence. Jake thought to ask Johnny what he had found out, but thought better of it after studying Johnny's demeanor. They tended to their horses, brushing them down and cleaning the mud from their hoofs.

Suddenly Johnny walked off heading for the small group sitting around the Captain who was sitting on a camp stool. Reaching the group, Johnny addressed the Captain. "If it's all the same to you," he said, "my companion and I figure to ride back and camp with the wagons."

The Captain studied Johnny. Obviously, he thought, the stories of the man's daring and courage were exaggerated or perhaps he had just lost his nerve. "Take word to Sergeant Stapleton if you will of my plan. Tell him I want him to head this way at first light. The battle won't be lengthy and we'll be wanting the rations and," he hesitated, "the wagons for the wounded."

Johnny touched his hat, turned and left to advise Jake of his decision.

As Johnny walked away, Captain Bates gave some thought to what had been said. Although he had served in the Civil War, Bates had managed to keep himself clear of the fighting by using his family's political connections to secure staff positions for himself. But after the war, many of the officers who had distinguished themselves and lived to tell about it, thought Bates, were seen in a favorable light. His father had suggested that he volunteer to serve on the frontier so he could see some action against the Indians. His father felt that he needed it for career advancement. In fact, the recent skirmish with the Indians had been his first time in action. He hadn't actually distinguished himself, but he thought, he was the leader and he had by God, led. Had he not? He had fired his revolver at several of the savages and had remained behind to check on everyone and monitor the situation when the troops had ridden off in pursuit. I am a trained military officer, and Black is another ruffian who thinks he knows a lot more than he does. He probably fought on the losing side and because he was in the war thinks he is an authority, thought Bates.

Sergeant Stapleton didn't seem surprised to see them approach, but when Johnny explained that the Tonkawas had located the Comanches and a morning attack was planned, his eyes narrowed. But before he could speak, Johnny explained he was confident of an attack on the wagons after dark and he had told the Captain, but the Captain had disagreed.

Sergeant Stapleton was chewing tobacco and he turned his head and spit. "The Captain lacks experience," he said, "Thanks for coming back with word."

THIRTY-FOUR

SERGEANT STAPLETON CALLED A MEETING and told everyone to finish dinner quickly and to put out the fires. He explained the Indians they were chasing were close and likely were watching them now. Everyone exchanged nervous glances. Soon everyone was in place and ready. Stapleton had appointed a guard, but there was little chance of anyone sleeping.

Expecting an attack by screaming Indians on horseback, two troops and one civilian died before anyone knew the assault was taking place. The moon and stars were largely hidden by cloud cover and using the dark, the Indians had crept into the camp and using knifes had killed the men, almost silently. One of the men had struggled, however, and a troop had fired his rifle, at almost point-blank range, at the intruder, alerting the camp. At the sound of the gunshot, the mounted Indians, screaming war cries, charged from the darkness.

Miles away, Captain Bates was awake, lying on his bedroll in the open air, going over his battle plan in his mind, when he thought he heard distant gunfire. Looking up at the sky, he decided it might be thunder. When he heard it again, a distant, dull sound, he felt a chill.

Jake had no time to think - only to act. Later, when he had time to revisit it all in his mind, he would remember how confusing the first fight had been when Hurricane had broken his legs, but fighting in the dark made the confusion much, much worse. As the raiders attacked on horseback, screaming and firing arrows at the wagons, the army troops maintained a firm discipline. The first shots came from panicking civilians, who fired into the dark at the noise, but the troopers held their fire until the Comanches were close. Men and horses screamed and fell. Gunshots and arrows split the darkness.

Wagons shielded the group on two sides, about thirty yards apart, and water barrels from the wagons had been set up on each end to form a defensive perimeter. There were too many horses to keep them all inside, but Loco and Blackie, along with the Sergeant's horse were there. The others had been tethered from a long rope that was tied to one of the wagons. If they were attacked, they planned to cut the horses loose. Maybe the Indians would chase them, maybe not. Sergeant Stapleton had placed the civilians under the wagons, three troopers behind each wall of barrels, and two troopers behind each wagon, with instructions to fire over them. Sergeant Stapleton told them he would stand in the middle if they were attacked to direct the defense. Johnny offered to post himself with him so they could stand back to back if the need arose. The Sergeant accepted gladly and everyone had bedded down to wait for dawn. Jake was lying under the eastern most wagon and as an Indian appeared out of the dark, his bow drawn, Jake aimed at his chest and squeezed off a shot. The brave jerked and dropped his bow but stayed mounted as he fell forward onto the horse's neck and then toppled off just feet from Jake as the horse veered right to miss the wagon.

As gunshots, screams and yells filled the air, Jake looked back to see Johnny standing alone in the center of the compound. Johnny's duster was gone and he was bare-headed, his hair blowing in the wind. An unlit cigarillo protruded from his mouth, and Jake realized he didn't want to make himself a target with a lit cigar. Holding his rifle, an 1866 model Winchester Henry Repeater, in his left hand, he was pulling cartridges from his pocket and reloading his rifle. A glint of light, caused by a gunshot perhaps, flashed off the yellow loading gate on the side of the rifle. Suddenly a horse filled the space in front of Johnny as a mounted Indian carrying a tomahawk leapt his horse over the water barrels, landing and heading for Johnny. The horse charged as the Indian screamed a war cry. Johnny quickly drew his revolver and fired two quick shots without moving from his position. The horse, his eyes white with fear, continued to charge even as his rider grabbed at his throat where one of the shots had hit him and toppled backwards off the horse. Johnny might have managed to jump out of the way, but when the charging horse was only yards from Johnny, it collided with a huge dark form, and the Indian pony was knocked sideways and off its feet before it could hit Johnny.

Loco, his nostrils flaring reared up on his hind legs and let loose a fearful scream seldom heard coming from horses as his front hoofs came down. The Indian pony no longer a threat, Loco turned right to circle the inner compound.

Flames lit up the sky as the wagon Jake was under caught fire from a lit torch thrown in it by an Indian. The extra ammunition had been buried, and the water barrels unloaded to be used on the perimeter, but the wagons held blankets, bags of oats, rations and cooking gear. As bits of burning wood fell on him, Jake looked to his right and left only to find himself alone under the wagon. He began to crawl backwards. After clearing the wagon, Jake began to rise and looked to his right to see an Indian in the perimeter holding a rifle pointed at him. As Jake brought up his own rifle, the Indian fired and Jake felt like someone had punched him hard in the head and his arms felt too weak to raise his own rifle. He felt like he was about to pass out and his vision blurred as he saw a trooper drive a bayonet into the Indian's back and the Indian, a look of surprise on his face slowly knelt down as his knees buckled. Is that real, was Jake's last thought as he saw the bayonet protruding from the Indians chest as though it had appeared there by magic.

The attack on the wagon detail had come about an hour before dawn. The Captain, realizing his mission priority was to recover the kidnapped boy, split his forces. It went against all of his training, but he intuitively felt it was what he should do. He led the attack on the arroyo with twenty-five troopers and he sent Lieutenant Angleton with the other twenty to assist the wagon detail. They were spread thin, but if the Indians had divided their forces they would also be at less than full strength. Starnes had estimated twenty Indians had raided his homestead, but there could be a larger force out here, waiting. Well, thought the Captain remembering his leadership training. Any decision is better than no decision. He decided to take the Tonkawas with him. At 0415 hours, the two groups galloped toward their destinations.

It didn't take long for the Captain's group to cover the three miles. He took eight of the troops along with the Tonkawas and approached from the north while the other 17 came at the Comanche camp from the south. The raid was a surprise, as the Indians had gambled that the entire force would respond to the attack on the wagons. A brief battle broke out, but there were only five braves watching the horses and the captured boy. Two of them had been hurt, probably in the raid on the Starnes ranch. These two moved slowly and were quickly shot dead where they stood. One of the other three stepped from behind a tree and drew his bow but was shot in the lower buttocks by the troops approaching from the south. The third one, a young warrior, perhaps too young to have made his first kill, made it to his horse and climbed aboard, but was promptly shot by at least two soldiers.

The young Starnes boy was terrified, but unhurt. As the troops gathered the horses and rummaged through the Indian camp, the Captain sat on his horse and pictured himself leading the troops back into the fort, the Commander waiting outside to congratulate him.

What Captain Bates didn't know, however, was the situation at the wagon camp wasn't good. Sergeant Stapleton had died moments after the battle started, an arrow burying itself in his heart. Six of the troopers were dead, and the other three were all wounded, one so badly it was doubtful he would make it back to the fort alive. Of the ten civilians, four were dead and two were seriously wounded. They might or might not live. Jake lay on his back, his face invisible for the blood. He had been left for dead, but Johnny had knelt, and feeling a weak pulse, had ordered one of the unwounded civilians to clean his head wound with water and try to stop the bleeding if possible.

Johnny was unhurt as far as he could tell. He was covered with blood and dirt but had no time to assess his own situation as he took charge and organized the recovery. One of the wounded troopers, a solider named Coleman offered his services and Johnny had given orders to the four unwounded civilians, including the farmer that Jake had visited with on the way out.

The wagon that had been on fire was almost completely burned up, two of the water barrels had been punctured by gunfire and they had cut the extra horses loose, but there was a medical kit in Sergeant Stapleton's saddlebag, so Johnny had an able-bodied force, more or less, of five. He put two to assisting the wounded, one to finding canteens and seeing that the wounded had water and the other two to moving the dead men's bodies to the center of the compound. With everyone at work, Johnny walked over to Loco and stood stroking his neck and talking to him for a few minutes before going back to check on Jake, who, Johnny was sure, would soon be dead.

"He's still breathing," said the man holding a bloody neckerchief to Jake's head.

Johnny nodded and walked over to the undamaged wagon. He rummaged around and found a bucket. After filling it with water from one of the barrels, he watered Sergeant Stapleton's horse, Blackie and Loco.

The fight had not been over long when the relief force, led by a Corporal arrived. The Corporal was an old hand; he had been a Sergeant several times before being busted down and quickly took in the situation before riding over to where Johnny squatted studying Jake.

Johnny looked up and spoke to the Corporal. "You need to gather the horses, we had to cut them loose. We're going to need to cut some wood poles and make some litters so we can put the dead on them. The wagon is going to be needed for the wounded."

"How many wounded sir?" asked the Corporal. The sir was automatic. There was no doubt Johnny had been an officer at one time. The man's very presence screamed officer, thought the old Corporal and he was happy to let the man take charge.

"Six at the moment," said Johnny, looking back down at Jake. "Eleven dead," he added somberly, then, "so far."

The Indians always tried to recover the bodies of their dead comrades so although Johnny was certain they had killed or wounded a fair number, the only Indian bodies they found were the ones in the compound. The one Johnny had shot with his pistol and the one that had been bayoneted in the back after he shot Jake.

Johnny recovered his duster, still neatly folded and tied over his saddlebags and almost by accident found his hat blown up against one of the barrels.

THIRTY-FIVE

WHEN THE CAPTAIN and his troupe of soldiers arrived, leading the stolen horses, litters had been cut from cottonwoods and the field mess tent, under Johnny's orders, had been taken out of the wagon and cut up to make beds for the three litters that held the dead. Of the six wounded, three felt they could ride, so Jake and one soldier and one civilian were carefully placed in the wagon along with the extra weapons. The horses had all been watered from the water barrels, the canteens filled. A fire had been built and coffee prepared. The old farmer tended to Jake and the other two wounded. Jake's bleeding had slowed to a slow seep, but he was still unconscious and his breathing was ragged.

Arriving at the wagon site, the Captain sat on his horse taking everything in. His emotions were very mixed. The attack on the wagon detail had been devastating and he quickly assessed how to avoid any blame. At the same time, he was very surprised at what had been done.

The Corporal approached, saluted and said, "Sir, there's coffee," pointing to the fire. Then remembering himself, he said, "Sir, Corporal reports eleven dead and six wounded due to an Indian attack. The dead include Sergeant Stapleton. The survivors say Sergeant Stapleton set up a really good defense and owe their lives' to his leadership."

This report was the one Johnny had coaxed him with earlier. He didn't really say it outright, but led the Corporal to it. Johnny also told the Corporal he had done a good job organizing the recovery and that he planned to tell the Captain just that. An old and experienced soldier, he realized Johnny wanted to be left out of the thing. Could be the man couldn't afford any attention be drawn to him, but no matter, the Corporal was more than happy to go along.

The Captain looked around for Johnny. Could he be so lucky Johnny was one of the dead and there would be no chance it getting out that he had warned the Captain. But he knew Johnny had taken charge upon Sergeant Stapleton's death. The man carried himself like an officer, a senior officer at that, thought the Captain. Damn the man. Things were too well in hand for the Corporal to have done it. He saw Johnny then, standing by the wagon. He seemed to be checking on one of the wounded men.

THIRTY-SIX

THE COMMANDER WASN'T WAITING OUTSIDE when the troupe returned to the fort. The Captain gave orders to Lieutenant Angleton and dismounted in front of headquarters. The wounded wagon was driven straight to the medical building and Johnny followed.

Johnny waited outside the small office while the doctor, a large, older man prodded and poked at Jake's wound. He cut away some of the hair and cleaned the wound. Finally, he packed it with dressing and wrapped Jake's head.

The doctor wasn't optimistic. "The bullet hit him high close to his hairline, shot away a part of the bone that covers his brain. Sort of a glancing blow if you will. I don't know if it damaged his brain or not. We'll know soon enough I suspect."

Johnny stared at him, his face hard. The doctor licked his lips. "Look Mr. Black, he may die at any moment or he might wake up at any moment. If he does wake up, he might have problems with his speech or walking. However, he might just wake up and be fine. Only God knows." The doctor looked at Johnny's bloodshot eyes, week's growth of beard and bloody clothes. "I think you should get a bath, a shave, maybe a meal and some sleep. Nothing you can do for your friend. For that matter nothing I can do either, truth be told. At this point, prayer is all that's left."

Early the next morning, feeling a lot better physically after following the doctor's advice, Johnny rode Loco up to the fort, Flop and Perro following. Arriving at the fort, he removed his hat and stepped into the small room where Jake was recovering. However, much to his surprise, the cot was empty. Johnny had seen a lot of death and suffered many losses in his lifetime, but still, he had come to enjoy Jake's company and enthusiasm for life. Johnny found the doctor in another, larger room, soldiers lined up outside the door for sick call. The doctor looked up and smiled. "You'll find your friend at the chow hall," said the doctor, still smiling.

"He woke up complaining his head hurt and he was starving. After giving him some laudanum for his pain, I told him the fare served up by the army cooks wasn't fit for man or beast, but he insisted."

Stunned, Johnny quickly uttered thanks, turned and left. Breakfast was over and the troops were on the drill field, but as Johnny entered the building where the troops were fed, he saw Jake seated at a table with the cooks and their assistants.

As Johnny approached, Jake saw him, smiled and said, "Morning Johnny." A cook, recognizing Johnny, ordered a helper to fetch Johnny a cup of coffee. Johnny stood staring at Jake, his head was wrapped in bandages, he was wearing a shirt several sizes too big for him. As Johnny stared, Jake said, "I borrowed the shirt from the doc, mine was thrown away, too bloody to clean." Then he added, "Head wounds tend to bleed a lot."

THIRTY-SEVEN

BAGGETT'S PLAN WASN'T FULLY FORMED, but he figured he would work on it as things progressed. Everybody in the area knew he wanted Anderson's spread, so he had to make sure he wasn't suspected in the events he planned to put in motion. Well, he thought, he'd be the first-person folks thought of, but he would make sure he didn't take any blame.

After a short meeting, Smith got to work carrying out Baggett's instructions. He personally removed the shoes from a spare saddle horse that no one rode and found an old feed sack. He had Kyle place it over his head so Smith could cut out holes for his eyes. It took some rummaging, but Baggett found an old serape poncho for Kyle to put over his clothes. The disguise probably wasn't necessary, but Baggett wasn't taking any chances. If anyone found his horse's tracks, they would think it was from an Indian pony and with the serape and feed sack, in the unlikely event someone spotted him, Kyle couldn't be identified. With everything in place, the next Saturday night, Baggett and Smith took the entire crew to town for dinner and then an evening at Shane's saloon.

While Baggett and his men were drinking, the Anderson's homestead came under assault. Hearing a crash and then rifle shots, Danny leapt from his bed, ordered everyone on the floor and grabbing his rifle he ran toward the barn where Alvin, wearing only his long-johns, ran out of the barn where he slept, holding a pistol in his hand. They met outside the now empty corral, a section having been pulled down allowing the horses to escape and helped along by the rifle shots. There was a single burning torch laying close to the barn, a piece of long dead cottonwood, wrapped with rope and soaked in oil. Either they planned to burn the barn or it was a warning. Danny picked it up and studied the tracks outside the corral. Although there were many, it was the unshod horse tracks that caught his eye. Could it have been Indians?

Back inside the house he found Rebecca sitting on the bed crying, Charity next to her, with an arm around Rebecca's shoulders, trying to comfort her. Pete was holding his old shotgun, but was white as a sheet.

"Was it Indians, looking to steal me?" he asked. After the Stapleton boy had been kidnapped, Pete had been obsessed with the Indians.

"No son," said Danny, "someone was after the horses."

THIRTY-EIGHT

ALTHOUGH HE INSISTED HE WAS FINE, Jake himself knew a head wound was unpredictable and he took the army doctor's advice and confined himself to his bed. Funny, he thought, how his and Johnny's roles were suddenly reversed as Johnny engaged the girl to look after Jake's needs while he rested and waited for his head wound to heal.

Two days later, Johnny sat on the room's chair reading the story Jake had written about the rescue. "Thank you for leaving my name out of it reporter," he said. "But I do kind of like this character that sounds like he's right out of a dime novel."

"I toned it down a bit," stated Jake. "People wouldn't believe it if I was completely forth coming about your skills." He grinned.

"You did a good job. It's just confusing enough nobody will realize the wagon detail and the main force were separated."

"Yes," said Jake, resignation in his voice. "I agree with you, there's no point in calling out the Captain and taking on the army. By the way, I was wondering. Where are the famous Indian fighters, the Texas Rangers?"

"The government hasn't seen fit to revive them since the war. There's talk of some sort of force, a State Police, but it don't look like the Rangers are going to be back, at least not for a while."

Jake spent a week dealing with his close call with death. It certainly gave him pause and something to think about. Physically he was doing pretty well. His head was healing, although it looked like he would have a sunken spot in his forehead about the size of a penny. He felt a great relief to be alive and was happy, but thoughts of Charity soon began to return. After a while, he decided to carry out his plan as soon as he felt strong enough to ride again. Occasional dizziness still hit him when he stood up and after finding himself feeling faint when he tried to walk down to the cafe yesterday, he'd decided to lay about for a few more days.

Johnny brought news the next day after breakfast. Danny Anderson had reported the theft of his horses to the army and word had spread like wildfire through the tiny settlement. Baggett's name was mentioned, but several folks recalled he and his entire crew were in town that Saturday night. Danny's mention of seeing some unshod horse prints was soon interpreted to mean his ranch had been attacked by a large group of Comanches. The fort Commander sent a Lieutenant out to look things over, but some of Baggett's men found Anderson's horses, rounded them up and drove them back to Danny's place. This didn't fit with Indians, and it was finally decided it was simply a gang of outlaws and they had been scared off and were probably miles away. Suspicion of Baggett was defiantly toned down, due to his help and cooperation.

"Nobody was hurt?" asked Jake.

"Well, I haven't personally spoken to Anderson, but according to rumor, everybody is fine."

Jake looking relieved, nodded. "That's good," he muttered.

THIRTY-NINE

EIGHT DAYS LATER, after the Lowery boys hadn't shown up for work for three days, Danny started riding to the farm the brothers share-cropped with their mom. When he saw the buzzards circling, he began to get a bad feeling. They were laying close together, but animals had already began to tear at their bodies. Even so, Danny could tell they had both been scalped. Choking off a sob, he mounted his horse and turned to return home to get a wagon, physically and emotionally distraught. After breaking the news to Rebecca, who didn't say a word, just turned away, Danny knew he had to report the murders to the army. The Indians hadn't been seen east of the Clear Fork of the Brazos for a year or more. Well, it must be a renegade band, thought Danny.

Jake, feeling almost himself, realizing it was a beautiful day, had decided to take a ride up to the fort to return the doctor's shirt to him along with a bottle of fairly decent whiskey as a thank you. Johnny, about to take his afternoon nap, had decided to ride along as Loco hadn't been out for a few days. Flop and Perro came along for the visit. They had visited with the doctor and were mounting up when they saw Danny Anderson riding toward the headquarters' building. Figuring it could only be bad news, they walked their horses in that direction without saying a word to each other, Johnny whistling for Flop and Perro who came running from the chow hall where the cooks had been feeding them.

Although Jake and Johnny considered themselves visitors to the area, they were troubled to hear that Indians had come east, killed and scalped two men, not many miles from the fort. While they were troubled, the Lieutenant Colonel was furious. He dispatched Captain Bates himself to take a patrol out to examine the bodies and then to begin a patrol of the area, looking for sign of the Indians or a fight, preferably a fight.

"I'll not stand for it!" screamed the Commander, normally a calm and controlled officer. "Get me the Sergeant Major," he shouted at Lieutenant Angleton. "I want every able-bodied man armed and outfitted, ready for patrol first thing tomorrow."

Johnny and Jake asked and were given permission to ride with the patrol. The Captain had started to object but thought better of it. Johnny had never said a word regarding the fact that he had warned the Captain about a potential attack on the wagon detail and he certainly didn't need it coming out now. He didn't want a confrontation with the man.

The patrol followed Danny, moving fairly slowly because Danny was driving his wagon, so he could use it to take the bodies' home, to their mother. Finally, they reached the place where the bodies were laying. After examining them, the Captain noted that they had been stabbed to death. While the Indians did occasionally get their hands-on rifles, it was uncommon and they had trouble getting cartridges. Both had been scalped and a soldier found a feather stuck on a bush close by. Captain Bates asked Danny if the boys were armed and at first he said no, but then remembered they did have one rifle between them and sometimes carried it for killing game. There was no weapon to be found which led the Captain to determine they had been run down and killed, possibly for their rifle. Danny mentioned they sometimes rode a mule, taking turns, but there wasn't a mule about.

As the Captain moved away from the bodies which were beginning to smell terribly, Johnny walked up, squatted down and examined them carefully. He poked at them here and there and noted marks and cuts on their faces and on one of the men's hands. Jake watched him from a distance, but when Johnny nodded just slightly with his head, Jake walked up and squatted beside him. Johnny pointed out the marks. Jake, seeing the animal claw and tooth marks, did not see the difference at first, but as Johnny pointed out the small bruises and cuts, Jake began to distinguish them from the damage caused by animals.

"Looks like they beat them."

"No," said Johnny, softly. "Those injuries were caused by a blacksnake."

They weren't far from the brothers' home, so after loading the bodies on the wagon, the army patrol, along with Johnny and Jake, headed that way. Not far from the little cabin where the Lowery brothers had lived with their mother, they came across the mule. They tied it to the back of the wagon. The scene at the shack was, Jake thought, heart wrenching. The boy's mother had screamed and cried. Both Jake and Johnny took turns with the soldiers digging the graves while Danny comforted the mother. The soldiers, Jake and Johnny stood with their hats in hand as Danny said comforting words and prayed as the mother wept uncontrollably. Danny, telling the mother he owed the boys some pay, gave her some money and after offering their condolences, they mounted up.

The Captain noted that he planned to take his patrol north in search of the Indians, so Jake, Johnny and Danny nodded and headed back to the southwest, towards Danny's homestead. As they rode in silence, Danny driving his wagon, he began to consider the practical issues he was now confronted with. The vaqueros who had been working for him when he had broken his leg had disappeared the morning after they were paid, leaving only the Lowery brothers to help Danny and Alvin with the ranch duties. Chase and Rusty had seemed like an answer to their prayers, but it turned out they were sent by Baggett to spy on them and see if they had any money hidden. For the first time, Danny considered selling out to Baggett and moving his family back east. He kept thinking Rebecca would come to love the area as he did and he had hoped having Charity around would help, but Rebecca was withdrawing inside herself. Maybe, he thought, this was God telling him to go.

Johnny was deep in his own thoughts regarding the bull- whip marks on the brothers, his search for the man that had killed his brother and how it all tied together. He thought about the Mexican who had been yanked down by a blacksnake, the man with the scarred face that the bartender in Shane's had seen playing faro late at night and now this. There was no doubt. The Lowery boys had been slashed by a bullwhip. Johnny wasn't sure how Kyle Stephens or whatever his real name was, fit into the death of the Lowery brothers, but he was certain of two things. Stephens was in the area and he, Johnny Black, wasn't leaving until he found Stephens and killed him.

As they plodded along, Jake watched Flop and Perro dashing about, but he didn't register them. He was deep in his own mind, thinking again about Charity. Although he had made up his mind to see Mrs. Anderson and explain his sudden departure after lunch, after his close call with death, he was thinking maybe he should just ride on out toward Dallas and then Mexico. His parents had raised him to act like a gentlemen and to, as his mother reminded him often, mind his manners, but there were certainly bigger issues than his leaving without saying goodbye and thanks for lunch. Charity would be a distant and faint memory soon enough he convinced himself. Now though, this stuff about the Lowery boys being cut with a bullwhip, that caused him to reconsider. He and Johnny had become friends and he found himself feeling guilty about leaving Johnny behind with someone in the area set on killing him. What the devil, he thought. He wasn't Johnny's keeper and he certainly couldn't follow the man around trying to keep him out of harm's way. It was then he heard Dandy barking and he realized they had arrived at the Anderson's place. Confusion flooded his mind. Hadn't he and Johnny planned to head back to town? What were they doing here?

Pete was standing in the yard, petting Flop and Perro as Dandy sniffed at them. As they approached the house, Alvin came out and took hold of the halters on the horses pulling the wagon. Johnny dismounted. Pete came over and took Loco's reins and began to lead him to the barn. Jake sat on Girl, still confused. He watched as Johnny and Danny unhitched the horses from the wagon and Alvin, leading them, followed Pete and Loco toward the barn. Flop, Perro and Dandy followed them, tails wagging. Johnny and Danny were talking as they walked to the well pump to wash up, but Jake continued to sit atop Girl.

"Are you going to sit there or get down and come in for supper?" asked Charity. "At the very least you should let your horse eat."

Jake looked out towards the house and there, as though a vision, stood Charity. Again, words failed him as he stared at her. She stood, hands on hips, staring at him. Finally, he realized he was staring and quickly dismounted. Charity walked up and taking the bridle, led Girl toward the barn. "Why don't you wash up, Mr. Evans, supper is waiting."

Jake was again seated on the opposite side of the table from Charity, but this time she was seated at the other end. After Danny offered a prayer of thanks, they began to pass the food. Everyone was careful to avoid conversation about the Indians and certainly the war.

Rebecca confided that she and Charity were working on a quilt, while Danny noted that the corn was growing well and he thought it might be ready for harvesting the middle of May. Pete invited Jake to come out and fish sometime soon. He and Alvin, he explained, had found a good catfish hole. Johnny commented on the food, declaring it the best he'd had since he could remember. Jake agreed and thanked Mrs. Anderson and Danny for sharing their meal. Jake took the opportunity to offer an apology to Mrs. Anderson for leaving without a word on his last visit, but she cut him off with a shake of her head and a look at Danny.

"Jake," said Rebecca. "You said you were from up north, but I can't place your accent." She smiled, then, "I hope I'm not being too forward."

"Oh no," said Jake quickly. "I grew up in New York."

"New York!" exclaimed Rebecca. "Oh my, please tell us about it. I've never been, but I've heard so much about it."

"Well sure, I don't know where to begin. It is like twenty cities all pushed together and it changes so very fast. I was gone for a while, and I hardly knew the place when I got back." Jake's face reflected the awe in which he held New York. "Hundreds of ships of every size from all over the world come in and out of its harbors. There is a brick lined street, Broadway, where thousands of wagons and buggies and people move up and down every day. There is a huge, fancy hotel, the Astor House that has eight hundred rooms and covers a whole block." He was quiet for a moment. "But it has its bad side also. There are terrible slums filled with disease. On the other hand, we have a great open area of over eight hundred acres, called Central Park that has lakes and trees and paths. Well, we have so many people of different cultures and our share of the poor, so there are clashes, but it is a place unlike any other."

Rebecca said, "I would like to visit it one day. Thank you Mr. Evans."

Charity was notably quiet, but then said, "Mr. Evans, I asked Mr. Black earlier why you were outside, sitting on your horse when everyone else had come in.

Mr. Black said you had suffered a blow to the head that it was minor, but left you a bit addled. Do you feel okay?"

"Charity!" chastised her sister, Rebecca.

"Addled?" asked Jake, giving Johnny a stern look across the table. Johnny was busy shifting his peas about his plate, but Jake could see the corners of his mouth turned up under his mustache. So, the man thought himself funny.

"I'm fine, Ms. Chapin," he said, "and thank you so much for your concern. It was, as Johnny said, a minor injury, and I was a bit disorientated for a day or two, but I'm fine now. I was just lost in thought earlier."

After dinner, Alvin went out to his place in the barn, Pete was tasked with feeding Flop and Perro on his way to slop the hogs. The ladies began cleaning up while Danny, Johnny and Jake took their coffee and walked out on the porch. Danny seemed lost in thought, then spoke. "Did you hear about the incident out here last week?"

"Yes, word gets around," stated Jake.

"Well, I was sure it was Baggett, man owns most of the land north of me. He's been pressuring me to sell and I suspected him of stealing my cattle, but his men rounded up my horses and last night one of Pete's friends, Adam Franklin, lives south of us with his mom and dad, came over to tell us someone was messing around their place. Whoever it was didn't get a chance to steal anything. The Franklins have five or six hands staying in a bunkhouse there and they heard them. Didn't see anybody, but they heard them and they found unshod horse tracks the next morning. Just like at my place. Now…the Lowery brothers. What is going on? Do you think the Indians are behind it all?"

Jake and Johnny looked at each other. Jake said, "We don't rightly know Mr. Anderson, ah, Danny. Could be outlaws."

Danny was holding his coffee cup, turned to look out over his land. "This is a dangerous place," he said. "Indians, outlaws, snakes, spiders, wild animals, tame animals, the land, disease and the weather, all of them with the potential to kill. Sometimes I ask myself what I'm doing here."

His statement didn't seem to require an answer, so Johnny and Jake sipped their coffee and waited. Finally, Danny turned and spoke again. "I didn't thank you properly for helping with taking the Lowery boys home and the burial. Thank you both." Jake and Johnny nodded. Jake looked over at Johnny, who moved his head so very slightly, but Jake and he had been together for a while now and Jake read the movement with

ease. It was Johnny saying it was time to go.

"Danny, we need to be getting back to town. We both thank you very much for the hospitality, do you think we could step in and say good-bye to the ladies?"

Danny held the door as Jake and Johnny entered and took off their hats. "Mrs. Anderson, Ms. Chapin," said Jake. "Johnny and I wanted to thank you again. We have to be getting on back to town."

"We are so happy you stayed for supper. You're both welcome anytime," said Rebecca. "We don't have much company out here and it is nice to visit." She smiled.

"Thank you both," said Johnny, backing out the door. Jake turned to look at Charity who was smiling at him.

"Good evening, Mr. Evans," she said sweetly. "It was very nice seeing you again."

"Ma'am," said Jake, smiling himself, "Thank you. Maybe I'll see you in town."

"Perhaps," said Charity, still smiling.

Jake was so surprised at this sudden friendliness, his smile became a small oval as he nodded and backed out the door Johnny had just existed.

FORTY

AS SOON AS THEY WERE OUT OF SIGHT of the Anderson spread, Johnny lit a cigarillo and Jake built himself a smoke. They rode in an easy silence, common to good friends who are comfortable with each other's company. They weren't far from town when Jake and Johnny heard Flop and Perro barking. Johnny pulled his Navy Colt and let his arm dangle down by his side. As they turned a bend in the trail, they saw what had excited the dogs. A man, a noose around his neck was swinging from a tree, the evening breeze pushing his body around. A crude sign hung from around his neck that simply said 'thief.' What he was accused of stealing wasn't mentioned on the sign, but stealing horses or cattle would get you hung quickly anyplace in the west. They halted the horses to take a look, but neither of them knew the man and it was clear he had been dead for a while. Although the Flat had no official law other than the army, vigilantes handed out justice as they saw fit.

The next morning over breakfast, Jake told Johnny, "I guess you found some humor in telling Ms. Chapin I was addled."

Johnny smiled. "I did, reporter, but really I was thinking maybe I might just save you."

There had been so much going on, Johnny said he was taking a few days off from his manhunt to relax. Jake stated that he really should be scouting out another story, the one about the rescue and resulting fight with the Indians had been well received, but he hadn't written another since. But Jake quickly decided to hang out with Johnny. Both men needed to plan out their next moves and both were worn down from the rescue, Jake's recovery and then the discovery of the Lowery Brothers' death. After breakfast they brushed down the horses and Johnny paid Whitt to trim Loco's hooves and replace his shoes. Flop and Perro were next, both getting a good combing with the horse brush.

The rest of the morning was spent in Johnny's room, cleaning weapons and Johnny took a while sharpening his knife. "This is what you call relaxing?" asked Jake.

After lunch, Johnny headed back to his room to take a long nap and as Johnny put it, "spend some time with my thoughts." Jake was glad of the chance to actually relax and nothing like a nap in the afternoon, he thought.

They met for supper and while they were eating, a fellow that had played cards with Johnny a time or two, stopped by their table to tell them there was a new player in town and he was winning. Most of the time he could be found at the Busy Bee.

After entering the Bee, Jake and Johnny stood for a minute, letting their eyes adjust to the dim light. Johnny was scoping out the place while Jake was looking for an open spot at the bar. Jake saw an opening at the end of the long bar and touched Johnny's arm as he headed that way. Johnny saw Clive at a poker table along with Birchfield, a buffalo hunter he knew to nod to, a rancher he had played with several times and a fancy dressed fellow he had never seen before sporting a bowler hat. Johnny smiled and headed for the empty seat.

The new fellow's name was Maxwell Porter and he was a talker. It didn't take him long to explain that he had been a drummer, selling a little bit of everything out of his wagon, but quite by accident he found that he had a knack for playing cards. No one asked, but as they played, he explained that he was out here on the frontier simply out of curiosity. He wanted to see some wild Indians. Oh, he knew they had moved many up to the reservations in Oklahoma, but he wanted to see them in the wild, not like animals in a zoo, he explained. No one responded except for the usual poker language, call, and raise, fold, or damn it. At least the man seemed to have been in the west long enough to know better than to ask questions.

As they played, Maxwell Porter apologized for winning and winning he was. He lost a number of small pots and one medium one, but there had been several large pots as almost everyone stayed in or tried to bluff. Porter won them all.

While the poker game progressed, Jake introduced himself to the bartender, a man he hadn't met before and they engaged in some pleasantries as Jake nursed his beer.

The bartender, a thin, hollow-faced fellow who said he was lately of the Kansas area, had introduced himself as 'Eli' and he was a friendly, talkative sort. Jake was enjoying visiting with him between his visits to customers. At one point, when a group yell went up from the faro game, Jake admitted he had never played and didn't know anything about the game, but noted that it was sure popular at all of the saloons in town. Eli offered to explain the basics to Jake if he was interested and Jake confirmed he was, because although he wasn't much of a gambler, he thought he might work it into a story.

"Well," began Eli, "the game uses a regular 52 card deck and if you look, the layout for the game has an imprint of the 13 possible cards on it; the suits of the cards don't matter. There's usually a spot for high card at the top of the layout," continued Eli, before excusing himself to serve a customer at the other end of the bar.

Jake turned to check out the saloon, but everyone seemed to be having a good time. Not a single fight had broken out the entire evening. Glancing over at Johnny, Jake thought to himself that the man was the picture of composure. A person couldn't tell by looking at him if he was winning or losing.

Eli returned to his spot in front of Jake, and said, "Okay, so as I was saying, players put their wagers on whatever card or cards they want to bet on. Then, the dealer burns a card, then deals what's called the 'banker's card' or 'losing card' and sets it on his right. Another card is dealt and this card is known as the 'player's card' or 'winning card' and the dealer sets it on his left."

Stepping away for a moment, Eli grabbed a whiskey bottle and moved down the bar, filling glasses and collecting money. Returning, he asked, "You following me so far?"

Jake nodded and responded, "I am."

"Okay then, if a player places a bet on the high card spot, he's betting that the 'player's card will have a higher value than the 'banker's card.' The dealer or banker as he's known, wins all the money bet on the banker's card. Anybody who bet on the player's card wins their bet."

Frowning, Jake asked, "How does the dealer, ah, the bank, hope to make money? I mean he might if he has a lucky run, but over time it would all end up pretty equal seems to me."

"Right you are my man," Eli said. "The house edge is that if the dealer lays out a pair, he gets half the money bet on the player's card."

"That makes sense, but it doesn't seem like much of an advantage," Jake noted.

Eli leaned forward, "That may be, but those are the rules." He smiled, exposing surprisingly even, but tobacco stained teeth.

Finally, in the biggest pot of the night, Porter had raised big and everyone, except Johnny folded. The game was five card stud. Porter had an ace showing. Johnny had a queen showing. Johnny wasn't bluffing and turned over a second queen.

"Damn," said Porter, "I feel bad, but a man can't help his luck," as he turned over an ace, hesitated a moment and with both hands, reached to draw in the pot.

Suddenly, Johnny's left hand slammed down on Porter's right hand and as Porter yelled, he twisted it backward, in danger of breaking the wrist, to reveal a card under Porter's sleeve, held in place by a rubber band. "You're breaking my wrist!" screamed Porter.

The players at the table pushed back their chairs and stood up as the room went quiet. Everyone in the saloon had seen this situation before and expected somebody was about to die. Everybody eased out of the line of fire.

Johnny let go of Maxwell Porter's wrist, slid his chair back and stood. "Let's put our guns on the table and go outside to discuss this, Mister sleight-of-hand man."

Porter smiled and stood up. As Jake watched he knew full well what had happened and he had a pretty good view of Porter and the man did not look particularly scared, but Jake wasn't concerned and watched with interest.

Birchfield and the other players slowly backed away, except for Clive, who had been seated to Porter's left. Clive was standing and pulled a plug out of his pocket. He tore off a piece and put it in his mouth and chewed.

Porter seemed to be trying to stare Johnny down. Finally he said, "Okay cowboy, tell you what, let's split the pot and I'm going to call it a night. I didn't have to cheat to beat you ignorant cattle herders. The card was there in case somebody tried to cheat me." He smiled.

"We can discuss it outside," said Johnny.

"I'm a salesman and a lucky poker player, not a cheat or a fighter for that matter."

In one motion, Clive drew his gun and swung it up into Porter's head, hitting him very hard in the left temple. Porter dropped like a rock.

"Sorry," said Clive to Johnny. "I got tired of waiting," as he stepped over Porter and stomped hard on the fingers of his right hand with his boot. "I don't think he'll be cheating anybody anytime soon." Silence still filled the room as Clive pulled a set of manacles, cuffs joined by a ten inch chain, from his coat pocket, leaned down and cuffed Porter's hands together. He quickly frisked Porter, removing his side-arm, a derringer and a knife, setting them all on the table. Stepping back, Clive reached into his inside coat pocket and pulled out a silver badge, holding it up for all to see.

"Pinkerton Detective Agency. This man is wanted for train robbery in Missouri," said Clive, "and he's under arrest." Then, turning to Johnny, "I'd say that's your pot. What say we split Porter's other ill-gotten gains with the table?"

As things returned to normal and the poker game resumed, Porter began to stir and Clive hoisted him up and half carried, half dragged him out of the saloon.

Next morning, early, Jake took a chance and knocked on Clive's door. When he answered he was dressed and on his way to breakfast. It wasn't a big surprise as Jake and Johnny had seen him often in the mornings at Kirk's. Clive looked at him with interest on his face and Jake offered to buy him breakfast.

As they ate, Jake explained that he wanted to write a story for the Dallas Herald about the Pinkerton Agency. Clive ate and looked at Jake for a bit, then said, "In my experience news stories tend to take on a life of their own."

Jake nodded. "I think I know what you mean, and I can't control it after I send it, but I'd be happy for you to read and approve my story before I send it off to Dallas.

Clive nodded. "Appreciate that, but as soon as I finish up and grab a bite for Mr. Porter, he and I will be heading out. But tell me a little about yourself."

Jake didn't know a lot about the Pinkerton Agency, but he did know they sided with the Union. "Well sir, I'm from New York and I volunteered to help during the war, on the Union side. I didn't fight; I helped with the wounded."

Clive smiled. Jake had guessed right. Clive wanted to make sure he wasn't dealing with a southern sympathizer that would be sure to paint the agency in a bad way.

"Okay," said Clive, "I'll give you a bit of background - some idea of what we do, but I'll be expecting you to show us in a favorable light. My name really is Clive, Clive Cole. I was named by my daddy. Momma wanted to name me after somebody in the Bible, but daddy thought Clive Cole had a ring to it."

"I've heard good things about the Pinkerton Agency," said Jake truthfully. "Well, mainly good things."

First, Clive explained that concerning the current affair, Porter and two other men had robbed or were accused of robbing a train in the north, with an army payroll of over twenty-thousand dollars. The other two men had been caught and about half of the money had been recovered. The agents had lost track of Porter, but had information that he was headed to Texas. The Pinkerton Detective Agency had scattered agents around Texas, waiting for Porter to surface. Jake listened intently and took notes.

Clive began to relate a bit of the Pinkerton Detective Agency history as Jake took notes. Later, back at the hotel, Jake read his notes and found himself interested. According to Clive, the Pinkerton Detective Agency got its start about 1850 when a Scot joined up with a lawyer to form a private agency with rules. Later Pinkerton left that partnership to join his brother. They worked undercover quite often, including as intelligence agents during the Civil War. Not only that, bragged Clive, the agency had provided protection for President Lincoln, but since he was assassinated, Jake thought that was a strange thing to admit to. They found themselves tracking train robbers on a regular basis. What made them different, according to Clive was the Pinkerton brothers' rules for agents and the agency. Included in the Pinkerton's regulations were a commitment not to accept bribes or rewards, a pledge not to compromise with criminals and a refusal to accept divorce cases. Adding to the unusual nature of the Pinkerton Agency was the fact that they had a number of female agents.

FORTY-ONE

JOHNNY AND JAKE SPENT a few more days generally enjoying the mild weather, taking note of the growing population in the Flat and napping in the afternoons. Sometimes they read and Johnny often took Loco, Flop and Perro out for a ride along the river. Jake usually read in his room or on the hotel porch.

Late one afternoon, sitting on the hotel porch enjoying a smoke, before they headed down to Kirk's for supper, Jake asked Johnny why faro was offered at every saloon. As he understood it, he told Johnny, there wasn't much advantage for the house or the banker. Johnny smiled and explained that Faro was popular with folks because it was easy to learn and play and a good many people enjoyed the action that came with gambling. The saloon owners offered it to bring folks in, but of course they wanted to make as much money as possible, so the fact was, it was very hard to find an honest game.

Jake frowned in thought. "So why would people keep playing?" he asked.

"Well, the cheating isn't on every hand nor is it blatant, at least most of the time. The banker will make sure he wins when he needs to, say when a large wager is on the table or if luck is running against him. So, sometimes folks win, but generally everyone loses if they play long enough, but they keep thinking they'll win next time," Johnny said.

That evening, Johnny wanted to play poker and Jake was in the mood to visit a bit, so the two made their way over to the Frontier. When they entered they were surprised to see the lawyer, Ladd at the poker table. Since they hadn't seen him for weeks, they assumed he had gone back to where ever he was from. After midnight the saloon had thinned out, as most folks had work or other duties to attend to the next morning. It had been a normal enough night, except Ladd cursed loudly several times and seemed to be getting drunk. Out of character for him. Jake was tired and catching Johnny's eye indicating he was turning in. As he passed the table where Johnny was playing, he noted that Johnny had had a good night and it looked like Ladd was almost broke. A bad night at the table then, that explained the cursing and drinking. Ladd lost a hand and cursing stood up and said he was going to the Busy Bee. Johnny and the other players continued for another half hour before deciding to call it a night.

Johnny stood outside, smoking a cigarillo and studying the stars as the other players bid him goodnight and walked out into the night. Johnny had been sipping whiskey all night and decided to walk over to the stables to clear his head. He would say goodnight to the boys, he thought, but then, he considered, he wasn't sure if Flop and Perro were in or not. They had been sleeping in the stall with Loco, but he only assumed they were there at night. Could be they were out catting around. He smiled to himself. He'd had a good night at the table, the whiskey had eased his aches and pains and hopefully soon, he would run down Kyle Stephens. He passed the Busy Bee, but it was dark. Continuing down the block, he walked behind Whitt's and suddenly felt something slam against the back of his head. He dropped to his knees, stunned, then felt like he was going to pass out, his whole body weak as he pitched forward, his nose slamming into the hard ground, instantly blood began darkening the dirt. As he tried to raise himself up another blow hammered him in the back of the head. Johnny saw red and black. He automatically tried to reach his revolver, but that act seemed to be beyond his power at the moment. He drew his knees up and felt he might vomit. If he could get his arm to work he could get his knife from his boot.

Ladd had been sitting in the dark outside the Busy Bee when Johnny had walked by without noticing him. He was somewhat drunk and in fact would be really drunk, but he was completely, totally broke and hadn't been able to pay for the last drink he had ordered at the Busy Bee, so they had thrown him out. People thought all lawyers were rich, but it wasn't true. In fact, Ladd had supplemented his income with some shady deals and illegal work, but it hadn't been enough. Some lawyers did well, but he didn't have the big clients or even a practice he could build on. The fact was, he had kept ahead of sheriffs and his debts by moving from one state to another as the need arose. On top of that, he gambled constantly. He lost, he always lost at faro, but he kept playing. He was a regular at the faro table at Shane's place. Sometimes he won at poker, but he was always drawn back to faro and tonight, down to the last of his funds, he had played poker hoping to improve his situation, but that damn Black had finished him off. When he saw Black walk by, alone, the idea came to him. He would knock him out and rob him. Hell, a lot of the money was his, wasn't it? As he followed Black he picked up a foot long, thick length of oak someone had meant for firewood, but had fallen beside the road.

As Black lay on the ground, Ladd squatted down and began going through his pockets, pulling out the cash. "Roll over damn it," said Ladd.

"That you Ladd?" said Johnny, his voice weak, but distinct.

Ladd jumped back. He hadn't counted on this. Black wasn't unconscious, he had recognized his voice. Struggling to think, Ladd realized that he had no choice now but to kill Black. He had seen the man in action. Black would kill him. His head cleared from the adrenaline. Taking the money and running was an option, but he'd never be safe. Not after what he'd just done. Better not to think about it, just get it done. Stepping over Johnny, Ladd raised the length of oak high over his head, posed for the killing blow.

He had actually started the downward blow when he was hit by one hundred and twenty-five pounds of snarling, crazed dog. The blow knocked him clear of Johnny and he hit the ground hard. There was no time to assess the situation as Flop, snarling and biting, went for his throat. Ladd managed to get his arms around his throat and face but the dog was tearing chunks out of his arms. He didn't completely understand, but it felt like the dog was biting him on the legs at the same time. There was no way he could see Perro, who had joined Flop in the attack. There was blood everywhere and Ladd was screaming when he heard a whistle and Flop, snarling, stopped biting him and backed off, watching him. He had shut his eyes, but as he opened them he saw Black's huge dog pad over to Black, who was sitting up and begin to lick his face. Another dog, a smaller one, came into view, growling at Ladd, who quickly raised his arms again.

Black shakily climbed to his feet and approached Ladd, who was still sitting on the ground. Ladd, soaked in his own blood, stood up, pulled out the stolen money and handed it to Johnny, some of the money falling on the ground, before folding his damaged, bleeding arms across his chest. There were bite marks on his head and one of his ears was mangled. Johnny, unsteadily, reached over and withdrew Ladd's revolver. After removing the shells he replaced it back in its holster and squatted down and gathered up the money that had fallen on the ground.

Straightening up, Johnny said, "I didn't expect that of you Ladd. Are you broke?"

Ladd nodded. Johnny reached over and pushed some money into his pocket.

"You need to head on up to the fort and locate the saw- bones before you lose too much blood." He was quiet for a moment, then, "I think it'd be wise if you left town in the morning and Ladd, if you say anything about my dog, I'll kill you."

Ladd nodded, stood and began walking toward the Frontier where he last remembered seeing his horse.

Jake wasn't asleep when Johnny rapped softly on his door. He had been reading by lamplight after finding he couldn't stop thinking about Charity. Opening the door and finding Johnny soaked in blood and swaying slightly should have shocked him, but Jake simply said, "Come on in and have a seat while I get my bag."

As Jake worked, Johnny told him the story. "I reckon I owe Flop - and Perro for that matter, a beefsteak," said Johnny. "I seem to recall Loco saving you during the fight with the Indians during the rescue," mused Jake, cleaning Johnny's head wounds.

"That's a fact, doc. But not only do I have some solid fighting buddies watching my back, I have my own personal sawbones," said Johnny, smiling, but wincing.

The next morning Jake went over to Johnny's room and knocked. In a moment, Johnny opened the door, but it was obvious he had just arisen from the bed and as he turned to return to it, he stumbled, then, reaching the bed, lay down and pulled the blanket over himself. "I think I'll skip breakfast this morning," he said, his voice strained.

Jake asked Johnny his name and where he was. Johnny answered correctly, but when asked about his vision, Johnny hesitated and said, "Things are a might blurry." Then told Jake his head hurt so bad he had trouble thinking. Jake gave him some laudanum, examined the wounds on the back of his head and told him he would be back after breakfast with coffee. Johnny didn't respond.

While he was eating alone, Jake saw Ladd on his horse, leaving town as ordered, at least if he's smart, thought Jake. After breakfast he found Brown, the hotel owner, at the general store and made arrangements for the girl to resume her duties assisting Johnny. Brown looked at him questioningly, but didn't say anything. Jake simply told him Johnny wasn't feeling well and required the girl's help again for a week or two, most likely. Brown said he would send word for her. Jake went down to the Whitt's livery and checked on Loco, Flop and Perro. He made arrangements with Whitt to feed and water the dogs every day when he fed Loco. Then he called for Flop to come, and of course Perro tagged along as they walked back to the hotel and up to Johnny's room. Flop went to the bed and licked Johnny's face.

Johnny opened his eyes and reached out and put his hand on Flop's head. Jake said he'd made arrangements for the girl and he'd be back later. He left the door cracked and looked back to see Johnny talking softly to Flop while Perro lay close by.

Things under control for the moment, Jake began walking down to Birchfield's. It was Saturday and maybe the Andersons would be in for supplies today.

FORTY-TWO

BAGGETT WAS VERY IMPRESSED with Lambert. The man carried out his assignments flawlessly. In fact, Baggett was beginning to wonder why he was paying Smith, when, it appeared to him, as soon as Lambert scared off the Andersons, he would be an excellent choice to ramrod the ranch. He followed orders, he was ruthless and knew horses. Smith ran a tight ship, but as they conspired, Baggett felt he had found a kindred spirit in Lambert. He would wait until the Andersons were dealt with, then he would task Lambert with getting rid of Smith.

What Baggett did not know was that his foreman, Charlie Smith and Kyle Lambert had something in common. A father. They were half-brothers and Lambert's real name was Kyle Smith. In fact, Charlie had sent word to Kyle that he was working for a man with money and thought maybe together, they might work the situation to their advantage. Kyle didn't really know why, but he had also kept his blacksnake and his ability to use it a secret. It was common among men in the west to provide little information about themselves and Kyle instinctively kept this fact to himself.

Baggett, Smith and Kyle were sitting in Baggett's den, drinking whiskey.

"Kyle," said Baggett. "You've been doing a hell of a job. Now, the other night, when you went down to that other place, the Franklins, you say nobody got a look at you huh?"

"Hell no," bragged Kyle. "I did what you said. Went in, made some noise and took off."

Baggett smiled and took a sip of his whiskey. "Excellent," he said. "An army patrol came by today, told me how they were looking for an Indian band that had killed and robbed two colored boys out east of here." Baggett began to laugh. "You did a damn good job. I like to keep up with my debts so in keeping with our agreement, here is one hundred dollars in gold twenty dollar pieces," he said as he tossed a small cloth bag to Lambert. "Now, for the next step I think we're going to need to bring in one more hand. Anybody you fellows trust?"

After a brief discussion, Charles and Kyle settled on Zimmerman, a fellow they knew was running from the law and was seriously lacking in morals. He constantly complained that he wasn't making enough money.

• • •

A few days later, just after dark, two cowboys headed into town were walking their horses slowly when a voice spoke behind them, ordering them to hold up. As they turned their horses, even in the starlight, they could see a man holding a rifle and wearing something over his head. The man told them to slowly ease their weapons out and drop them in the dirt along with their vests. Like most men, they carried their money in their vests and the thought occurred to them they might see a way out of this fix, but a horse neighed to their left and out of the corner of their eyes, they saw a form they figured was a third rider holding a rifle on the other side of the trail.

"We ain't carrying no pistols," said one. "Just rifles," said the other.

"That's fine," said a voice coming out of the potato sack. "You boys just drop them rifles down easy and then the vests."

The cowboys did as ordered. The voice told them to head on into town.

"But we got no money now," complained one. "Git!" shouted the voice, waving the rifle.

Arriving in the tiny town, the two cowboys headed straight for Shane's where they were able to buy a couple of drinks on credit and a few were bought for them as they told their story. A great majority of the clientele in Shane's had committed criminal acts, but were horrified at the idea that someone might rob them. As men moved to other saloons and out to the buildings where ladies of the night entertained, the word spread. It was becoming apparent that an outlaw gang was in the area.

As soon as the cowboys rode off into the dark, following Baggett's orders, Kyle, Charlie and their newest member, Zimmerman, picked up the rifles and vests, removed the money, threw the vests and rifles into the bush and headed home, their job done.

• • •

Three days later, Baggett, sitting in his parlor, sipping whiskey, thought it all through again, trying to make sure there weren't any flaws in his plan, which had come together nicely. As he saw it, Anderson had no help and had to be struggling. Added to that, the fear factor. The attack at their house, the Franklins getting hit, death of the Lowery boys, bushwhackers in the area, he laughed out loud. There was no way they could blame him. The Andersons weren't the only ones getting hit. It appeared there were outlaws and Indians in the area and no one was safe. Now, he'd show them real fear. The two women, the boy and sometimes the one-armed fellow went to town regularly, early, every other Saturday. They would be the bushwhacker's next target. After that, thought Baggett, Anderson will be begging me to buy his land so he can get his family the hell out of here.

FORTY-THREE

PETE SAT ON THE WAGON SEAT, between Rebecca and Charity, holding the horse's reins loosely in his hands. Pete was lost in thought, hoping that Adam would be in town and wondering if his mom would buy him a piece of candy as she sometimes did when he rode into town with them and helped load the wagon. Alvin had stayed back to help Danny with the ranch work. Danny had asked Rebecca to leave word with Birchfield that he was looking to hire some help.

They were still a ways from Collins Creek which ran east and west just north of the Flat, rounding a curve on the road cut through oaks and cottonwood when Pete noticed a tree log lying in the road. He eased the horses to a halt, confused. It took a moment for Rebecca and Charity to understand why Pete had stopped and just as they registered the downed tree, two men on horseback walked out of the woods with feed sacks or maybe potato sacks over their heads. The men were pointing rifles at them. No one spoke and no one moved. Pete, Rebecca and Charity were all aware there had been stories of outlaws in the area, but were shocked to find themselves facing them on an early Saturday morning.

Smith, his voice muffled because under his hood he had a handkerchief tied over his mouth, said, "Get out your money, nice and slow," as he waved the rifle at them.

Rebecca slowly reached under the seat and grabbed a small bag filled with their money for supplies. She held it up for the riders to see.

Zimmerman looked at Smith and asked, "Should we take the boy to sell to the Indians?"

Rebecca gasped and involuntarily almost shouted, "No! Please. Here's the money." She waved the bag of money at the two riders.

Smith said loudly, "We can always grab him later."

Zimmerman, nudged his horse forward to get close enough to take the money from Rebecca.

• • •

One Christmas during the war, Charity's fiancé had made it home to see her. He was there for a week and spent one full day making forty-two caliber cartridges for a Confederate manufactured single action revolver called a LeMat. It was a large, heavy weapon weighing in at three pounds and wasn't particularly accurate. But what made it unique was a second barrel located under the main barrel that fired a single sixteen gauge buckshot round when a lever on the weapon was pressed down and the trigger pulled. He insisted on not only showing her how to use the weapon, but had her practice with it and had left it with her, telling her it made him feel much better. Just in case.

• • •

As Zimmerman reached for the money, Charity pulled the huge LeMat revolver from under her wrap, and in a smooth motion that came from practice, pulled the hammer back and pushed the lever beside it down. Raising the gun with both hands she pointed it at the center of Zimmerman's chest, but when she pressed the trigger the kick of the sixteen gauge shell caused the barrel to lift. Because he was so close, the pellets didn't have time to expand very far. The main force of the buckshot hit Zimmerman high in the chest blowing a hole the size of a plum in him, not far below his windpipe.

Zimmerman was flung backward by the force of the blast, and his boots were jammed hard into the stirrups. His horse reared, turned and ran as Zimmerman's dead body bounced against its back. Kyle, a coward at heart, had stayed hidden in the trees, and seeing Zimmerman shot, had turned his horse and spurred it hard. His half-brother Smith hesitated, in shock, but Charity calmly pulled the lever on the pistol up and swinging it around, pointed it at Smith and fired a .42 caliber bullet which missed him only because he was already moving. Seeing Kyle and Zimmerman galloping away he had quickly turned his horse and slammed his spurs into him.

Two miles west of Baggett's cabin, they caught Zimmerman's horse, who, exhausted, had finally stopped running. Zimmerman's boots were still lodged in the stirrups, but his body had slid sideways and dangled upside down from the right side of his mount. They argued about what to do, but finally they decided to tie the horse, with the dead Zimmerman aboard, a mile or so from the house and then ride in and ask Baggett what to do. The hands had all been tasked to work in the eastern part of the ranch today, looking for calves and taking inventory, so they should all be gone.

The three of them were seated in Baggett's study. Baggett had been very calm, too calm, thought Smith. They had told him what happened. Now they were awaiting orders.

Finally, Baggett said, "Okay, so you three were headed to town and three bushwhackers jumped you before you could get to town. They killed Zimmerman, but you two got away.' He smiled. "I guess the same three attacked the Anderson family, of course, we don't know that yet, and when we hear about it we'll be surprised. Can you two handle that?"

Baggett sent them out to get Zimmerman and to bury the potato and feed sacks. As soon as they returned he made them dig a grave for Zimmerman because he didn't want anyone seeing how he died. Insisting they 'get their story straight', he also made them go over it again and again until they almost believed they had in fact been attacked rather than what had really happened.

When he went in to tell Baggett everything was done, Smith asked, "You okay boss?"

Baggett said," Oh yes, good. Oh, did you get in the part about selling the boy to the Indians?"

"We did, before, you know."

"I think it all worked out well. There's no doubt you scared them bad and that part about stealing the boy, the mother will have nightmares. Zimmerman would have had to go anyway, the sister did us a favor killing him."

FORTY-FOUR

REBECCA DIDN'T STOP SHAKING on the way into town. She had wanted to immediately return to the Rocking J, but Charity had prevailed. Pete couldn't wait to see Adam to tell him what happened. Arriving at the general store, they saw the Franklin's wagon, but Adam had heard that Whitt had mounted a real Indian arrow on the wall at his livery and he had headed there to look at it. Rebecca didn't want to let Pete out of her sight, but again Charity intervened and soon Pete was off to see if he could find Adam and the arrow.

After they explained to Birchfield what had happened, he said, "That's it. I'll talk to some of the men. We're going to have to take some action."

Seeing the Anderson wagon in front of Birchfield's made Jake's spirits soar. He saw Adam, across the street, running toward Whitt's. Jake took his hat off and dusted it on his leg before replacing it. Good thing he had taken time to shave this morning and he had put on his clean shirt. It was a good decision he thought as he smiled.

As he entered the store, Jake saw Charity and removed his hat, but when she turned to look at him, her face solemn, fear grabbed at him.

Seeing Jake, Charity smiled, "Good morning Jake." "Good morning, Ms. Charity."

"Is that offer of coffee still good?" "Yes, for sure," said Jake.

"Just a second," said Charity, moving over to speak quietly to Rebecca who was talking to Birchfield. After a brief conversation, Charity walked over, slipped her arm inside Jake's and they walked across the street to Kirk's café.

Neither spoke until Maybelle had brought them coffee and dashed away, dealing with the late arrivals for breakfast.

"How have you been?" asked Jake.

"I am doing well, thank you Jake, but, as I'm sure you noticed, my sister is a little upset."

Jake looked at her, his face expressing his interest as Charity began telling him about the morning's adventure. Jake forgot he had coffee nor did he speak as Charity recalled the attempted hold-up. When she finished, she sipped her coffee and studied Jake who sat like a stone, looking at her as though, she thought, he was trying to figure out if he should stay or run.

"You shot him," said Jake.

"Yes, Jake, I shot one of the men who were trying to rob us."

Returning to the store, they found Rebecca had finished her shopping, and Birchfield's helper was loading their wagon. Rebecca told them Birchfield suggested they visit the fort and speak to the fort Commander. Jake offered his sympathy to Rebecca and as if on cue, Pete showed up. While the wagon was being loaded, Jake walked over to the livery and saddled Girl. He had grown fond of her and purchased the gentle mare from Whitt the week before. As soon as he finished, he rode over to the general store and followed Rebecca's wagon up to the fort. Jake led them to the Headquarters building and Pete secured permission to explore the fort after being warned to be on his best behavior. It irritated Jake that Captain Bates took an immediate interest in Charity as soon as Jake introduced her as Ms.

Chapin. After a brief explanation, the Captain disappeared into the Lieutenant Colonel's office. Emerging minutes later, he ushered Rebecca and Charity into the office, telling Jake he would have to wait outside.

Jake cooled his heels for almost an hour before the women emerged, all smiles. The Captain was talking to Charity and Rebecca seemed to be recovering from the shock and fear of the morning. When Charity joined them, Rebecca said, "Since we're here I thought I would visit the sutler's store. Jake, Charity has never been to the fort, do you mind showing her around?"

"I'd love to," said Jake, looking over at the Captain who was engaged in conversation with Lieutenant Angleton.

"I think a half-hour should do it and if you two see Pete, please grab him." She smiled.

A few minutes later, as they walked about the fort, Jake said, "Mrs. Anderson seems to be feeling better."

"She is," said Charity. "The Commander promised to find the outlaws and he was very understanding and supportive. Plus, she's southern born and bred. We southern girls are taught to maintain our dignity and our emotions in public."

The troops were at fatigue duty, so various working parties were engaged around the fort. Charity was surprised to see the washerwomen at work and amazed at the size of the hand dug well. "Oh," she said, the Captain offered to escort us home." Jake's mouth tightened. "But I told him you were going to do that. Did I speak out of place?"

"No, not at all. I do plan to escort you home. Mainly to protect the bushwhackers."

Charity looked surprised, then realizing Jake was joshing her, punched him hard in the arm.

"Such a gentleman," she said, smiling.

They found Pete sitting in the middle of a group of soldiers tasked with scrubbing pots, regaling them with the story of the morning's events. When they had all gathered back at the wagon, they found Rebecca was thrilled to have located some canned condensed milk at the sutler's store. They decided to meet for lunch in town and Jake said he would meet them there as he had to make a stop at the hotel.

On the way back to town, Jake's thoughts turned to Johnny and his prognosis. There had been any number of head injuries during the war and the recoveries had been mixed. Many of the soldiers had no physical signs of injury, but suffered from dizziness, blurred or double vision and other maladies like Johnny. Most of these were the result of being caught too close to an explosion. Some with head injuries never lost consciousness, others, like Jake, had seemed asleep, but awoke at some point. Many though, had, like Johnny, suffered physical blows to the head. Sometimes they were clubbed by a rifle butt or they fell from a horse and hit their head on a rock. Jake tried to remember. It seemed to him that those who had suffered from weakness, dizziness and blurred vision, recovered fairly often. But not always.

As he approached Johnny's room, Jake could see it was dark inside and the door cracked. He entered quietly to find Johnny asleep, Flop and Perro lying on the floor, watching him. The blinds had been pulled and a quilt nailed over the window, darkening the room. Jake listened to Johnny's breathing, touched Flop and Perro on the head, and eased out of the room. He stepped across the hall, entered his own room and found his pommel holster and pistol.

The trip back to the Rocking J was uneventful. When Rebecca told Danny what had happened, Jake could see him struggling to control his emotions, but Rebecca's calm demeanor seemed to settle him after a few minutes. Over supper, Jake told them that Johnny had been hit in the head by a disgruntled gambler and would be lain up for a bit, but he was sparse with the details. Johnny was a private person and Jake didn't want to say too much. Everyone expressed their sympathy and asked Jake to tell Johnny he was in their prayers. After supper, Jake and Charity walked away from the house, talking and enjoying the mild March weather. There were some natural, large flat rocks on a small ridge overlooking the rolling landscape some one hundred feet from the house.

"Let's sit there," said Charity, pointing to the rock for- mation. "It will be proper, everyone can see us from the house."

"Rebecca seems to be doing okay," said Jake, hopefully. "She's not," stated Charity, without further explanation. Their discussion turned to more pleasant subjects, as

Charity talked about life in Atlanta before the war. Jake wasn't surprised to learn that their family had not owned slaves. "Papa was a very successful lawyer. I don't know a lot about his business, but I know he did work for the railroads and the lumber industry. He was often away on business in Savannah."

Jake nodded. "Father was a trader. He hated the idea of slavery."

"Papa and mother had only us two girls. Papa taught us to ride and to shoot. Sometimes I think he forgot we were girls." She laughed. "Mother taught us manners and our lessons."

"We have something in common. My father taught me to ride, to shoot and to hunt."

They looked at each other and smiled. This providing of information, small pieces related to their parents was a way of testing the reaction of the other as they became better acquainted on a personal level.

"We had a large library and we all read most evenings after supper."

"Now we didn't have a library, at least not one to speak of, but I am a reader myself."

"Jake Evans are you saying that to please me?" teased Charity.

"No ma'am! Test me if you'd like." "Pride and Prejudice," she challenged.

Jake laughed. "I'm not sure you're playing fair, but written by English author Jane Austen, about sisters…" It was Charity's turn to laugh.

"I am impressed. You see, I love English authors, and was writing myself, until, until I came out here. One day I hope to visit London." Charity looked away, lost in thought, and then turned to Jake, her face serious.

"Jake, I want to tell you about the war and then maybe not talk about it anymore."

Jake nodded, "Sure," he said.

"I was seventeen, in love and engaged when the war started," said Charity. "Papa felt the war was very wrong, but didn't think it would last long or at least would not affect us in any real way. Rebecca moved home with Pete who was about six years old when her husband joined the confederate army. He and his family didn't believe in slavery, but he said Southern honor was at stake and my fiancé looked up to him and listened to him and later followed him into the army. Truly I don't understand men."

She was quiet for a while, but Jake waited.

"The war didn't affect us so much at first. Things were pretty normal. We were getting by with our garden and our food we had canned. We had money to buy what we needed, although of course there were shortages, the army needed to be supplied and much went to them. When we got word Rebecca's husband had been killed, well, it was a bad time. Somehow I knew my fiancé wouldn't return so when I got word I didn't even cry, at least for a while. Mother and father discussed leaving many times, especially when the union army began to move south, but we were there when they began to shell Atlanta in the summer of '64. It was horrible. We hid in the basement a great part of the time for over a month, but our home was spared. After the army occupied Atlanta, the soldiers were pretty well behaved and father began to feel that everything would be alright. But then word came that we had to leave Atlanta, we couldn't believe it. They only let us take what we could carry. One of my uncles and his wife and kids lived on a small farm near Gainesville. He came and helped us, took us in. It was very crowded and so distressing, to be disrupted from one's life. But we left Atlanta in September and in December we heard that people could return. So we went back, just before Christmas of '64. We had a nice home and a small barn for the horses. The barn had mostly been dismantled, stripped of its wood and tin by the soldiers. The house was intact and most of the furniture, but the silverware and valuables were gone. We blamed the soldiers, but found out later it was probably our fellow southerners. Thieves."

Tears began to run down her face. Jake became anxious, but didn't know what to do or what to say. Afraid of saying the wrong thing, he just sat quietly, but he reached over and put his hand over hers.

She turned her head to look at him. "The books had all been thrown on the floor. Every single book, but they were all there. Father was so happy."

Taking a deep breath, she continued, "Of course business goes on and there is so much to be rebuilt, he has actually prospered, but Georgia has refused to honor the new Fifteenth amendment to the United States Constitution, the one that says all men can vote, even Negroes. So Georgia can't be readmitted to the Union until it agrees. There is a lot of unrest in Atlanta."

"I think the entire country is healing and adjusting," said Jake. "It's going to take a while I think."

"Am I talking too much?"

"No, no, not at all," said Jake. "I want to know about you." "After the war, when things began to return to normal, young men called on me and I went to dances, but I have never been drawn to anyone, in a romantic way, since the war. That's why I consider myself a product of the war. It has occurred to me that I may die an old maid."

Jake looked at her. "I somehow doubt that," he said with a smile.

"Mother was, well, is worried about me, so when she got the letter from Danny, mother thought it might be good for Rebecca and me if I came out here for a while. I had lost my zest for life, like part of me died when my fiancé died." She paused. "Somehow I don't think mother really understands the hardships and dangers, but strangely, coming out here brought me out of my melancholy. The hard work, the strange sights, it doesn't give me time to dwell on the past."

Jake nodded.

"Now, meeting you, has given me someone to visit with." She smiled at Jake.

"The letter from Danny?" Jake asked. "Did he ask you to come out?"

"No, he just told mother Rebecca was okay, but didn't seem happy." She was quiet for a moment, then, "So here I am. How about you Jake Evans, if that's really your name."

Jake laughed, glad Charity had finished her narrative and returned to her outspoken self.

"As a matter of fact," Jake began, "Jake Evans is my name. As I mentioned before, I'm a Northerner, born and raised in New York. My papa is a successful trader. My mother is a wonderful person who taught me to read as a child. My brother works with papa in the family business. It was a disappointment to my folks when I told them I wanted to go to school. Medicine and science interested me much more than the price of cotton and the cost of cargo insurance, all things papa obsessed over."

Charity stared at him with interest on her face. "I did work for papa for a bit, but eventually he agreed it might be best for me to go to school. Maybe because my heart just wasn't in the business. So off I went and did finish up."

"Where did you study?"

"Harvard, medicine," said Jake studying her carefully.

She was quiet for a moment, surprise showing on her face, then asked, "In the war, did you work as a doctor?"

"Yes," said Jake. "I was a volunteer. I learned a lot about doctoring, but it, the wounds I mean, were so horrific, it, well, I have nightmares."

Charity stared at him. "I am so very sorry Jake."

Jake smiled. "Thank you. You're right you know. The war has altered everyone's lives. We're all on a different course because of it. I wasn't engaged like you, but I did have a girl." Charity tilted her head, her interest obvious. "While I was away with the army, she married another fellow. A banker."

"Oh my," said Charity softly.

Jake, smiling now, said, "I must admit, it took me by surprise and I guess hurt my pride a bit, but after I thought about it I realized it was all for the best. Anyways, when the war came to an end I wanted to forget doctoring for a while, so I started drifting. Met a fellow in Dallas who hired me on as a reporter and sent me out here to Fort Griffin and the Flat."

"Where you got shot in the head," Charity reminded him. "Well, there's that, but it's also where I met you," said

Jake, "Course that might be worse than getting shot in the head, according to Johnny Black."

"What?!" Charity almost shouted, feigning anger.

It was dark now, so Jake stood, realized he was still holding her hand and helped her stand. A spark of light flashed by the barn. "That's Alvin," said Charity, "He smokes out back of the barn in the evenings. Danny and Rebecca know of course, but never mention it." They walked back to the house in silence, both wondering where this friendship might lead.

Danny told Jake he could bunk for the night in the barn, but Jake begged off as he wanted to look in on Johnny. Arriving back in town, Jake took care of Girl and then walked to the hotel where he found Johnny's room dark, but the door cracked. He eased in to find Johnny sleeping. Loco and Perro were in the corner watching him. Anybody comes in here will be in for a surprise, thought Jake looking at the two dogs. A quick check of the room confirmed the girl had been doing a good job. He just couldn't remember her name, but he made a mental note to ask. Everything was clean and neat, there was water for Johnny and the dogs and the chamber pot was empty and clean.

Jake went to his room and turned in, sleeping soundly and nightmare free.

FORTY-FIVE

CAPTAIN BATES WAS IN A GOOD MOOD. This outlaw business would give him an opportunity to show the Commander how versatile he was and to show off his leadership abilities. But it was Charity Chapin that had really had an effect. She was gorgeous and he considered - of his class. Not the usual uneducated rough females one encountered on the frontier. It wouldn't be long before she realized what a catch he himself might be, he thought. Yes, he would have to call on the Anderson homestead, very, very soon. It would be easy to convince the Commander he needed to check on them and that he had a few more questions about the bushwhackers. He would time it so that he arrived there just before the noon meal. They would be sure to invite him in to eat and he would have a chance to visit with Ms. Chapin and then set up a future meeting.

That friend of Black's, what was his name, oh yes, Evans, another young, uneducated cowboy who thought himself irresistible to women, had some idea of a claim on Ms. Chapin. It was so damn obvious. The man did cut a bit of a figure, he thought. With his blonde hair and blue eyes. But that hardly mattered in the case of a lady like Ms. Chapin when a man had no future prospects. A reporter, what did they earn. Not much he was sure, while he would soon be a major on his way to an eventual generalship and station in Washington, where he would attend parties and rub elbows with the powerful. Although his family had fallen on hard times financially, they still had political connections. Yes, he thought, he might have met the future Mrs. Bates, the wife of General Bates, he laughed out loud, startling Lieutenant Angleton who stared at him, but didn't say anything.

FORTY-SIX

BAGGETT WAS FEELING PRETTY GOOD. Part of his good spirits could probably be attributed to the whiskey he was drinking, but it was late March, the rains had ensured an abundance of grass and he had a large herd of longhorns ready for the market. His contract with the army allowed him a steady income furnishing beeves to Fort Griffin, which he did year round, but he had a huge surplus. In recent years he had partnered with a half-dozen local ranchers as they combined their herds and crews. They would only drive the cattle as far as the old Fort Worth settlement. There would be other, larger herds stopping to rest there and he would find a buyer. He could get more money if he drove his herd on up to the new yards in Kansas and he might do that next year, but he wanted to stay close for now. He was confident Anderson would be wanting to discuss selling his land soon.

He leaned forward and poured himself another bourbon. Sitting back, he considered his new plans. It was all coming together. Smith had done him a good job and he had come to enjoy Kyle's company, he reflected, but as soon as they got back, they were both going to have to go. Permanently. In fact, he had a plan for that. The issue was, they knew it was him that had put the bushwhacker plan and the killing of the Lowery boys in motion. They might get greedy and try to blackmail him or let something slip when they were drinking. No, unfortunately, they had to go, soon. He had meant to have Kyle Lambert kill Smith and then promote Lambert to foreman, but after thinking about it, a better plan would be to get rid of both of them. Hire a new man who knew nothing about what had happened.

As he sipped his drink, he thought about it again, just to see if there were any holes. When the hands get back from their trip, he'll give them their pay for the trip and they'll head into town. He'd make sure everybody went including the cook. He'd ask Kyle Lambert and Smith to stay back and play some poker with him, tell them he wants to talk about his plans for the future. Then, at the table, in the middle of the game, he would shoot both of them. When the hands got back, he'd explain that Kyle had got drunk, started arguing with Smith and shot him so he had shot Kyle. An unfortunate event. They would bury them and he'd pick a new foreman. Laughing, he said out loud to himself, "You are one smart devil!"

Meanwhile, Charles and Kyle Smith were sitting on horses in the northern area of the ranch watching cowboys branding and ear-marking cattle. They were starting the drive to Fort Worth at the end of the week. Baggett was going along, to make the sale and collect the money, but Smith would head up the drive to Fort Worth and Lambert would be his second in command. It would keep the two of them out of the area for a few weeks while the search for the bushwhackers died down.

The half-brothers, Charles and Kyle sat, Kyle chewing, Charlie smoking. Kyle wasn't too enthusiastic about going on the cattle drive. He had never been on one and wasn't worried about the trip, but he had come through the Fort Worth settlement on his way out to the Flat and he certainly wasn't impressed. One of the benefits of a drive for the cowboys, was the chance to let loose at the end of it, but Fort Worth had dwindled after the war began and had not recovered. It had been a sparsely populated, dreary place. However, Charles explained that cattle drives were stopping there on the way to Abilene, Kansas and it being the season, they could count on a number of saloons being in operation. This caught Kyle's attention and considerably cheered him up. He missed not going into town and thought every day that if Black didn't give up and leave soon, he would have to find a way to kill him. The fact was, Kyle was absolutely terrified of Johnny Black. He had heard the stories; the man was almost a legend.

His luck hadn't been all that good for a while, but maybe it was changing. Baggett had paid him well for killing the Lowery boys, the attacks on the cowboys and the Anderson wagon. To add to it, he had been planning to ask Clive, who everyone said was a famous killer and gunfighter, what it would cost to kill Black. Lucky he didn't, considering Clive turned out to be a Pinkerton man. The more he thought about going on the cattle drive, the better it sounded. When they got to Fort Worth, he could drink and visit, hopefully play some faro and if his luck held, Johnny Black would be gone when he got back to the area.

"How long you reckon we'll be gone?" Kyle asked.

"Well, depends on the weather, the creeks and such, but we can cover about ten or twelve miles a day, so figure on two weeks or so to get there. Generally we lay in for a few days, selling the cattle, re-outfitting and resting the horses. It'll be quicker coming back of course, so figure on maybe three weeks or a little better."

"So tell me a bit about it," said Kyle. "I don't want to look like no greenhorn."

"Well, Baggett has made me trail boss, even though he's going. I guess he don't want to do no work. I been getting sixty-five a month as foreman, but I'll make a hundred as trail boss. We'll take the cook and a chuck wagon with supplies. The cook will get double pay. There will be ten or twelve cowboys and damn near as many wranglers handling the extra horses. Like I said, we'll cover maybe 10 or 12 miles a day. Switch off on night watch. It ain't bad unless it rains a lot."

Smith suddenly threw his cigarette butt into the grass, pulled a plug out of his pocket, pinched off a large chunk and stuck it in his mouth. Kyle watched him. The man has something on his mind, he thought. They sat. Kyle chewed and spit. Smith chewed and spit. Finally Smith said, "Brother, you remember when I contacted you, said maybe we could take advantage of the situation here?"

"I do," said Kyle. "You got something in mind?"

"Well, as I got to know the hands, even the cook and housekeeper, I realized there wasn't one single person working for Baggett that had been there when he got started, built his cabin and barns. He pays well and he treats the hands fair, so that got me to wondering. When he was in town, I poked around, just out of curiosity."

He spit and gazed out at the cowboys, yelling, "Damnit! Quit jawing and start branding!" They had branded and ear- marked all of their cattle, but they were adding a trail or road brand that all of the cattle in their drive would have, no matter who owned them. The other ranches were doing the same thing.

"Didn't have any idea of what I was looking for really, but one day, after I had poked around the place a few times, I went into the man's bedroom. Hadn't been in there, you know, kind of a private place. But after standing in there I realized something was wrong. Didn't take long to figure it out. He's got a storage area walled off, but it has a fake wall in it." He looked at Kyle's surprise and smiled.

"Yep, I reckon you got an idea what was behind the wall. A safe. It would take a few strong men to move it. It's a heavy damn thing. He's got it hid and I'm thinking he didn't want anybody around what knew about it. Probably killed anybody knew about the secret area. Wouldn't surprise me."

"If it's that heavy how are we going to get it open?" Smith spit, "I been thinking about that. The quickest way was if we could just open it. But the combination is for sure in Baggett's head. He ain't likely to give it to us at gunpoint. He's smart enough to know we'll kill him. I figure we can try to catch him when he's got it open or we can shoot him a few times where it ain't likely to kill him, see if he'll give us the combination to stop the pain, but failing that I figure we pick up some chisels and hammers in Fort Worth."

"No need, interrupted Kyle, "I saw a couple of chisels and hammers in the tool room out at the barn."

"Okay, then. Now, when this drive is over, some of the boys will take their pay and move on. But quite a few will go back with us and as soon as we get back, they'll be heading into town to spend their money. Soon as everybody's paid, well he ain't gonna leave all that money laying around."

Charlie Smith and Kyle Smith grinned at each other.

"So, we just hang back for a bit, surprise Baggett when he opens the safe, kill him, or maybe kill him and break the safe open ourselves, take everything in the safe, the bag of money from the cattle sale and head south," said Kyle, in awe. "Got to hand it to you brother, you are one smart cowboy."

FORTY-SEVEN

JAKE WAITED UNTIL HE HAD FINISHED breakfast before he stopped by the hotel desk and learned the girl's name was Sarah. He walked up to Johnny's room and announced himself by saying "Good morning," before easing the door open enough to walk in. Surprise registered on his face as he walked in to witness Sarah sitting in the chair beside Johnny's bed, reading to him. As Jake entered, she stopped reading, lowered the book and smiled.

"Morning reporter," said Johnny.

Jake took off his hat and glanced around the room.

"The boys are off to the livery, Whitt's been feeding them their breakfast," Johnny said. "Come on in."

Sarah rose, placed the book on the dresser and said, "I'll ask the barber to come by and I'll be back at lunch Mr. Black."

"Thank you," said Johnny as Sarah smiled and left. Jake sat his hat upside down on the dresser and as he walked up to the bed, Johnny sighed. "I already know all the questions. My headache is gone, but the back of my head is still a mite sore. I can walk okay, but I get dizzy when I stand up, so I have been avoiding going downstairs."

"Are things still blurry or do you just like the sound of the girl's voice?" asked Jake.

Johnny looked at him. "Well," he said, "I still find it hard to make out the words, but I can see things better, like you for example."

Jake sat in the chair by the bed. "You're doing fine. I saw a lot of this during the war and most men got back to normal. Sometimes in a few days, sometimes it took a couple of weeks." "Okay then," said Johnny. "Although my sight is still a little off, I can tell you're feeling better. I wonder what could be the source of your good spirits."

Jake shook his head. "It's no wonder you're good at poker. Yes, I do have some news and if you're not going to give me a hard time, I'll share it with you."

"Little touchy are you," said Johnny grinning. "Okay, reporter, I am getting a little bored. What's been happening?"

Jake told Johnny about the attack on the two cowboys and the attack on the Anderson's as they were headed into town in their wagon, including the threat to kidnap Pete and sell him. When he told him about Charity shooting one of the men in the chest, Johnny looked surprised and acted like he was about to comment, but he remained silent, listening intently.

When Jake had finished, Johnny didn't respond, just sat, staring at the ceiling, in thought. Then, Jake said, "Almost forgot, the Anderson's said to tell you they were praying for you."

"Please tell them thank you. I can use all the help I can get."

The two men were silent for a while, then Johnny took out a cigarillo and lit it. Following his example, Jake took out the fixings and built himself a cigarette. "The rules say no smoking in the room on account of fire," said Johnny, taking a drag on his smoke. "But as I can't get down the stairs, I figured an exception could be made."

After Jake promised to take Loco, Flop and Perro with him the next time he went up to visit the Andersons and telling Johnny he would look in on him before bedtime, he took his hat from the dresser, nodded at Johnny and walked down to the street, lost in thought.

FORTY-EIGHT

ALVIN HAD BEEN IN THE CORN PATCH since first light, picking the ears that were ready for harvest and most were. He had filled several baskets already as the sun fully appeared, announcing full dawn. Pete and the girls would be gathering eggs and milking the cow. They had a new foal in the barn and Danny would be out there checking on it and tossing some hay for its mother. Breakfast would be ready soon, so he finished filling up the basket he was filling and headed toward the house, stopping by the well pump to wash up.

After Danny said grace, they ate in silence. Strain had been evident on Rebecca's face since the attack and the threat to kidnap Pete. This added to the stress and worry Danny had already been under, and it was showing in his manner. On the other hand, noted Alvin, after a couple of weeks on the ranch, Charity had seemed to come out of her shell. Although he couldn't seem to force himself to utter words, Alvin's mind worked fine and his powers of observation seemed keener than it had before the war. He had noticed Jake and Charity's attraction to each other and he felt it was a good thing. They both seemed to him to be fine young people.

As Alvin ate, he pondered the future. Life on the ranch was everything he had ever wanted. It was something he had taken to as a young boy, much like Pete, he thought. People tended to ignore him, almost forget he was there, like a servant because he was mute. For some reason, folks thought because he couldn't speak he must be slow. Why he couldn't speak he didn't know, but he awoke night after night, reliving the nightmare of Shiloh where he had been severely wounded in his left arm, the surgeon taking it without a thought. He had awoken after the surgery, confused and had tried to speak, but no words would come out. He felt a tremendous guilt for living. So many had died. Why had he lived? He wasn't sure what he could have done, but surely he might have done more, saved more lives. The Lord knew he had tried. After a while, seeing the death, he had decided he was as good as dead, so he had begun to risk his life over and over. But it hadn't been enough. So many good men dead.

He said a silent prayer for the dead on both sides of the conflict. His thoughts turned to Danny. His brother Danny who people in the street called a coward. It enraged Alvin every time, but Danny had asked him to please, please, not interfere. It was, according to Danny, God testing him. If only those fools had seen him in action! Danny risking his life dozens of times to protect his men or to pull wounded men to safety. He had been wounded twice, but was fortunate that he didn't lose a limb.

Alvin couldn't imagine living anywhere else or doing anything else. He thought constantly about Baggett's threats. But that wasn't the only thing that threatened their life on the ranch. Surely Danny knew how unhappy Rebecca was and the latest events had brought it all to the surface. Danny had told him Rebecca had been a little melancholy, but was hopeful her sister Charity coming out would make things better. It had in fact seemed to help a little, but Alvin listened to the conversa- tions and he knew Rebecca missed the city life. The funny thing was, Danny worked hard and tried to be cheerful, but Alvin knew he had missed his calling. If ever there was a man who should be preaching the gospel, it was his brother, Danny Anderson.

As breakfast finished up, Danny told Rebecca he and Alvin were going to ride up north to check on their herd and they could use Pete's help. Rebecca didn't speak, then said, "He needs his lessons."

"We thought to be back by mid-afternoon," said Danny, then, "He won't be out of our sight."

Rebecca nodded and began clearing the dishes. Danny closed his eyes and silently asked God for his guidance. Alvin and Pete helped clear the table, then Rebecca told them to go before it got too hot, so they all walked out to the barn, saddled up and rode out, but not before Alvin and Danny had checked their weapons and Danny told Pete to fetch his shotgun.

Communication among the ranchers was spread by visits to town and by the wives as they got together to can or quilt. Most ranchers would be joining up with Baggett for a drive to Fort Worth in a few days, but Danny, the Franklins and a few other smaller ranchers had decided to band together and make a drive in about a month. They reasoned the cattle would fatten up in the next month and the grass itself would be better. Danny still needed to hire some help and cowboys and hunters were arriving at the Flat every day. He figured he would find some help soon. Baggett couldn't keep hiring every able-bodied man that showed up. He smiled to himself when he remembered that Jake had volunteered to help around the place and when Danny discussed the need for some experienced hands for the drive to Fort Worth, Jake said he would accompany them. When he had said that, for some reason Charity had broken out laughing.

FORTY-NINE

CAPTAIN BATES DIDN'T WAIT LONG to make the trip out to the Rocking J to visit the Andersons with the real goal of seeing Charity Chapin. He timed it well, arriving a bit before lunchtime. He was welcomed and invited to lunch, which he thought later, couldn't have gone better. He had regaled the entire family with stories of his accomplishments including the two battles with the Indians and he impressed them, how could they not be, with his family's status in political circles. As he was preparing to leave, he saw his opportunity and asked Charity if she would like to join him for a ride, perhaps on Sunday afternoon. She had readily agreed to the engagement inviting the Captain to take lunch with the family first. Captain Bates couldn't wait.

Charity watched Captain Bates ride away and as he turned to wave, she smiled and waved back. Oh my, she thought, as a string of descriptive words came to her mind, pompous, conceited, pretentious, arrogant and vain. He had caught her totally by surprise when he asked her to go riding. Certainly, she could have said no, but the army was a powerful force on the frontier and the settlers depended on them. Danny and Rebecca had enough problems right now, without her adding to them by offending an army officer. As she considered the situation, she decided she would go for the ride and be polite, but use the opportunity to let the Captain know she was not interested in being courted.

That evening Captain Bates, dressed in civilian clothes, rode into the Flat. Troop's visits were restricted except for the non-commissioned officers and commissioned officers. Sometimes Bates, in uniform, would lead patrols through the town, but he frequently rode into town alone, advising the fort Commander one day that he felt it his duty to keep an eye on things in the Flat and to let the non-commissioned officers know he was around. Bates did patrol the town including the prostitute's huts on the edge of town, and he never drank or gambled, however, he was both known and feared at the huts where he secretly engaged the services of the girls who lived and earned their livelihood there. He had his favorites and he paid the going rate, but he was feared because of his violent tendencies. He was physically rough with the women and one girl had left the area after he choked her into unconsciousness. This night, his favorite girl begged off sick, but Bates was able to corner his second choice and took his excitement over his future with Charity out on the girl in an exceptionally rough encounter.

FIFTY

TEN DAYS LATER, much to Jake's relief, Johnny was his old self. A week before, Jake had entered Johnny's room and found him reading a letter. This came as a pleasant surprise and it also made Jake curious seeing Johnny had received a letter. Jake just didn't know anything about Johnny's past other than the fact that his brother had been killed.

Not only had his vision cleared, but so had the dizziness and Johnny had been walking distances to get his strength back. Loco had been ecstatic to see him, almost breaking down his stall in the livery. Johnny had taken him for a long ride accompanied by Flop and Perro and brushed and talked to him when they returned. One night, Johnny had played some poker while Jake sipped beer and visited with Jones at the Frontier. There had been a fistfight at the bar and a drunk had passed out and collapsed as he was making his way out of the saloon. Such was life in the Flat.

At the moment Jake and Johnny were finishing breakfast. Johnny wanted to ride out to the army range to do some practice shooting and then come back and clean all of the weapons. He hadn't said, but Jake inferred that Kyle Stephens was weighing on Johnny's mind. They were wearing their pistols as usual, so Jake was going to the hotel to fetch their rifles while Johnny picked up some cartridges at the general store before they met at the livery.

Johnny was approaching the store when he saw two ladies, he thought them to be army wives, being confronted by three young men. The three had the women hemmed against the wall of the store. A rough crew thought Johnny. As he walked up, Johnny smiled and said, "Please step aside gentlemen, so the ladies can do their shopping. You seem to be impeding the sidewalk."

The three young toughs looked at Johnny, studying him. "You gonna shoot us old man?" asked one, "For im…whatever you said." The other two laughed. The two women crowded closer to each other and the building.

"Oh, I don't think that'll be necessary," said Johnny amiably. "I am confident that you young scholars will assess the situation and act in accordance with your best interests, which, I assure you, would be to get far, far away as fast as possible." He smiled.

The largest of the three stepped close to Johnny. "It sounds like you are making fun of us, now get the hell out of here before we kick your old ass into heaven."

Johnny looked disappointed, stepped back, turned away to his right and grabbed a brand-new shovel Birchfield had placed outside for sale. As he turned away and grabbed the shovel he just kept turning, going full circle, but as he came around to face the three men the metal end of the shovel was moving at an alarming rate and caught the big tough square in the face. As the big man screamed and staggered backward he tripped and fell on his back as Johnny reversed the shovel and jammed the handle end hard into the stomach of the second man who bent double, dropped to his knees and began to vomit. Johnny stepped around the two, dropped the shovel, faked a right and hit the third man with a left hook that might well have felled a horse. The man dropped like a stone and didn't move. Walking over to the man on his knees retching, Johnny said,

"Stand up." The man responded with a vulgar retort and Johnny said, "Suit yourself," and kicked the man hard in the head with the heel of his boot. Satisfied that the three no longer posed a threat, Johnny turned to the women, opened the door and said, "Ladies." The two women, in danger of inhaling flies because their mouths were gaping open, never took their eyes off Johnny as they entered the store. Johnny picked up the shovel, checked to make sure it wasn't bent and stood it back in its place before entering the store to see about the cartridges he needed.

A few days later, when Jake and Johnny were back at the Frontier, Jones was telling the story. Jake was confused because Johnny hadn't said a word about it, but there had been a number of witnesses and the legend of Johnny Black grew.

FATE RIDES A TALL HORSE

FIFTY-ONE

DANNY AND REBECCA WERE SURPRISED when Charity told them the Captain would be coming for Sunday lunch and that he and she would be taking a ride in the country. They had been horrified at the Captain's bragging and his domination of the conversation. Rebecca asked Charity if she was sure about going for a ride with Captain Bates, but Charity told her it would be fine. He had asked and she wanted to be polite.

Rebecca had given it some thought and had sent Alvin into town with a note inviting both Mr. Evans and Mr. Black to join them for lunch on Sunday. He had returned with an acceptance. Rebecca smiled, but decided to keep the surprise to herself.

On Sunday, his spirits soaring, Captain Bates rode into view of the Anderson homestead only to see Black's huge horse grazing. He wasn't sure, but there was another horse that he thought belonged to Evans. Did the man invite himself out here, he wondered. Of course he did. No manners and trying to woo Ms. Chapin. He had to fight to control his anger. Did the young dolt not grasp the fact that he was a commissioned army Captain? Damn it.

Then it occurred to him, what he would do. He would bring up subjects of conversation well beyond Evans' education and understanding, totally embarrassing the man. As he approached the Anderson's cabin, Pete came out to take his horse.

"Thank you, young man," said Captain Bates, stepping from his saddle. "Are there others here for lunch?"

"Yes sir," responded Pete. "Mister Evans and Mister Black are already inside. Lunch is about ready."

Bates put a smile on his face, stepped upon the porch and knocked on the door.

Lunch was, thought Danny, a very strange and uneven affair. How they came to have Captain Bates, Johnny Black and Jake Evans as guests all on the same day, he wasn't quite sure. Certainly everyone was polite and well mannered. Rebecca and Charity, southern ladies they were, worked hard to include everyone in the conversation and to keep everything civil, but he saw and felt a tension between Captain Bates and Jake. Johnny was respectful and polite to the Captain, but Danny felt that Johnny was barely tolerating the man, although Captain Bates didn't seem to notice. The tension was all due to Charity he felt sure. Out here on the frontier, men far outnumbered women and attractive, educated women were scarce.

Johnny saw the issue between the Captain and Jake instantly. There was no doubt both gentlemen were interested in the attentions of Ms. Chapin. But as lunch progressed his assessment of Captain Bates continued to evolve and not in a good way. He already harbored serious doubts about the man's abilities to lead troops in battle after the two encounters with Indians they had shared. And he could understand the man's interest in Ms. Chapin, a very attractive and sophisticated young woman, but the conversation at lunch provided Johnny with clues to the Captain's personality and it was of a type he held in great contempt. Obviously the man considered himself more than an officer and a gentlemen, as he constantly alluded to an aristocratic background and tried very hard to impress with his knowledge on a number of subjects. Also, the man talked incessantly. Black had known women who were inclined in that way, but Bates' constant chatter, most of it about himself, was beyond the pale.

Jake was smiling and listening politely, but he wasn't comprehending much. Shortly after he and Johnny had arrived, Charity had told him that she had agreed to take a ride with Captain Bates. He and Charity seemed to have connected, at least Jake thought they had. It had never occurred to him that other men might be pursuing Charity. It wasn't like he had a claim on the woman, but just like that, she had agreed to a ride with Bates. He wasn't jealous, he told himself, he was just irritated. There was a big difference he thought.

For his part, Captain Bates continued his rhetoric, but channeled it in an attempt to embarrass the other two guests, especially Evans. He was however, becoming frustrated. Black didn't speak, but Evans seemed to be an encyclopedia of knowledge. Regardless of the subject, Evans seemed to have a comment on it and often it seemed to counter what Bates had said. It was almost like a verbal jousting match and would have been had not the ladies often stepped in to make a comment or change the subject.

Finally, out of character, Captain Bates actually asked Danny why he hadn't seen any hands about. Danny was diplomatic, saying things were competitive, that it was hard to find ranch hands, but Charity, outspoken young lady she was, said, "There is a bit more to the situation Captain. We are engaged in a bit of a struggle with a rancher to our north. He would like to purchase our property, but Danny and Rebecca aren't interested in selling. It seems that every time Danny hires someone, Mr. Baggett, our esteemed neighbor offers them more money to work for him."

Captain Bates looked very surprised. "I know Mr. Baggett. The army has a contract with him to provide beef to the fort. Are you sure that he's intentionally trying to undermine you?"

"No," said Danny. "As I said, Baggett runs a large operation and requires a good many hand."

"Excuse me brother-in-law, but you are sometimes too polite for your own good. Captain, Mr. Baggett has made it clear it would be in our best interest to sell to him and he makes no secret about trying to keep the pressure on the Rocking J."

"Danny," said the Captain, "What Mr. Baggett is doing may not be illegal, but certainly I plan to have a word with him." He smiled at Charity.

Johnny ate, while Jake fumed.

After lunch, Charity invited Johnny and Jake to join herself and Captain Bates on a ride to the river, Johnny politely declined, thanking everyone for lunch and saying his goodbyes. Jake was torn, but accepted the invitation. At first irritation was evident on the Captain's face, but only for a few seconds before he smiled and said, "Excellent, I've heard there have been some turkeys spotted around the river, perhaps we'll see some."

As the three walked their horses away from the house and toward the river, the Captain kept up a stream of conversation all addressed to Charity as though Jake wasn't present. When they returned to the cabin an hour later, the Captain struck up a conversation about religion with Danny, lingering so long, out of good manners, Jake finally excused himself, thanked everyone, told Charity he looked forward to seeing her again soon and left, frustrated by the day.

For his part, as he prepared to leave, Captain Bates assured Charity that he fully intended to speak to Baggett and invited her to a soiree to be held at the fort the following Saturday night. Caught off guard, but still feeling encouraged about the Captain talking to Baggett, Charity said, "That would be wonderful, Captain Bates."

On the way back to the Flat, Jake talked out loud to Girl. He was angry with his own lack of performance as much as he was with Captain Bates. Why didn't he shut the man down, tell him he was a Harvard grad, a doctor and that he had studied in England and well, truth be known, he was fairly wealthy. His dad had seen to that, investing money for both him and his brother, which had multiplied many times over.

He knew why he had not. There was no way he was lowering himself to the kind of self-serving chatter that seemed to be second nature for the Captain. Charity knew he was a Harvard trained doctor and that was what mattered. Besides, he and Charity had connected. There was no way Charity would allow herself to become involved with that pompous, self- centered, egotistical pea brain. At least he didn't think so.

FATE RIDES A TALL HORSE

FIFTY-TWO

THE ENTIRE ANDERSON CLAN CAME TO TOWN the following Saturday morning and Jake stood wearing a clean shirt, bearing a fresh shave and haircut, when the wagon pulled up in front of the general store. Danny clapped him on the shoulder as he strolled into the store, Pete showed him a tiny snake he had caught, Alvin waved at him, Rebecca greeted him warmly and Charity walked up and said hello. But he could feel that something was wrong. "How about treating me to a cup of coffee?" Charity asked.

They were on their second cup of coffee when Charity told Jake she had agreed to attend the Saturday night soiree at the fort with Captain Bates. She quickly explained that she felt perhaps that the Captain might have some influence with Baggett and she didn't want to alienate him while he was offering to talk to Baggett.

During the extremes of stress during the war, as wounded were being hastily brought into the large tent, seemingly without end, many of them with horrific wounds, Jake had quickly managed to bring his emotions under control. The chaos that ensued when Jake found himself part of a group defending themselves from the Indians was a different emotional experience, but again, Jake's natural abilities took over and he had reacted with a reasoned calm. However, now, as his thoughts raced and his imagination soared, he found himself unable to control his emotions at the thought of Charity in the arms of Captain Bates.

Although Jake didn't respond immediately, Charity looked almost frightened at Jake's reaction, as his face seemed to harden. Unable to speak, Jake finally lifted his coffee cup to his mouth and sipped, in an effort to buy some time to process his thoughts.

Finally, he said, "I understand. Can't say I'm thrilled about it, but I understand." He thought he smiled, but it was so forced it looked as if it was painted on his face. "Of course, it's not like you and I are courting or anything," he continued, "I just don't much like the man's attitude."

"That's right, Mr. Evans," Charity said, secretly thrilled at Jake' reaction. "We are not courting, at least not that I am aware of."

Saturday night found Johnny playing poker at his usual spot at the Frontier, while Jake stood at the bar nursing a beer and his emotions. Jake always limited himself to three beers, but tonight, after two beers he switched to whiskey and it wasn't long before the liquor began to show itself. In fact, Jake not only confided his deep dislike of Captain Bates to the bartender, Jones, but he was loud enough that the men around him were soon privy to Jake's complaints. When he began to state that he would like to punch that egotistical ass right in his fat head. Johnny looked up, excused himself, rose and walked up to the bar. Jake was saying he would like to stab the man so all the hot air could escape and Jones was laughing. Taking Jake by the arm, Johnny escorted him out the door and to the hotel.

On the night of the soirée, Captain Bates picked Charity up in a buggy and horse rig, decked out in his finest uniform. Charity looked beautiful in the one gown she had brought out west from Atlanta. She wore it with her hair up and a small broach her late fiancé had given her.

The soirée, a small private party held at the fort was a success. Some of the army band members had formed a small ensemble and provided music for dancing. There was food and wine. In spite of herself, Charity enjoyed the event. Captain Bates was every bit the gentlemen and she danced and visited with all of the young officers present. Because everyone circulated and visited, Charity was spared the Captain's self- centered conversation. However, Charity thought constantly about Jake and cringed when, as they reached the Anderson cabin after the party, the Captain asked her to join him for a picnic lunch on Sunday week. She smiled and agreed, knowing she would further alienate Jake, but she so wanted to help Danny and Rebecca and they needed the Captain to talk to Baggett, who she understood was out of town at the moment on a cattle drive to Fort Worth.

FATE RIDES A TALL HORSE

FIFTY-THREE

CAPTAIN BATES KNEW THAT Charity had enjoyed the soirée and he could tell the Lieutenant Colonel who commanded the fort was impressed with Bates having brought her. The Captain had hinted that the two were in fact courting and it might not be long before he wasn't on the market anymore. There was no doubt whatever that every one of the officers was jealous. Having a sophisticated and beautiful wife was always helpful to an officer's career.

However, at the moment Captain Bates was unable to enjoy his fame. He had a problem. Urinating was extremely painful and his male organ was dripping a greenish tinted discharge. There was no doubt of his condition. It was a common problem among the troops, but the Captain could not have it known that he had contracted it. He waited until sick call was over before entering the doctor's office.

"Captain, am I behind on my reports?" asked the doctor. "I'm not of a mind to change them if that's what the Commander has in mind. I've said time and time again, the conditions here are deplorable. It's a miracle we're not all suffering from any number of maladies."

Captain Bates held up his hand. "Nothing like that. This is personal. One day the officer's latrine was engaged and unfortunately my bowels were in distress, so I used the troop's latrine. It appears I have contracted a disease from the encounter."

The doctor looked at the Captain. He struggled with his emotions. As a doctor it distressed him to see anyone take ill or to suffer an injury, but he could not stand the arrogant Captain Bates. So, the man had the clap, well, well. Toilet seat my ass, thought the doctor. The great, at least according to himself, Captain Bates had been romping with the ladies of the Flat, no doubt. "Why don't you lock the door and have a seat. Let me have a look at your symptoms."

After examining the Captain, the doctor prescribed the usual treatment which sometimes seemed to work and sometimes did not. Pulling a bottle from his medical cabinet, the doctor handed it to Captain Bates. "This is what we've had the most success with. It is medication mixed with some liquids, just take a dose three times a day and I'll check you in a couple of weeks."

FIFTY-FOUR

CHARITY AND CAPTAIN BATES DID ENJOY a picnic lunch the following Sunday and Charity had to admit, the Captain was a well-mannered and educated man. He seemed to relish exhibiting his knowledge of various subjects. The only issue occurred when she and the Captain returned in mid-afternoon. Rebecca told her Jake had ridden out after lunch to call on her.

Charity shut her eyes in dismay, but Rebecca said Jake had expressed his regrets on not catching her at home and had spent a pleasant hour visiting with herself and Danny. He had also promised to go fishing with Pete and Alvin the following Friday evening after the chores were done, so Rebecca had invited him for supper on Friday.

"Charity," Rebecca said, "Danny and I appreciate your trying to stay in the Captain's good graces so perhaps he will intervene with Mr. Baggett, but we like Jake and don't want you to jeopardize your friendship. That is, unless you're getting on with the Captain?"

Charity laughed. "Oh my, no, no," she said. "Captain Bates is polite, but so full of himself. Hopefully Jake understands."

Friday evening was pleasant, but a bit strained. Jake was polite, but Charity could tell he was unhappy about her outings with Bates. When he left to go fishing with Pete and Alvin, she told him they would all be in town the next morning and perhaps they could have coffee. This seemed to cheer him up and they said goodnight.

FATE RIDES A TALL HORSE

• • •

Saturday morning, Jake was up early for breakfast and was waiting outside the café watching for the Andersons. He turned to visit with House, a local rancher who was in town for supplies and when he looked back, the Anderson's wagon was there and he saw Charity climbing down. He was only two steps into the street when he was knocked sideways by a horse. His hat went flying and after he chased it down, he saw the culprit had been Captain Bates, who was now dismounting to talk to Charity. Fuming, Jake waited until Charity had spoken to Bates and excusing herself had entered Birchfield's. He stalked over to Captain Bates and let loose the anger that had been building. At first, Jake took Bates to task for running him over, but his emotions soon boiled over to rather ungentlemanly terms regarding the Captain's pursuit of Ms. Chapin in complete disregard for her feelings and the fact that she and he were courting.

"I think that fact would come as a surprise to Ms. Chapin," responded the Captain coldly. A public confrontation with someone of Jake Evan's status was embarrassing to Bates and he held his tongue. Finally, when Jake said something about kicking his pompous ass, Bates responded, "You might want to be careful about threatening a United States Army officer," before turning and walking away. The dispute had been witnessed by dozens of people beginning their day and it left Jake feeling angry with himself.

FIFTY-FIVE

WHEN CAPTAIN BATES WAS ABSENT from the morning roll call, an army patrol, led by Lieutenant Angleton was dispatched to locate him. The guard reported that he had not returned to the fort after leaving late the night before. The soldiers were working their way through the early risers, asking if anyone had seen him. After an hour, they hadn't found anyone who had seen the Captain after about ten the previous evening. There had been a few men who remembered him walking his horse through town, dressed in his uniform. However, at least one noted that he couldn't be sure if it was last night that he had seen the Captain or maybe the night before.

"Damnit man!" exploded Lieutenant Angleton, this is important. "Think, will you."

"Sorry sir," said the man, "but I saw the Captain many a time, just riding around the town, so I don't really notice him. Sir," he added again. Two men standing with him nodded their agreement.

In two hours they had covered the Flat twice and found no sign of the Captain or his horse. It occurred to Lieutenant Angleton that perhaps he had been accosted by the bushwhackers that had been active in the area, but why would the Captain have left the Flat? The Lieutenant sent a man back to the fort to report and ask for further instructions. While they were waiting a mill worker at the army mill located on Mill Creek, rode into town leading a horse with an army brand, on his way to the fort. Seeing the Lieutenant, he stopped and told him that he had found a body and the horse down by the creek. Leaving one man to wait on the returning trooper, the Lieutenant and his patrol followed the wood mill worker to the site of the body.

Captain Bates' body was face down in the mud on the edge of the creek. Unmounting from his horse, Lieutenant Angleton handed the reins to a trooper. Kneeling down by Captain Bates, he slowly rolled his body over. The Captain's uniform was literally soaked in blood and mud. The Lieutenant saw that his throat had been slashed and it appeared the man had been stabbed repeatedly, judging from tears in his coat. It was apparent to the Lieutenant that Captain Bates had been the victim of a robbery. Most likely he had put up a fight and been killed for his efforts or perhaps he had recognized his attackers and he was killed so he couldn't identify them. The soft bank was a sea of horse hoofs and boot prints from people and animals watering at the creek. Lieutenant Angleton had never conducted an investigation, but he was an intelligent man and knew that the murder of a federal army officer was a major event. Establishing that Captain Bates was beyond help, he ordered the patrol back from the area and told them to form a perimeter. He tasked the Sergeant with ensuring no one got through until the Commander arrived and the body was removed. Another trooper was dispatched to alert the Sergeant Major and the Commander with all haste.

• • •

The fort Commander and the Sergeant Major stood over Captain Bates' body, staring at it. He still wore his saber, but his revolver was missing. Finally, the Lieutenant Colonel spoke, "Sergeant Major, are we still holding that man for the Pinkerton agent?"

"We are sir," replied the Sergeant Major. "I want you to dispatch some men to locate the agent and have him brought here. I don't care what he's about when he's located. My orders are to bring him immediately."

"Yes sir!" responded the Sergeant Major, raising a hand in salute before turning away to issue orders to the troops. The Commander did not acknowledge his salute, he simply continued to stare at Captain Bates' dead body.

Clive Cole had enjoyed a late breakfast and was lingering over a third cup of coffee, having risen late after playing poker into the early morning hours, when several troopers appeared at his table, led by a Corporal that he knew from the fort. "Good morning, Corporal," Clive said.

"Sir, we've been ordered to escort you down to Mill Creek.

The fort Commander is waiting for you there."

Clive didn't respond for a moment, sipping his coffee, then asked, "What's this about?"

"I believe it concerns Captain Bates, sir, he wasn't at roll call this morning."

Arriving at Mill Creek to find a number of army troops and a small group down by the water's edge, Clive dismounted and spotting the Commander, approached him. Clive glanced at the dead body before turning to address the fort's commander. "Good morning, sir, I believe you wanted to see me."

"Yes," said the Lieutenant Colonel, "if you're the Pinkerton man."

"I am," responded Clive. "Clive Cole at your service."

"Mr. Cole pleased to make your acquaintance. Do you have much experience in investigations?"

"I have sir. As a matter of fact, I did some work for the army involving an officer that absconded with army funds, and I was involved in investigating a shooting involving a non- commissioned officer."

"That man," said the Colonel, pointing to Captain Bates' body, "is or was a commissioned officer in the army. He has been murdered. It is my intention to engage you and your agency to look into his murder pending any counter order I may receive from higher headquarters. My First Sergeant will provide background information and assist you. I will personally guarantee your payment and expenses if the army does not, although I am confident they will be pleased that you were in the area and available. The Pinkerton Detective Agency has a sound reputation. Do you accept?"

"I do sir," said Clive, holding out his hand and shaking the Lieutenant Colonel's hand.

FIFTY-SIX

CLIVE SPENT A LONG TIME poking around on Bates' body. He borrowed a kerchief from a trooper and wiped away mud. He removed a small pad from a pocket along with a pencil stub and took notes. Finally, satisfied, he walked over to where a trooper held the Captain's horse and studied the blood-soaked saddle and the blood on the horse. A canvass of the area by a dozen troops resulted in the discovery of the Captain's revolver in shallow water at the creek's edge.

As the body was loaded in a wagon for transfer to the fort so that the doctor could examine it more closely, Clive spoke to the First Sergeant. "It's all very preliminary, but it appears he was killed somewhere else and thrown over his horse's saddle. The horse was likely led down to the creek and turned loose. The Captain could have fallen off or been pulled off. Whoever did it threw his revolver into the creek. Cause of death can be confirmed by the doctor, but it's apparent his throat was cut. The unusual thing is that the man appears to have been violently stabbed at least twenty times."

Later, at the fort, Clive examined Bates' body and discussed the wounds with the doctor. The doctor felt sure the wound to the throat had resulted in Bates' death in a matter of minutes, but many of the twenty-two puncture wounds discovered by the doctor could have, by themselves, resulted in death. The two men pondered the body for a bit, then agreed that whoever had killed Captain Bates had done so in a rage or with extreme hatred. There was no doubt, this was a crime of passion. It did not appear he was robbed. His watch, money and saber were all with him. The only further information the doctor would furnish was that the knife wounds were wide and fairly deep. Most about six inches deep, and an inch or so wide, indicating a medium sized weapon, possibly a hunting or skinning knife.

"The sort of knife one might sheath and carry on his belt or carry in a boot," noted Clive. One thing the search of the creek where the body was found did not turn up was a knife, thought Clive, so it is likely our culprit still has it with them, well, if they didn't throw it out into the creek.

"Somewhere is a lot and I mean a lot of blood," said the doctor, interrupting Clive's thoughts. "Blood would have pumped, literally pumped out of the artery in his neck, not to mention the puncture wounds. Our killer would have been soaked in blood. He would have to be after standing close enough, long enough to stab the man twenty-two times. I feel sure his throat was cut first, otherwise it wouldn't have been possible to continue to stab him."

Leaving the doctor, Clive was let into Captain Bates' quarters and he quickly found what he was hoping for. The man had, like many men had during the war and during times of loneliness, kept a journal. Clive sat in the room's chair and started reading.

Although Clive had seen the Captain around town and had spoken to him a time or two, he didn't know the man. However, as he read the diary, he began to gain a sense of his personality. While the majority of the entries were the normal recordings of a man's life in the army, the two encounters with the Indians, the first after the buffalo hunter had arrived back at the fort after being horribly disfigured and the second when the Stapleton boy had been kidnapped, were very interesting reading.

What stood out after an hour of reading was that Captain Bates held a very high opinion of himself. According to the Captain's journal, he had been instrumental in the successes regarding both encounters with the Indians. It would have been difficult for the Lieutenant Colonel to manage the fort's affairs if not for Captain Bates, according to Captain Bates.

Clive laughed out loud. "Well, maybe it's all true," Clive said to the empty room. The Captain had confided to his diary his conviction that it was important to 'show the flag' in the Flat, to maintain a semblance of order. There were entries noting that he had taken a small patrol into town and many others recording his experiences patrolling on his own. Clive was almost through the journal and hadn't found anything he thought was helpful, when he reached the first recordings that mentioned Ms. Charity Chapin.

His interest began to grow when he reached the parts describing Jake Evans, who according to the late Captain, was extremely upset at the attentions that Ms. Chapin showered on himself. Bates had described Evans as very jealous and noted that he had threatened the Captain only the day before. 'I must keep an eye out for the man' Bates had written. Clive knew Jake and had never thought of him as the murdering type, but when a woman was concerned, men would do unlikely things. Leaning back in the chair, he gave it some thought. A crime of passion. It fit. The thing to do now was to find out where Jake Evans was on the night Captain Bates was murdered.

Clive found Johnny and Jake at breakfast the next morning. "Mind if I sit?" Clive asked.

"Pull up a chair," responded Johnny. Clive pulled up a chair and Maybelle appeared to take his order for coffee.

"Don't mean to impose," said Clive, "but reckon you boys heard I'm looking into the death of Captain Bates at the army's request."

"Word gets around," agreed Johnny.

"Well, I'm trying to track the late Captain's movements the night he died by asking folks if they saw him. If they didn't, then at least I know where he wasn't." Clive smiled at this bit of insight. "Do you fellows remember seeing him, the night he went missing? He didn't leave the fort till after nine that evening according to the logbook, so it would be after that."

"Nights kind of run together," offered Johnny eating his breakfast while he looked at Clive.

"So they do. But I've found that in the saloons in this town, something memorable happens every night. Now I know you favor the Frontier, would it be safe to guess that that's where you were this week?"

Johnny and Jake looked at each other in thought. Then Jake said, "I don't think we've been anyplace else in the last week."

Clive pulled a notebook out of his pocket and after consult- ing it, said, "The night of the Captain's demise, at the Frontier, a wrestling match broke about midnight between two buffalo- hunters arguing over which one was the better shot. According to witnesses, the two were so drunk they could hardly see each other."

Johnny laughed. "That's right. I was there. The poker game broke up just after they were thrown out. I stepped over them in the street on my way back to the hotel. They had both passed out, but I don't recall seeing the Captain."

Clive looked confused. "You not with him Jake?" he asked. "I was, but I don't remember the fight, that must have been the night I turned in early. Yes, that's right, one night I left maybe eleven, the beer was hitting me kind of hard, and so I went to the hotel and went to bed. I didn't see the Captain,

I'm sure of that."

Clive scratched in his notebook. "Can't thank you enough," he said, rising, he placed a coin on the table. He nodded, turned and walked out.

FATE RIDES A TALL HORSE

FIFTY-SEVEN

FOUR TROOPERS, THE SERGEANT MAJOR, a Lieutenant and Clive Cole banged on Jake's hotel room door just before six in the morning. When he didn't answer they entered using a key from the front desk. They found the bed made and the room tidy. On top of the dresser, along with some coins, lay a leather-sheathed, skinning knife. Clive picked it up, pulled out the knife and looked at it. It was clean, but in the crease between the blade and the handle, Cole could just make out what had to be dried blood. A few minutes later, the group entered Kirk's and placed Jake under arrest for the intentional murder of a federal officer, to wit, one Captain Earnest Abraham Bates, USA.

Jake didn't say a word. As ordered, he stood, unbuckled his gun belt, answered that he didn't have a knife or another gun on his person and held out his hands. A Sergeant placed manacles on him. Jake wasn't surprised; he was in shock. He had been questioned about his whereabouts the night Captain Bates disappeared and he had told the truth. How the army could have reached the conclusion that he had killed Captain Bates was beyond him. Then it occurred to him. Somehow the competition between him and the Captain for Charity's attention must have something to do with this.

Johnny asked calmly, "Who ordered Mr. Evans' arrest?" "The Lieutenant Colonel, the fort Commander, Mr.

Black," said the Lieutenant who liked both Jake and Johnny.

"I'll be up to see the Commander in a bit, Jake," said Johnny, as though he planned to meet Johnny at the general store. "We'll get this straightened out quick."

Jake nodded, then said, "Will you take my gun and see to Girl?"

Johnny nodded and watched as Jake was led out the door while everyone in the place stared. Captain Bates' death wasn't something Johnny had given much thought to up until now. He assumed the army would find the killer and he would be hung. The word around the Flat was that the Captain had been robbed and his throat cut, so he probably recognized the robber, and had been killed as a result. Now, for reasons Johnny couldn't fathom, Jake had been arrested, so he was suddenly very interested in the Captain's murder.

Jake was taken before the fort Commander who advised him he was being held on suspicion of the murder of Captain Bates. Jake started to speak, but the Lieutenant Colonel held up a hand. "Lieutenant Angleton will be assigned to act as your legal advisor until you can make arrangements for an attorney. I would advise you to hold your counsel until you do so. I feel that I have full authority to try you by military tribunal, but I am inclined to transfer you to Waco or Austin to the jurisdiction of the federal circuit court. In that case you and the evidence against you will be presented to a grand jury. If indicted you will be tried by the circuit court and I feel sure hung until dead if found guilty. I am requesting guidance on the matter and I expect a response in two weeks or less, but in the end I think you will be tried by the federal courts. In the meantime you'll be held in the fort's stockade. Dismissed."

The fort's Commander returned to the paperwork on his desk and the Sergeant of the Guard ordered two troops to take Jake to the stockade.

It was three hours later, before Jake was led from the stockade, his legs and hands shackled, to a small room in the headquarters building where he found a somber appearing Lieutenant Angleton and Johnny Black. After he was seated, the two troops who had escorted him from the stockade departed, but left him wearing the manacles. "Colonel's orders," one of the privates said, indicating the chains.

"That bad?" Jake asked. "Could be," answered the Lieuten- ant. Holding up a single sheet of paper, Lieutenant said, "Jake, the Colonel wants to keep certain matters, well, secret I guess, until the grand jury hearing. However, you have a right to know why you are being held, so the Commander let me summarize the official reports. I'm not a lawyer, so you need to make arrangements for one." Jake looked at the Lieutenant and Johnny.

The Lieutenant handed Jake the sheet of paper and Jake began to read.

• • •

'Captain E.A. Bates was murdered on or about late April, 1869 in the vicinity of the settlement known as the Flat or Hide town established just below the confines of Fort Griffin, Texas. Cause of death was cutting and stabbing by a sharp instrument, likely a knife. There was no evidence of robbery, as the Captain's revolver, saber, horse, gold watch and twenty dollars in coins was recovered on or near his person. He was killed in a violent and personal manner, having his throat cut and suffering twenty-two stab wounds. These facts are indisputable and suggest the Captain was killed by someone he was acquainted with.

The Captain's personal journal notes that he had been threatened by one Jake Evans, known locally as a reporter for the Dallas Herald. According to the journal, Evans was upset and jealous over a relationship between one Charity Chapin and himself. A number of witnesses, listed in the official report, attest to the fact that Evans had suggested he would like to stab the Captain and that Evans and Captain Bates had a loud argument on Main Street regarding Ms. Chapin. The lady in question has confirmed her acquaintance with both Captain Bates and Mr. Evans. On the night of his disappearance and murder, Captain Bates was last seen about midnight on his horse turning east on the road by the river, apparently to turn back toward the fort. Two witnesses, named in the official report, saw a man on foot walking east of the Busy Bee saloon, and both attest that upon reaching the next road, the man turned to follow the road toward the river. Assuming the Captain was following the same road, this would have meant the man would have intercepted Captain Bates. Both witnesses stated the man in question was of the same build and height of one Jake Evans. Given the history of the two men, the investigator questioned Mr. Evans and found he had no alibi for the night in question, stating that he had turned in early and not left his hotel room again until early morning. A knife, of the skinning type was discovered in Mr. Evans room. After removing the handles, the investigator found dried blood. It is the opinion of the investigator that Mr. Evans confronted Captain Bates on the deserted road, slashed his throat and stabbed him repeatedly in a fit of anger and jealousy. Having murdered the Captain, he covered the bloody ground with dirt, placed the Captain's body over his saddle, led the Captain's horse down to Mill Creek and then returned to the hotel, slipping into his room unseen.'

• • •

After reading the summary, Jake looked at Lieutenant Angleton. "Well, if this is so, wouldn't I have had blood all over my clothes?"

"Yes, but I don't think the Commander thinks it's important to speculate on every detail of what you did after the murder."

"Doesn't matter," Jake said, "I didn't kill the man."

For the first time, Johnny spoke. "Fact you didn't kill him won't matter. It's likely you'll hang unless we can discover some new facts. Men have been hung on a lot less evidence."

FATE RIDES A TALL HORSE

FIFTY-EIGHT

THE MURDER OF AN ARMY OFFICER, especially in Texas, couldn't go unanswered. It had been almost two weeks since the death of Captain Bates and a full Colonel had arrived at the fort to take over supervision of the investigation. He explained to the fort Commander, a Lieutenant Colonel and outranked by the full Colonel that he was sent to assume full control and responsibility to oversee the investigation.

When Lieutenant Angleton related this new development to Johnny, he added that with no witnesses and no other suspects the army and the federal government would press hard to convict Jake. Johnny knew that many a man had been convicted and hung on less circumstantial evidence than what was being used to charge Jake. But, although he knew Jake was innocent, he had to admit the facts did point to Jake as a suspect.

Captain Bates wasn't popular, but no one seemed to have any cause to kill him. Jake certainly had a motive, he had made his dislike of Bates well known and of course, he like most men, owned a knife. But the fact that he had no alibi for the night of the murder, well, that was the sticking point given the other facts. Certainly it was all circumstantial, but the problem was, the stakes were high. It was like betting the ranch on a pair of deuces; very risky.

Johnny had been granted an audience with the Colonel out of respect for his part in the two Indian skirmishes. The Colonel, impressed with what he had heard about Johnny, explained to Johnny that an army detachment would be escorting Jake to Austin in a few days. Johnny asked to visit the Captain's quarters and the Colonel had looked at him with sympathy and granted him permission. The Colonel didn't even ask Johnny what he expected to find. It wouldn't have mattered because Johnny didn't know himself. He did have an idea that he might find something that might provide a clue to Captain Bates' life. Surely a man like Bates had secrets and maybe one of those secrets had gotten him killed.

He found some letters and normally he would never read another man's correspondence, but he didn't flinch or hesitate now, not when his friend was looking at a death sentence. Although some of the letters confirmed what Johnny had always suspected, that Bates had exaggerated his family's situation for one thing, he didn't find anything that would help. As he scanned the letters, it became apparent that the Bates family was struggling financially. The father had written that he was pursuing his connections in an effort to find some backing for a new venture that he felt would, in a relatively short time, restore the family fortunes. Although he didn't explain the new venture, there was mention of railroads. After quickly scanning the rest of the letters, Johnny replaced them and continued his search.

Using his foot to push Bates' extra boots aside, floor boards were often removed and items hidden under them, he heard something or felt something. Not sure, Johnny picked up the boots and shook them. Something was rattling around in the toe of one of the boots. As he turned it upside down, a bottle of medicine fell into his hand. Why would a man, particularly one who had private quarters, hide his medication? Because he didn't want anyone to see it, even someone cleaning his quarters. But why not?

The first Sergeant had to talk to the Sergeant Major who had to talk to the Commander who agreed to let Black visit with Jake. The guards shackled Jake's hands and feet before leading him out into the sunlight, thirty yards from the stockade where he sat on the ground with the sun warm on his back. Johnny squatted next to him and after a bit of small talk, Johnny pulled out the bit of paper he had written the name of the medicine on and handed it to Jake who studied it for a moment, then looked at Johnny with some alarm on his face.

"Balsam of copaiba, it comes from trees that grow in South America. The army doc prescribe this for you?" asked Jake.

"No," said Johnny, "I found a bottle of it hid in Captain Bates' quarters. I figured it odd the man hid his medicine, so I figured I'd ask you about it."

Jake smiled. "It is used to treat the clap."

So, the late, great Captain Bates had the clap. Now that was interesting because no one, in any of the reports or testimony had mentioned the Captain frequenting the cribs at the edge of town and Johnny had never seen the man even speak to any of the women in the saloons. Well, he thought, he could have gotten together with one of the washerwomen. It was common for them to supplement their income and convenient due to their location on or close to the forts. On the face of it, that seemed way too risky and Johnny had noted in the testimony that Captain Bates had often ridden into town when he wasn't on duty. As he thought about it, he remembered the Captain riding about town alone, often in uniform, but he hadn't thought much of it.

After Jake was led back into the stockade, Johnny wandered over to encampment of washerwomen and found the woman who did his laundry. He stepped close as if asking her a question and slipped her a dollar coin. She palmed it and smiled. "Just a question, between you and me," said Johnny. "By any chance was Captain Bates, you know, seeing one of the women here?"

"Ha!" said the woman, who Johnny was pretty sure was German, given her accent. "The man was above speaking to us, much less, ah, visiting with us." She smirked.

"He sent a troop to deliver and pick up his laundry. Never has he set foot in this area of the camp. I would know," she said with conviction.

"Thank you," said Johnny, touching his fingers to his hat.

Johnny's next stop was the Frontier where he found Jones restocking the bar from some wooden crates. It didn't take long to find out that Jones, as Johnny had guessed, was part of a network in the tiny settlement. He visited with the other bartenders, saloon girls, shop owners and all of his customers. Yes, he had told Johnny, it was common knowledge that Captain Bates circulated through town, but no, he hadn't ever heard a word about the late Captain entertaining any of the working girls. Johnny thanked him and walked back to the hotel where he took a seat outside the door, fired up a cigarillo and dropped into deep thought.

After an hour, Johnny decided his best move would be to involve Clive. He felt himself a good judge of men and it seemed to him that Clive was as interested in finding the right man as he was in closing a case and getting paid. It was a matter of pride, thought Johnny, as well as seeing justice done. If he could convince him he might be on to something it would make it a lot easier to investigate. Having made a decision, he stepped into the street in search of Clive.

It was dark in the Frontier and almost empty, but Clive was sitting at a table, sipping on a whiskey. Seeing Johnny standing in the doorway, waiting for his eyes to adjust, he hollered, "Johnny Black, come on in and have a drink."

Johnny, spotting Clive, walked in, waved at Jones and sat at the table with Clive.

"I know it's early," Clive said, "but I'm picking up my prisoner and heading out today. Thought I would fortify myself a little first."

Jones set a glass on the table and Johnny poured himself a whiskey. He held it up in a toast to Clive and drank it down. "I came looking for you," Johnny said. Clive frowned.

"I didn't come to try to get you to change your report, not exactly anyway." Johnny pulled out a cigarillo and lit it. Clive watched him cautiously. "Did you know Bates had the clap?"

Clive was surprised. Johnny saw it in his face, but Clive took his time answering, mulling this new fact over and what it might mean. "I didn't. What are you thinking?"

"I have been trying to reason out if a woman could have killed the Captain."

"Well, I have to admit, I briefly considered the Chapin woman, given all the emotion in the killing, but quickly ruled her out."

"I'm wondering if a working girl might have given the Captain the clap, he reacted badly and she killed him. I've asked around about the washerwomen and the saloon girls. Not a whisper about Bates, but I got to thinking about the women that do business out in the cribs at the edge of town."

"Now that's something I should check on. He picked it up somewhere," Clive said.

The cribs as they were known, were clustered just outside the eastern most part of the Flat. Twenty minutes later, Clive and Johnny stepped down from their horses and began beating on doors. The women entertained late at night and slept late. Finally one of the women, pulling a robe around herself opened her door. Clive took off his hat. "Sorry to disturb you ma'am," he said pleasantly, but I and my associate," he said, pointing at Johnny, "are here on official government business."

In the third hut, the woman living there mimicked what the other two had said, that Captain Bates regularly came by to check on things and had on more than one occasion straightened out a drunken cowboy or made sure one paid. As the woman talked to Clive, Johnny glanced about the room, but as sunlight poured through the one window, he began to despair. As they stepped outside, Clive said, "Well, nobody seems overly nervous."

Johnny had to agree as they continued to move from hut to hut, but as they left one, Johnny looked back to see the curtains move. Someone was watching to see if they had left. It was at the fifth or sixth room, when no one answered the door. They waited, finally, they heard a noise. "Government business, open up, now!" yelled Clive, pounding on the door. A woman opened the door, but only a crack. She was clearly hostile.

"What do you want?" she asked.

"Ma'am, I am here on authority of the fort Commander and we want to come in to visit with you for a minute."

"I'll come out," said the woman, trying to step outside and close the door behind her, but Clive grabbed the edge of the door and pushed hard. The door swung open just as the woman stepped outside. She gasped. The window curtain was drawn, but enough light entered the room so that Clive and Johnny could see the dark stains on the floor and the wall. It appeared everything had been scrubbed clean, but dark stains remained in the wood. The woman reached back, grabbed the door handle and slammed it shut. "You got no right to go in my place uninvited," she hissed.

Clive took her into custody on the spot and told Johnny he would discuss authority to search the hut with the Colonel, but the woman suddenly broke into hysterical sobs.

The story came out in starts and stops. Three other women joined the small group. The crying woman was having trouble speaking, but through sobs and tears, told Clive she had killed 'the monster' in self-defense. The other women began to nod in agreement. The Captain it seemed, had been very rough with the women, often striking them and enjoyed choking the women until they passed out. The crying woman was his favorite and the last time he had visited, he walked in and seemed to be in a rage as he began to choke her before even taking off his uniform. She had grabbed the epaulette on his left shoulder and held him as she slashed his throat with a knife she held in her right hand. He had grabbed his throat with both hands and she had stabbed him and stabbed him - she began to sob again, recalling the incident.

"By any chance do you suffer from disease?" asked Clive gently.

The woman's head jerked up and her sobs suddenly stopped. "I'm taking medicine," she said, before once again breaking into convulsing sobs.

After a minute or so, when she had regained some control, she continued explaining what had transpired. After she had slashed his throat and stabbed him repeatedly, Bates had tumbled to the floor in a huge pool of blood. She took a deep breath and told them how blood was dripping from the walls after it had spurted from his neck. Some of the other women had helped her drag his body outside and put him over his horse's saddle. They led the horse down to Mill Creek and let it go. The Captain's pistol had fallen out and the woman had picked it up and then realizing she couldn't sell it, or keep it, she threw it in the creek. While she and two of the women were moving the Captain's body, others mopped up the blood and burned the bloody sheets, but the floor and walls were stained dark. In response to Clive's prodding, the woman admitted she was holding the knife when Captain Bates came in, but she said she was only going to threaten him, to ask him to leave, because she was tired of being struck and choked, but he surprised her, grabbing her before he had even undressed.

Clive told the woman he didn't know what would happen, but warned her not to leave or the army would run her down and the penalty would be severe. He had to talk to the army, he told her. In the meantime, he cautioned the women against saying anything about what had happened, explaining that he would convey the circumstances to the Colonel in charge of investigating the Captain's death. "We'll just have to see what he says," Clive said.

FIFTY-NINE

CLIVE AND JOHNNY STOPPED at Clive's room so an addendum report could be written up for presentation to the Colonel. Arriving at the fort, they were shown into the small room the Colonel had commandeered to use while he was at the fort conducting the investigation of Captain Bates' death. The Colonel sat behind a small desk reading the new report Clive had written. Johnny stood by the wall as Clive sat in the only other chair in the room. As they watched the Colonel read, they saw his face tighten. Finally, the Colonel looked up.

"Mr. Cole, I appreciate your efforts to be thorough. The Pinkerton Agency has a well-deserved reputation. As you may or may not be aware, not only am I in charge of overseeing this matter, I have been conducting my own investigation into the Captain's death. I have charged a Lieutenant with interviewing the people named in your report as well the local citizens. As to the idea that Captain Bates, a highly respected officer, would have acted in the manner suggested by these prostitutes, is simply, ludicrous on its face. Although I was personally not acquainted with the late Captain, his reputation is spotless. Now, you say here in your report that the woman who claims she murdered the Captain is suffering from a disease. She is doubtless suffering from syphilis. A common thing among these type women and the men that engage their services. During the war I saw a great many men suffering from syphilis and found that it often affected the mind. There is no doubt the woman knew the Captain, as his regular patrols have been well documented, but it is clear her mind has been affected."

Johnny and Clive stared at the Colonel in silence.

"I want to be clear gentlemen, I will not stand for one disparaging word to be uttered regarding Captain Bates. He had a stellar reputation as an officer and a man and he will be buried with his reputation in tack." The Colonel looked at both men before continuing. "Now, Mr. Black, you will be happy to know that as a result of my investigation and purview of the reports submitted by Mr. Cole, it is clear to me that Mr. Evans had no role in the death of Captain Bates and will be released immediately."

Johnny had been listening to the Colonel's dismissal of the woman's admission with horror, but suddenly he realized what the Colonel was planning, and relief flooded him.

"I'm glad to hear it," Johnny said quietly.

"It is my finding that the Captain was the victim of one of the outlaw groups operating in the area. Now, gentlemen, I assume I can count on your discretion." Clive and Johnny both affirmed their agreement. The Colonel stood and the three men shook hands.

After Johnny and Clive left, the Colonel picked up the addendum report containing the woman's confession and striking a match, set the paper on fire, dropping it on the floor as the flames neared his hand.

Sitting down and opening a folder on his desk, he removed another report. Glancing down the report, he read, 'After a thorough investigation, it is apparent the murder of Captain E.

A. Bates was carried out by an individual named Jake Evans who is currently being held in the fort stockade.' The Colonel struck another match and setting this report on fire, he turned and when the flame reached his hand, he dropped the paper on the floor and watched it until its destruction was complete. Turning back to his desk, he removed some paper and began to write a new report. 'After a thorough investigation, it is apparent the murder of Captain Bates was carried out by one of the outlaw gangs operating in the area.'

After completing his new and final report, the Colonel ordered the Sergeant Major to take a patrol down to the cribs and make it clear to all of the women they were to be out of the Flat prior to sundown and if he heard one despairing word about the Captain, he would personally see that every one of them were charged with a number of crimes. Of course it didn't take long for the void left by the departed women to be filled by other females looking to earn a living in a wild and dangerous area, so there wasn't much notice that the women had even left.

His investigation complete, the Colonel returned to his post in the east. Captain Bates was buried with honors.

• • •

Jake was unshackled and led out of the stockade into the sun, unshaven and pale. He was escorted straight to the Commander's office. His two guards stopped at the door and indicated he should enter. He was surprised to see the Sergeant Major, the First Sergeant, and Lieutenant Angleton standing in the office. They were all smiling. The fort Commander looked up. "Come in Mr. Evans," he said. "I want you to know that I am very happy to inform you that all charges against you have been dropped. Dismissed."

Stunned, Jake walked outside to find Johnny Black wait- ing, standing between Loco and Girl. He could see Flop and Perro dashing about twenty yards away.

"I'll explain over lunch, your treat," said Johnny, as though it was just another day like any other. On the ride down from the fort and into the Flat, Johnny noted that maybe Jake should stop for a bath, a shave and a change of clothes before lunch. Jake readily agreed and while Jake was cleaning up, Johnny would catch up on some letter writing as Clive was heading out the next morning and Johnny planned to entrust some mail to him.

Later, they met at Kirk's and as they ate, several folks stopped by the table to say hello to Jake. He hadn't been out of the stockade for three hours, yet word had spread through the grapevine like wildfire. The word was that the investigation had at one time cast some suspicion on Jake, but he had been completely vindicated and the army had caught the killer and he had been ushered out of town to stand trial in San Antonio or somewhere.

Jake was anxious to get out to the Rocking J to tell Charity he had been cleared. He and Johnny knew the "official story" as the Colonel saw it and felt no need to sully the Captain's reputation. While they were eating, they saw Clive Cole riding out with three extras horses loaded with supplies behind him and sitting, manacled and tied to the saddle horn of one of the horses was Maxwell Porter.

SIXTY

CHARITY WAS SO RELIEVED THAT JAKE had been cleared and released she couldn't stop crying. He had spared her all the details, simply telling her the army had solved the crime and released him. She didn't think the Captain had talked to Baggett, because he was still away on the cattle drive to Fort Worth, but Danny had hired two new hands. Birchfield had told two cowboys who had showed up in his store that Danny was hiring, and they seemed like good men. Danny had told them up front that Baggett would likely offer them more money, but they had said money wasn't everything, loyalty was something and since Danny had hired them, by golly, they would work for him come what may. They were branding cattle for a drive to Fort Worth and Danny was feeling so much better that even Rebecca seemed less blue. Now that Jake had been cleared and released, the future looked brighter. The threat of Baggett hung over them, but they were all praying and felt that it would all work out.

SIXTY-ONE

REBECCA, CHARITY, PETE AND ALVIN were almost to town when one of the wagon wheels hit a hole and the wagon axle broke. There is no way to tell if it would have mattered in the end, but that event would alter Alvin's life in many ways. Since they were only a mile from town, Alvin and Pete unharnessed the horses and the four of them walked into town leading the horses. Alvin and Pete stopped at Whitt's livery while Rebecca and Charity walked on to the store. Rebecca was informed that the blacksmith was visiting his brother's place some twenty miles to the south but was expected back the following morning. However, Birchfield kept a buggy and horse at Whitt's and offered it to Rebecca and Charity. They gladly accepted as Danny would be overcome with worry if they didn't return today. They walked to the livery and found Pete and Alvin still unharnessing the horses. The buggy was secured and the horse hitched to it and Alvin agreed to sleep at the stable and see the blacksmith the following morning. The girls would go home and return in two days, reasoning that the wagon would be fixed and they could return the buggy and complete their shopping. Whitt was more than happy with Alvin staying as he indicated he would work for his board. There were always horses and mules that needed brushing, feeding and exercising. There was also a great deal of time involved in mucking out the stables. Rebecca thanked Whitt as she, Charity and Pete climbed into the buggy and headed back home to tell Danny what happened. Alvin spent the day assisting with the animals and cleaning stalls.

Johnny and Jake had breakfast as they did most mornings. As they were eating, Johnny confided to Jake that he felt he was pushing his luck waiting for Stephens to make another move. The more he thought about it, the more he felt it was Stephens that had killed the Lowery boys and yanked the vaquero off of his horse. To add to it, his intuition told him Stephens was behind the bushwhacker attacks. There was, he added, a common factor. Somehow it all tied into the Andersons. When he mentioned the Andersons, Jake's attention focused.

"How do you figure?" asked Jake.

"We know Baggett was pressuring the Andersons and hiring away their help. The Lowery boys didn't own anything worth killing for, but their deaths added to the pressure on Danny and they were killed up north between the Rocking J and Baggett's spread. Remember, I'm sure there were whip marks on them. The vaquero was also traveling down through Baggett's land. I realize two cowboys were robbed, but the attack on the Anderson's wagon, especially in daylight didn't make sense. Add to that the threat to kidnap Pete, it seems to me it all might have been set up by Baggett to scare the Andersons."

"If that's the case, it worked. Rebecca has been upset since the attack and doesn't like Pete being out of her sight," responded Jake.

"There haven't been any more attacks," said Johnny. "No Indian attacks or robberies. I can see Stephens hiding out at Baggett's and doing his dirty work for him, until he gets the chance to kill me or earns enough money to move on."

"Do you have a plan?" asked Jake, tentatively.

"Well, I think I'm just going to have to visit the Baggett homestead."

"That might not go well," offered Jake. "Might not," agreed Johnny.

After breakfast, they walked back to the hotel so Jake could write a letter to the editor of the Dallas Herald resigning his position as a reporter. He had decided to focus on helping out the Andersons, even though he wasn't sure how much help he would be. Johnny waited for him and then they both visited the barber for a shave before riding up to the fort. The army had been carrying the mail between the forts and the major cities, traveling in small patrols and Jake wanted to post his letter. Johnny, ever factitious about his appearance had left his laundry with the washerwomen and wanted to pick it up. They ended up spending the morning at the fort and staying for lunch with the Lieutenant Colonel who commanded the fort and in spite of the official reports, knew Johnny had saved his patrol during the rescue of the Stapleton boy. Realizing the reports didn't make sense, he had invited the old Corporal into his office for a few drinks and some off the record conversation. It was quite a story. Too bad Black wasn't one of his officers.

Both Jake and Johnny enjoyed lunch and decided on a nap after returning to town. They met for dinner and afterward walked over to the Frontier. It was crowded, but there wasn't a poker game to be had, so they wandered over to the Busy Bee. Johnny found a game and Jake settled at the bar.

• • •

The cards weren't treating Johnny very well so after an hour he bid his goodbyes and finding Jake at the bar where he had just ordered his second beer, explained that he thought he would try Shane's. Jake looked at him in surprise, then realized that Johnny was thinking just maybe Stephens would put in an appearance.

The place was crowded, but Johnny found a spot at the one poker game in progress, although he didn't know any of the players. Jake pushed up to the bar and ordered a beer.

It didn't take long for Jake to gather from the conversation that Baggett's cattle drive crew had just returned from their trip to Fort Worth and with their pockets full of money had headed for town. They had only been there for a short time, but some had obviously started celebrating on the way in using flasks hidden in their boots or saddlebags, as most ranchers didn't allow drinking on the job.

Jake listened to some interesting and some humorous stories about the trail drive and finding himself in conversation with one friendly, but very drunk cowboy, said, "Hey, a friend of mine came out here a while back and said he was going to try to get on with Baggett. I don't see him though."

"What's his name?" asked the drunk cowboy.

"Well, you know, he was running from a mad woman" The cowboy laughed. "I hear you. What's he look like?" "Last I saw him, he had a dark beard, but you can't miss

him. He has a scar on his face and one of his ears is jacked." "Oh hell," said the cowboy. "You're talking about Lambert.

Yeah, he's with us. Thick as thieves with the boss and Smith. Smith is the foreman. The cowboy turned to look around the saloon. He didn't come in with us. He and Smith are coming in with Mr. Baggett. They'll be here soon I reckon."

"Great," said Jake. "Let me buy you another drink," he said waving at the bartender.

As soon as the cowboy had his drink and was involved in conversation with another man, Jake eased away from the bar, stepped through the crowd and reaching Johnny's table, stood, holding his stomach. He waited until the hand ended, then he stepped up, leaned over and whispered in Johnny's ear.

Johnny frowned, said "Dang it," in disgust. Angrily, he told the table, "Deal me out for now, I have to make sure my buddy here gets home okay." Picking up his money, Johnny took Jake's arm and escorted him to the door.

Jake glanced back and saw the cowboy he had been talking to was laughing and drinking, paying no attention to Jake as he and Johnny eased out the door.

As they walked down the sidewalk toward the hotel, Johnny said, "You are a jack of all trades, Jake. Doctor, reporter and now, actor. Good work."

They stopped by the hotel, so Johnny could pick up his rifle and they took a minute to check their revolvers. Turning to Jake, Johnny said, "Jake, it would be best if I deal with this myself."

"Not going to happen," said Jake.

"You've got a lot going for you doc. A fine girl and a bright future. Anything can happen in a deal like this, especially when you're hunting a back shooter."

"Johnny, let's not waste time. I'm going to try to have your back. Not that you need it mind you. I think you're on to something and if I can help the Andersons I have to go."

When they got to the livery they were surprised to find Alvin. Whitt, looking sleepy and irritated came out of his room, but seeing Johnny, became helpful. He quickly explained Alvin's presence and when Jake told Whitt they were headed to the Baggett spread on personal business, Alvin began to motion his desire to accompany them. Johnny was in a hurry and just shrugged his shoulders. Alvin stepped away and was back in an instant with his scattergun and Whitt helped him saddle a horse. It didn't take long for the three to mount up and head out.

SIXTY-TWO

AS THEY NEARED THE RANCH HOUSE after their drive to Fort Worth, Baggett rode up beside Smith and Lambert. "I guess you boys are in a hurry to get to town, but after you wash up, come on in and have a drink, maybe we can play a few hands of poker."

Smith and Kyle stared at him. "I want to talk to you boys about the future," he said smiling. "I think you're going be real excited about my plans. It's early, we'll have time to go to town after we talk."

"Sure thing boss," said Smith and Kyle nodded.

After they reached the ranch's bunkhouse, Smith and Lambert washed up, changed shirts and brushed their boots off. "We're going to have to leave our holsters in the bunkhouse," said Smith. "He don't like guns in the house and it would make him suspicious we show up wearing our iron. We'll have to stick them in our pants and make sure he don't see them."

The first thing they saw when Baggett opened the door, was the saddlebags with the money from the cattle drive. It was laying on a small sofa that hugged one wall.

"Come on in and sit," said Baggett cheerfully, pointing to the table where a deck of cards, a bottle of whiskey and three glasses sat. "I appreciate you boys hanging back. I do believe you're going to like what I have in mind."

After settling at the table, Baggett passed the bottle around and encouraged them both to drink up. Baggett insisted they play some poker, a warm-up, he stated, as he planned to play in town tonight after their little talk. They played and drank for an hour. Neither Smith nor Lambert could concentrate and both lost steadily to Baggett. Finally, Smith lost patience.

"A couple of things you might find interesting, Mr. Baggett," said Smith, "is that Kyle here and I are brothers."

"What's that?" asked Baggett.

"Well, actually we're half-brothers. The other thing is we quit." Smith reached behind himself and pulled out his revolver and pointed it at Baggett.

There was a second of silence, then a gun exploded, Smith jerked, and blood began to soak his shirt as he dropped the gun and clutched his stomach. Baggett had been holding a gun under the table and after shooting Smith, he tried to get it in position to shoot Kyle, but Kyle jumped up and pulled his gun from his trousers and shot Baggett in the chest, the bullet hitting with such force, the chair skidded backward several inches. When he looked over at his half-brother, Charlie Smith, he saw he had expired. He walked around the table and asked Baggett for the combination to the safe, but blood bubbled from Baggett's mouth and his eyes closed.

"Damnit," said Kyle. He stuck the revolver in his waist- band and went outside to fetch the hammer and chisel. He was hammering and cursing the safe when he heard Jake at the front door. Grabbing Baggett's fancy scattergun he had discovered in the storage area, Kyle went out the back door and after pressing himself against the outer wall of the cabin was shocked to see Johnny Black walk by in the dark.

• • •

Lamps burned inside the big cabin. As the three walked their horses up close, they stopped and dismounted. Johnny asked Jake to knock on the front door and talk to Baggett while he went around to the back of the cabin. He had turned Loco loose, but asked Alvin to hold the other two horses. They had decided against any kind of a story. Jake would simply tell Baggett that he had ridden out with Johnny Black and Black wanted to have a word, a personal matter, with the man with the scarred face and the bad ear. Jake was nervous. He had complete faith in Johnny's skills, but on the way Johnny asked him to look out for Loco, Flop and Perro if things didn't go his way.

Johnny felt sure Kyle would head out a back door the moment he heard Black was asking for him. As Jake approached the front door, Johnny headed around to cover the back and wait for Stephens.

Jake pounded on the door, but when no one answered and he couldn't hear anything, he tried the door. It swung open. "Mr. Baggett, are you home?" yelled Jake as he walked into the cabin's main room. He was met with silence, but he could see two figures sitting at a table; no they were slumped there. Drawing his gun, Jake said, "Mr. Baggett," in a low voice. As he got closer he could see the two men were dead.

He recognized both Baggett and his foreman, Smith. There were playing cards scattered about on the table, but no money. A half-empty bottle of whiskey sat on the table and Jake realized, three glasses. His mind processed the scene. Three men had been playing poker. Two of them had been shot where they sat. The third man was gone. His gun held out in front of him, Jake checked the rooms. They were empty, but in Baggett's bedroom he found a storage area. When he poked his head in he saw a mess of broken wood torn from a wall to reveal a safe whose door had been battered and bent, but was closed. A chisel and hammer lay on the floor. He was walking back toward the door so he could find Johnny and tell him what he had found, when he heard an unfamiliar voice shout.

• • •

Johnny was almost to the back of the cabin when he heard someone yell.

"Jo…Johnny!!!" screamed Alvin.

Johnny instinctively dropped and rolled, turning his body around to face behind him as two shotgun blasts exploded, in quick succession, lighting up the night. Although Johnny had dropped the instant Alvin had screamed, a dozen buckshot pellets hit him in his left shoulder and back causing him to drop his rifle. It made no difference. Johnny, as he fell, had drawn his revolver and lying on the ground, calmly fired two shots, so quick it almost sounded like one shot. The first shot hit Kyle Smith, also known as Kyle Stephens and Kyle Lambert, in the center of his heart. The second shot hit one inch directly above the first one.

Jake heard the two quick scattergun blasts and following them, the two quick pistol shots. As he stepped from the house, his rifle at the ready, he saw Kyle standing in the dark, a double-barrel shotgun dangling from his right hand. As Jake swung the rifle towards Kyle he saw Kyle's knees buckle as he pitched forward on his face.

Alvin walked into the scene and told Jake, "Don't shoot, it's me, Alvin."

"Don't shoot me either," said Johnny standing. "What about Smith and Baggett?" he asked Jake.

"Dead," said Jake, who was staring at Alvin. Turning to look at Johnny, Jake said, "Alvin spoke."

Johnny was standing over Kyle's dead body, staring down at it as he used his boot to turn Kyle over. "He did," said Johnny, "and he picked a good time to do it. Otherwise I would likely be visiting with my dead brother right about now." Looking over at Alvin who seemed to be in shock, Johnny said, "Thanks Alvin." As he studied the now dead Kyle, he took a look at the double-barreled shotgun he had fired at Johnny. It was a beauty, with gold inlays. Must have belonged to Baggett, thought Johnny. Kyle wasn't wearing a holster, but had a revolver stuck in his waistband.

They found the saddlebag full of money in Baggett's bedroom. It was getting late and Jake had put a pot of coffee on the woodstove. They drank coffee as Alvin puffed on his pipe, Jake drew on his handmade cigarette and Johnny enjoyed a cigarillo. They were waiting. Finally the first group of cowboys rode into the yard. After a brief explanation, Johnny selected the two that appeared to be the most sober and sent them to the fort to ask the guard to awaken the Commander.

Several hours later, an army patrol arrived led by Lieutenant Angleton. Johnny, Jake and Alvin showed them around, told them what they had found and gave the Lieutenant the saddlebags of money for safekeeping until Baggett's next of kin was located. When the three left, the Lieutenant had hungover and still drunk cowboys loading the three dead men into a wagon for transfer to the fort and ultimately the area graveyard.

SIXTY-THREE

JAKE AND CHARITY WERE MARRIED on a warm May afternoon at the Rocking J in front of a large crowd. Social activity was limited on the frontier and marriages were a great opportunity to gather. Charity looked beautiful in her wedding dress the ladies who gathered to quilt, had created. After the nuptials, everyone drifted to an area where tables, under some very large oaks, covered with food had been set up for the celebration. The fort's Commander was in attendance and after offering his congratulations he asked the happy couple about their future plans.

They looked at each other as Jake said, "We're going to make a stop in Atlanta to see Charity's parents then we'll be traveling up to New York so I can introduce Charity to my folks. After that sir, we will be moving to London."

The Commander was more than a little surprised and interested in how they came by the decision to move to London. Jake explained that he had attended the Royal College of Physicians there and given his status as a former student and his experience as a doctor during the Civil War, the school was thrilled to have him as a professor. Also, Charity planned to write and London seemed an excellent home for writers.

Although he was confused by Jake's status as a doctor, he had interviewed the Commander for stories when he had been working as a reporter, the Commander simply stated he wished them all the best and excused himself to allow others to visit with the couple.

Trying to get to the food, Alvin had been cornered by a number of young widows who all sought his attention. Several were offering to fix him a plate and giving each other rather hateful looks. After he regained his ability to speak, the word had spread through the town and Alvin, who had been largely ignored, was now always spoken to by both men and women when he was in town. Many were sisters or daughters of local women, and some were widows whose husbands didn't return from the war. The unmarried ladies in town began to see him in a new light. He wasn't one of the rough buffalo-hunters who were flooding into the Flat, nor was he a poor cowboy, but in fact, they had heard he was a part-owner of the Rocking J ranch. A man with prospects.

The truth was that regardless of Alvin's strong objections, Danny had signed the deed to the ranch over to him, making him the sole owner. Alvin had argued that they should remain partners; that he would send Danny his share of the profits as the ranch prospered, but his brother wouldn't hear of it. Danny had been accepted at the Newton Theological Seminary in Massachusetts and he and Rebecca were headed there. Rebecca's father was happily funding Danny's education with the hope that they might move to Atlanta when Danny graduated.

The only issue had been Pete who had just turned fifteen and was shocked and upset when he was told the news of the move to Massachusetts. Many a young man might have welcomed the move to a city, away from the long hours and hard work of a ranch, but Pete had lived in a city and as far as he was concerned, the ranching life was near to heaven. Alvin and Pete had become close and Alvin was also disappointed. When Danny and Rebecca relayed their distress at Pete's unhappiness to him he quickly offered to let Pete stay with him. In fact, he argued, he needed the help. Pete knew the animals and the ranch. He would prove invaluable to Alvin.

After much discussion, the sticking point was Pete's education, but that was resolved when they discovered that Bill Franklin's brother and his wife, a former teacher were joining the Franklins and would be teaching the Franklin's children and would welcome Pete as a student. This would allow Pete to see Adam regularly.

After a good thirty minutes of accepting congratulations from well-wishers, Jake excused himself to look for Johnny. He finally found him sitting cross legged under a tree chewing on a corncob while balancing a plate full of fried chicken, gravy, potatoes and beans.

"Congratulations doctor, to you and Mrs. Evans," said Johnny.

Jake smiled and looked out over the landscape where Loco was grazing and Flop and Perro were happily chasing chicken bones thrown by the kids. "Thank you, Johnny. I'm a happy man, but truth be told, I've kind of gotten used to you. Guess what I'm trying to say is, I am going to miss your company."

"Well, you know, I reckon I'll miss you, but we all have to follow our chosen path."

"You never said what your plans are," said Jake.

"Next stop for me is San Antonio. I haven't been back there for a while and I have some kin there. I guess me and the boys will head on down there and check out the lay of the land."

"Hmm," said Jake, "It's good to catch up with kin. By any chance you planning on catching up with anybody else, a woman friend maybe?"

Johnny's face registered surprise. Jake smiled.

"You remember when I came in to check on you after your vision had cleared? Well, if you remember you were reading a letter. I didn't mean to get in your business, but the envelope was sitting on the chair there by the bed and when I moved it I noticed it was from San Antonio. After I finally got your attention, and it took a minute because you were totally engrossed, it occurred to me that the letter was in Spanish and you had a very happy look on your face."

Johnny laughed. "Maybe you should take up poker after all, doc."

SIXTY-FOUR

DANNY, REBECCA, JAKE, CHARITY AND JOHNNY all traveled together until they reached Dallas. They found rooms in the Crutchfield hotel, a fine two-story wood and brick establish- ment on Houston and Main streets. As darkness fell, Charity sat brushing her hair as she prepared for bed. Jake was standing, staring out the window, lost in thought. Finally, Jake asked, "Charity, do you think, I don't know exactly what I'm trying to say, but does the Lord send messengers or something to advise us or maybe help us?"

Charity stopped brushing her hair and looked at Jake. "Like angels?"

"Maybe, but I was thinking about regular folks, strangers even that come into our lives or touch our lives in some way."

"I do think the Lord talks to us through our conscience so why couldn't the Supreme Being touch us through others?"

"Well, I've been thinking about my fate, you know, where I find myself, right this moment."

"Are you thinking about Johnny Black?"

Jake turned to look at her, smiling. "Now you're scaring me. If you can read my mind like that. Yes, I've been thinking about Johnny. The man is almost not human. There's no doubt he's had a hand in how things have turned out, he's a part of my fate."

The next morning Jake and Johnny had breakfast in the hotel's dining room. As they ate Jake looked at Johnny and said, "You've never mentioned the war."

"I haven't?" Johnny asked, an innocent expression on his face. "Reckon the subject never came up." Johnny smiled. Jake understood that not only had Johnny never mentioned his role in the war, he wasn't likely to.

"Well, I have to ask you one thing Johnny. Why did you name Flop's friend Perro? I mean what kind of name is that for a dog?"

Johnny smiled and explained, "Truth is Jake, a name just didn't come to me, so I started calling him Perro and just got used to it. Perro is Spanish for dog."

It was Jake's turn to smile.

After breakfast they walked around to the livery where Johnny saddled Loco, fed Flop and Perro, mounted Loco, raised a hand to Jake and as the two dogs ran ahead, Johnny Black, man and legend, and perhaps an agent of fate, turned and rode away toward San Antonio.

THE END

Special Bonus Content
Opening Three Chapters of
Cimarron Jack's Real Wild West
A Novel

GP Hutchinson

CHAPTER 1

St. Louis, Missouri, September 1888

"Haven't I always treated you fair and square?" Jack Wheatley threw his hands wide and then let them fall again to his sides. "I thought I had."

"That's your problem, Wheatley," the sinewy Charlie Tuft said. "You got your head so deep in your own concerns, you don't know what's fair and what ain't."

"May seem that way to you, Charlie, but you don't sit in on meetings where we work out the business side of this show."

Red O'Malley, another of Jack's trick riders, stood hip-cocked just inside the entrance flap of Jack's canvas dressing tent. "We know enough to say one thing for sure—you been givin' us the short end of the stick."

Jack opened his mouth to respond, but Red cut him off. "Fact is, you oughta be grateful we're givin' you notice before the show pulls outta St. Louis. Town this big, maybe some Johnny-fresh-off-the-farm will come to you, hat in hand, and beg to ride for you."

Charlie pointed. "And maybe you'll learn from this and start payin' talented and able hands what they're worth."

"That's right." Red nodded emphatically.

Jack drew a deep breath and let it out slowly. Would it do any good to tell these two that *he* sure as blazes wasn't getting rich off ticket sales? Certainly not at his employees' expense. True enough, they were performing before packed houses every night. But practically everything he personally earned was going right back into running the show. Meanwhile, he paid his people everything he could, plus room and board.

He cocked his head. "By any chance has Stu Portman been bending your ears?"

"What if he has?" Charlie said.

"For eighteen months now, things have been harmonious, I'd say. Traveling together, drawing bigger and bigger audiences, adding new acts. Far as I know, everybody getting along just fine. Then we hit St. Louis. Within mere days, Portman quits over money. Then, Diego Camacho and Beto Vega come to me and quit—although I've gotta say, they weren't all horns and rattles like you two. Two more days, and here you come. What's stirred all this up?"

Red gave Jack a cold stare. "Let's just say yours ain't the only show in town."

Charlie turned for the tent opening and said over his shoulder, "We'll ride for you tonight, Wheatley, and that'll be that."

Before Red let Charlie lead the way out, Jack said, "No need. Stop by Mr. Birch's tent and tell him I said you can draw full pay for St. Louis. I don't need performers who don't have their heart in it."

Charlie scowled at Jack, and the two stunt riders exited.

Jack shook his head. What was going on?

He pulled his watch from his vest pocket. *Sweet Jezebel!* Half past three already. He had a parade to ride in at four o'clock and a show at six. While he dared not put off getting to the bottom of all these unexpected resignations, he certainly didn't have time before the parade to dig into the matter in earnest. He didn't even have time now to clean his revolvers as he'd planned to do. And given his line of work, he wasn't simply obsessing over a little extra unburned gunpowder.

In three brisk strides, he was at the tent flap to check the afternoon air. The notion of sweating in a heavy buckskin jacket didn't sit well with him. He had a lighter-weight jacket, but he preferred to save it for performances. At least there was a nice breeze today.

Just as he was about to tie the flap shut and change into his showman's attire, he caught sight of the darling of the show, the lovely Miss Adelia Flynn, "The Pride of the Prairie." She was marching directly for his tent, and judging from her expression, she plainly wasn't happy.

His heart gave a peculiar thump. *Tell me she's not coming to resign, too.*

CHAPTER 2

A delia glowered. "When were you gonna tell me?"

Jack deliberately remained close to the tent opening. The lithe blond sharpshooter never would let him know just how old she truly was, but he guessed no older than eighteen — if that. He, being over thirty already, thought of himself as a much older brother figure to her. And he didn't want ugly rumors regarding the two of them floating about.

But, *land o' Goshen*, was she pretty! Already dressed for the parade in a fringed sapphire-blue riding skirt and blouse, her golden hair was fastened below the back of her Stetson with an oversized matching blue bow.

"Tell you what?" Jack tilted his head.

"About this sudden spate of resignations — the bunch of ingrates!"

"So . . . you're not planning on resigning too?"

"Don't be foolish, Jack. 'Course not."

He breathed a sigh of relief. "Of course not. Anyway, it's not a 'spate.'" He looked her in the eye. "Five performers, that's all."

Arms folded, she said, "Five who've quit and a whole trainload of grumblers over in the big show tent."

Jack trusted she was exaggerating. He found it hard to believe that, overnight, any considerable number of his cast and crew had suddenly become truly disgruntled. Not like Charlie and Red. The season had gone well — no, *exceptionally* well. Most likely, it was just one lone malcontent over there in the big tent, sowing seeds of dissatisfaction.

"Listen," he said, "we'll sort this out after tonight's performance." He tugged at the lapel of his vest. "Look at me, I'm not even dressed for the parade yet."

Adelia unfolded her arms and trooped over to his wardrobe chest. "Leave the jacket behind today," she said. "I know how you detest being overly warm."

"I can't ride in the parade without a jacket. People expect a scout of the Western frontier to wear a beaded and fringed buckskin jacket."

"You were never a scout." Adelia shuffled through his clothes.

"They don't know that."

"Some do, and they love you just the same. Here." She turned around holding up a bib-front, fringed shirt of lighter buckskin with fancy stitching on the chest and cuffs. "This is perfect."

Having bigger things to worry about, Jack said, "Well, go on and pick out a tie for me then. Something colorful."

"A bandanna," she said. "A tie's too formal."

"Not for Custer."

"Custer's dead." She dug deeper into the trunk.

"But isn't that a big part of what the show's about? Keeping all the heroes of the West, like Custer, alive in the hearts and minds of the people?"

She sighed aloud. "You win—this time." Buckskin shirt and scarlet, cravat-style tie in hand she traipsed up to him. "I've got to fetch my gun belt. See you at the remuda." She pressed the clothes into his hands.

Jack tied the tent flap behind Adelia and made quick work of changing into his parade costume.

Minutes later, he emerged from his tent and made his way through the staging area behind the main performance pavilion. A huge, colorfully painted canvas banner with the words CIMARRON JACK WHEATLEY'S REAL WILD WEST EXTRAVAGANZA covered a large portion of the side of the venue. In a big golden oval at one end of the banner was a fairly accurate likeness of him: shoulder-length auburn-brown hair, straight nose, and a long, well-manicured mustache. In the image, the front left quarter of his sand-colored Stetson's brim was curled up a bit. *In dashing fashion,* as Adelia often said. Most days, admiring that banner on his way over to the corral filled his chest with a healthy dose of optimism, and some days, a gratifying measure of satisfaction with the show's success. Today, it left a knot in his stomach. Was this enterprise beginning to unravel just as it was getting started?

"Nothing to be done about it at the moment," he murmured.

Putting on a showman's smile as he passed a large red-wheeled cage, he waved at Hitch Porter and Ty Simmons. "Priscilla all fed and happy?" he asked.

Ty waved back. "Happy as a housecat."

Jack caught a quick glimpse of the beautiful, tawny-coated mountain lioness the two men were tending.

As he approached the wranglers and horses, he spied his seal-brown paint mustang, Fuego, already saddled and ready for him.

Lefty Braddock, wearing his signature Montana peaked hat, handed over Fuego's reins. "There you go, boss," he said.

"Much obliged, Lefty."

Jack had one foot in the stirrup when Adelia came a-running. She wore the fancy gun leather and six-gun she had gone to fetch. Customarily she carried her trademark Colt Lightning rifle in the parade too, but she didn't have it with her.

"Where's your Lightning?" he asked.

She stopped and put a hand to her forehead. "I don't know what's wrong with me today."

Before she could turn away, he told her to saddle up, and he sent Lefty back for her long iron. Once she was situated astride her horse, he asked, "You'll be all right for tonight, huh?"

She nodded. "Of course."

Lapses like this weren't typical of Adelia. A peculiar feeling flitted through Jack's innards, and he had to tell himself—more emphatically this time—that a few performers quitting on him didn't necessarily augur full-fledged disaster for the whole show, nor even for its most popular act.

Lefty returned in no time with Adelia's rifle, and before long, the cavalcade was on its way—colorful cowpokes driving a dozen particularly handsome longhorns, then a bold yellow stagecoach pulled by a team of bay geldings. The massive trio of buffalo that followed was always popular with the crowds. Then came the Indians with their painted ponies and feathered war bonnets, and the Cowhand Brass Band right behind them kept things lively.

Jack waved to the eager crowds lining the street. Now, he was in his element. The enthusiastic response along the parade route lifted his heart and boded well for a full house at tonight's performance. Gaze still on the crowd, he said to Adelia, "I'm glad we've ended the tour in St. Louis. Nice town. I've enjoyed it."

"Me too," she said.

When he glanced her way, he found her smile genuine. And when she waved, the onlookers responded with animated applause.

Sun out, a fresh breeze blowing, Jack at last began to let go of the annoyance he'd felt since this afternoon's meeting with the discontented trick riders.

Then he spotted a pair of smiles in the crowd, the owners of which he'd prefer never to see again.

CHAPTER 3

Jack said nothing to anyone—not to Adelia, nor to his business manager, Albert Birch, not even to his closest amigo, Billy Douglass—about having spied James and Loftus Stilton in the crowd along the parade route that afternoon. Last he'd read about them in the newspapers, the rival Stilton Brothers' Wild West Show was performing somewhere back East—Baltimore, he thought. He'd have to look into the brothers' unexpected presence in St. Louis, but not until after tonight's performance.

Despite having lost five troupe members, the final show of the season was going along swimmingly for Cimarron Jack Wheatley's Real Wild West Extravaganza. With oohs and ahhs and fervent applause at all the right moments, the audience seemed to be as thrilled and delighted as any during the course of the tour. The fancy-roping and stunt-riding acts had been well received. The dramatic reenacted stagecoach robbery had gone flawlessly. Folks seemed to love the Indian dancers in their feathered headdresses.

Comanche Joe Tucker, whose mother had in fact been an Indian princess until she married Joe's Kentucky-born father, was just finishing up his highly popular tomahawk-throwing act.

On cue, Jack touched spur to his prized pinto and trotted into the center of the pavilion. "How about another big round of applause for Comanche Joe Tucker, ladies and gents?"

The crowd's response brought a broad smile to his face.

Next came bronco riding, bull riding, and the running of the show's half-dozen buffalo. Brief moments within each dangerous act had the crowd holding its collective breath. Then, following a more lighthearted segment of the extravaganza, when cowhands and Indians engaged in horseraces across and around the arena, Jack resumed his role as the show's host and announcer.

"And now, one and all," he intoned, "from the untamed land of the Apache, may I present to you a noble warrior whose skill with the bow and arrow remains unequaled in any quarter of our great nation. Archers from around the world have challenged our brave hero and have walked away with heads hung low, unable to match the incomparable talents of this legendary Apache bowman. Ladies and gentlemen, I present to you Junipero!" He doffed his hat with a flourish.

As Junipero appeared at the far end of the arena, mounted on a boldly painted Indian pony, the audience erupted with cheers and clapping.

With a war cry that pierced even the animated applause, the Apache goaded his mount into a full gallop. While Junipero made a lap around the perimeter of the arena, a crew of cast members hastily set up a series of bright-colored vertical hoops on stands. The hoops were arranged in a line down the center of the arena. The largest ring was placed at one end, and each successive hoop was smaller, until the final one, which was hardly the breadth of a grown man's hand. Beyond the final ring was a wooden target board.

After completing his circuit of the pavilion, Junipero rode at full speed to the middle of the arena, skidded his pony to a halt, and vaulted from the animal to his feet.

More applause.

To the beat of Indian drums, three Apache maidens brought Junipero his bow and two quivers of arrows.

Junipero nocked an arrow, took aim, and released the missile, which sailed through the row of hoops and exited at the far end, embedding itself with a sharp thwack in the target board.

He repeated the feat from greater and greater distances.

Finally, one of the Apache maidens dashed to the edge of the arena and returned to Junipero with a flaming torch. Junipero nocked another arrow and then held its tip in the flame until it caught fire.

While this was being done, a second Apache maiden walked to the far end of the series of hoops. She formed a circle with her hands and, standing just to the side, she held out her hands in line with the series of wooden rings. As the crowd realized what she was doing, a murmur arose.

Jack sat saddle at the edge of the arena. At this point in each performance, he whispered a brief prayer for both Junipero and Liluye, the girl at the far end who held her hands out as a final hoop. Without question, bull riding was dangerous — and he prayed for his bull riders, as well — but for some reason, this act made Jack hold his breath.

Junipero took aim with the flaming arrow.

Jack kept his eyes on Liluye.

A hush fell over the crowd.

The warrior let the arrow fly.

Waiting to hear the familiar snap of the arrow striking the target board, Jack instead heard a shriek.

Liluye fell to the sawdust, and Junipero's arrow veered off to the opposite side, ultimately piercing the ground at the base of the low wall that separated the audience from the performers.

Jack gave Fuego the rowels and raced for Liluye.

Many in the crowd were on their feet. A cascade of chatter spread throughout the arena.

Jack swung down from the saddle before his horse even came to a full stop.

Liluye was on her knees. Before Jack reached her, he could see blood on both her hands, on her buckskin dress, and on the sawdust.

"Where'd it hit you?" he asked.

The other Apache girls arrived at Liluye's side.

Liluye showed Jack her left hand. The arrowhead had sliced the flesh between her thumb and index finger all the way to the bone. "It will be all right," she said, tears glittering down her copper cheeks. She bit her lip and drew in an uneven breath.

Jack pulled the cravat from around his neck. "Here, use this to slow the bleeding. Let's have the girls help you to your tent and get you cleaned up. Can you make it?"

She nodded and accepted the cloth tie.

"I'll check on you as soon as I can, OK?"

Liluye's friends helped her to her feet and on toward one of the performers' exits.

When Jack looked back for Junipero, the warrior was already on his pony and riding out the far end of the arena.

Jack mounted up and rode to the center of the venue where he had Fuego wheel so that everyone in the audience could see his sober expression. "Ladies and gentlemen," he said, "every day in the West is dangerous. These Indians, cowhands, scouts, teamsters, and trailblazers have known perils by day and threats by night. One and all, they are a brave lot. I am proud to inform you that the Apache maiden, Liluye, having stood only a whisper away from calamity, remains unwavering in her courage. She's going to be quite all right. Meanwhile, let us show her our admiration and appreciation with a hearty round of applause."

The audience's response was immediate and seemed to Jack quite genuine. As they clapped, he wondered whether an entire season's luck had at last run out, or whether something else had been at work, causing Junipero's unfortunate miscue. He scanned the crowd until the ovation died down.

"And now, my dear friends, young and old, the moment so many of you have been waiting for," he called out with a broad smile. "With all due respect to Miss Annie Oakley *and* to Mr. Billy Dixon, let's give a warm welcome to the most astounding, the most prodigious sharpshooter our great nation has ever seen—'The Pride of the Prairie,' the lovely Miss Adelia Flynn!"

Adelia galloped in on a handsome blue-roan gelding that perfectly complemented the sapphire-blue shooting outfit she had selected. Her act was flawlessly executed and wonderfully received. With her Colt Lightning slide-action rifle, she shot and shattered twenty-five consecutive glass balls, without missing a single one, as each was tossed into the air. Then, from horseback, on the move, she used her Colt Model 1877 revolver to shoot specifically designated bottles from intricate stacks set up on tables.

Jack returned to the center of the arena and swung down from Fuego. "How about that, ladies and gentlemen?" he called with heartfelt exuberance.

Effusive applause filled the tent. Adelia rode to Jack's side and stepped down from her saddle.

Jack turned to her and said in a stage voice, "You know, I'm not such a bad shot myself, Miss Flynn."

She smiled broadly, and Jack had a sense it wasn't only for the audience. "Are you challenging me, Cimarron Jack?"

"I am, Miss Flynn." He teased her with his eyes. "I'll bet I can shoot a tossed silver dollar dead center. It's smaller than those glass balls you shattered."

"Well, then, let's see you do it."

"Would you like to see that, ladies and gentlemen?" Jack called out.

The crowd responded with cheers and clapping.

With a flourish, Jack drew a brand-new silver dollar from his pocket, held it for all to see, and turned in place. Upon completing his turn, he flipped the coin into the air, drew his Colt revolver, and squeezed the trigger.

An assistant caught the falling coin and held it up to show that the formerly flat silver disk was now bowl-shaped. As the applause continued, he offered the bent coin as a souvenir to a redheaded little girl in the front row.

"That was pretty impressive," Adelia called, "but I can do the same with a *half*-dollar."

"Can you?" Jack said. "I think I'll have to ask you to prove it. Right, ladies and gentlemen?"

More applause.

The assistant tossed Adelia a shiny fifty-cent piece, which she held high.

"Show 'em what you've got, Miss Flynn," a fan shouted.

Effortlessly, Adelia tossed the half-dollar, drew her revolver, and fired. Her bent coin went to a young boy in the front row on the opposite side of the audience.

"How about a quarter?" Jack challenged. "I'll go first."

Hands on her hips, Adelia said, "If you really want to challenge me, then why don't we make it a dime?"

Jack stood there rubbing the back of his neck while murmurs rippled through the crowd. At last, he said, "Can even the talented Adelia Flynn do that?"

"I believe I can."

"Then, by all, means . . . " He extended his hand and took a few steps back.

Adelia marched to another section of the audience and asked whether anyone had a dime they could lend her. A rotund fellow in a gray suit was only too eager to offer her one from his pocket. She thanked him politely and returned to the center of the performance area.

The snare drummer from Wheatley's Cowhand Brass Band commenced a tension-enhancing drumroll.

Adelia tossed the dime high, drew her Colt revolver again, and took the shot. The assistant caught the now-bent dime and returned it to the overstuffed fellow in the gray suit.

Jack held his arms wide. "My apologies, Miss Flynn. I did not think that shot was possible."

"I dare you to try it," she said with a twinkle in her eye.

Jack feigned reticence. But at the urging of the audience, which only escalated when Adelia folded her arms and smiled as though she doubted Jack could match her skill, he gave in.

He shook his head, extracted a dime from his own pocket, and attempted to match Adelia's feat — and missed.

With an immediate, deep theatrical bow to Adelia, Jack brought the charmed audience to its feet for a prolonged ovation.

The program then drew to a close with a boisterous and colorful display of all sorts of riding and roping skills and tricks by dozens of cast members.

Cimarron Jack Wheatley made a final circuit of the arena, smiling, waving his hat, and thanking the fine people of St. Louis. As he rode, he again scoured the audience, convinced that he'd spot the faces of his competitors, James and Loftus Stilton. But they were nowhere to be seen.

He left the pavilion perplexed. *Here for the parade but not for the performance. What, if anything, did that mean?*

Cimarron Jack's Real Wild West

Available Now on Amazon.com

Made in United States
Orlando, FL
05 January 2022